Otter Dumpkin

Stephen Vandergrift

Stephen Vandergrift
12/15/02

Lion's Paw Press, Inc.
4039 NE 57th Street
Seattle, WA 98105
www.lionspawpress.com

This is a work of fiction. Names, characters, places and incidents are either a product of the author's imagination or are used fictitiously, and any resemblance to actual persons living or dead, business establishments, events, or locales is entirely coincidental.

Cover Design by Tom Buffington
www.SaveAsProductions.com

Library of Congress Control Number: 2001118034
ISBN 0-9712400-0-0

Printed in the United States of America

To my son Nathan, whose life is just beginning, and to my father, Donald, whose life recently ended, I dedicate this book. In a way, they are the bookends to my life. Between them one can find all my stories.

Chapter One

Millard Fillmore Dumpkin. He sat back and looked suspiciously at the name he had carefully printed in the space at the top of the genealogy worksheet. Then he leaned over and erased Millard Fillmore, and wrote in *Otter*. My name is *Otter*, Otter Dumpkin, he thought to himself. He would defy anyone to convince him otherwise, even Mrs. Newburg, his sixth grade teacher.

Otter's given name meant little to him. As far as he knew, the Dumpkin family had no connection to the thirteenth president of the United States. Otter's naming had been the whim of a troubled, pregnant sixteen-year-old, whose only attraction to school was her American history teacher who passed on to her his fascination with President Fillmore. On May 22nd, just over twelve years ago, as she stood in front of her class to read her report on his presidency, her water broke, signaling the beginning of labor. To Katie Dumpkin, Otter's mother, it was a sign. From that moment there was no question in her mind what to name the baby.

Otter tapped his pencil rhythmically on the dining room table. Spread out before him lay the contents of his backpack. "I should be down at the lake fishing, not here doing stupid homework," he whispered to himself. He was a little miffed at Mrs. Newburg and all the other teachers in the county that had gone out on strike at the beginning of the school year. At the time it was like a dream come true to have the summer vacation extended. When the strike was settled, almost a week after Labor Day, there had been talk about make-up days. But nobody thought much about it then. Now it was almost the middle of June, and there was still two weeks of school remaining. He was paying the price—and it seemed a little steep.

Otter usually put off doing his homework until after supper, but this evening he and Dee had made plans to gig for frogs. Addison Dumpkin, known as Dee to his friends, was Otter's grandfather and the owner of *Dee's Diner* in the small central Florida town of Lacey where they lived.

He continued the nervous tapping of his pencil and inspected the worksheet. It bore a faint outline of a tree surrounding a series of short lines arranged in a triangular shape. His assignment was to fill in the spaces with the names of his ancestors as far back as his family had record or memory.

Otter leaned forward and wrote *Katie Dumpkin* in the the first space on the right designated for his mother and her family. The space on the left, reserved for his father and his family, he left blank. Next, under his mother's name, he wrote his grandfather Dee's name and beside it, his grandmother's name, *Ruth Fisher*. He sat back and looked at the worksheet and shook his head. That was all he knew.

It was embarrassing. So many empty spaces. He really knew very little about his family history. On his mother's side of the family there were the Dumpkins and the Fishers. As far as Otter could remember, Dee had never spoken of the Dumpkin family roots. Of the Fisher family, Otter knew only of his grandmother, Ruth. He thought he remembered something about her being from Georgia, but he wasn't sure.

As for his father and his family, he didn't have a clue.

Otter put down his pencil and pushed his chair back from the table. He would ask Dee about the family this evening.

Otter reached down beside his chair and grabbed his backpack. A skeleton key fell out onto the floor, making a tinkling sound. He leaned over and picked it up and felt the cold steel in his hand.

"Dang it!" he said out loud to himself. "How could I have forgotten?" The key reminded him that he did know of another member of his family. Two weeks earlier, due to a bizarre chain of events, it had been necessary for him to stay for the weekend in the home of a great-uncle he barely knew. Otter recalled with some anxiety the morning after the first dreadful night he spent in the house. His great-uncle announced he needed to run an errand. After the man left, Otter's curiosity got the best of him, and he set out to explore the old house. He hadn't expected he would make such a startling discovery.

Otter looked down at the key and closed his hand tight around it. He knew what he had to do. Suddenly, the screen door off the back porch slammed, causing him to jump. A little surprised at how tense he had become, he took in a slow deep breath.

"Otter? Anyone home?" It was Dee.

"I'm in here!" Otter replied. He stuffed the key into his pocket then quickly scribbled *James Fisher* next to his grandmother's name. He would ask Dee later more about his great-uncle.

Dee walked into the dining room with gig in hand. "Ready to go?"

Chapter Two

Splash! "I got another one, Grandpa!" Otter secured his grip on the long bamboo pole, then leaned into the darkness to see if the gig had indeed hit its mark. The weight of it signaled that he had a frog on the other end. Seated on the front bench of the aluminum flat-bottom rowboat, he planted his feet firmly on the floor. Slowly, he began pulling the pole, hand over hand, toward himself. It was heavy and was becoming entangled in the cattails. Instinctively, he started to stand trying to gain better leverage.

"Sit back down, Otter. Take your time," his grandfather admonished wisely. "He's not going anywhere."

"I know, I know, Grandpa," Otter replied, embarrassed that he had to be reminded. He smiled and sat down. He knew that standing up in a flat-bottom rowboat was not a good idea. It was only a tad safer than standing in a V-hull, but when you're gigging frogs in the middle of the night on a lake full of gators you can be none too careful. Just last summer he had gigged a frog about to become the late-night-snack of an eight-foot bull gator. The gig had pierced the frog cleanly just before the gator had clamped his teeth down on it. Thinking he could snatch it from the gator's jaws, Otter held tight to the pole, stood up, and yanked hard. Before his grandfather could issue a warning, the boy found himself scrambling to get back into the half-swamped boat, having been pulled head-over-heels into the black water.

Dee was remembering the very same incident and offered a silent prayer of gratitude. Close calls are blessings in disguise, he told himself. Remembering them could save the boy's life some day. He was glad Otter was learning to respect the lake and its more unforgiving inhabitants.

Dee Dumpkin had grown up in the same house that he presently lived in with his grandson. The small wood-framed structure was built on a hill rising from the shore of Spring Lake, one of the few lakes west of Orlando unaffected by Disney World's sprawl. It faced west overlooking the lake. A large picture window framed the lush landscape of the lake's opposite shore where ancient live oaks with beards of gray leaned low over the water to shade the cattails and lily pads.

The spring-fed lake was crystal clear, due in no small part to the fact that it remained free of the pollution of powerboats. Its incredible natural beauty led the collectivity of people that lived nearby, not to want to foul it. Dee was committed to keeping it that way. In his mind the lake was the home of the wildlife that inhabited it. He felt privileged to share it.

Of all the inhabitants of the lake, Dee found the otters to be the most fascinating. The graceful animals that swam so effortlessly through the water, played with one another as if they didn't have a care in the world. Often, in the early evening just before sunset, he would see them journeying across the lake in groups of three or four to play in the springs on the south shore.

It didn't take long for Dee to recognize that his grandson had inherited his love for the lake and his fascination with the otters. He recalled one summer evening when the boy was just a toddler, the otters appeared near the shore where he was playing. What attracted them, Dee didn't know. As he sat and watched the boy splashing in the shallows, it amused him that the child was enjoying the water as much as the otters in their dance around him. They had no fear of him, nor he of them. In that amazing moment, almost twelve years ago, Dee was inspired to give his grandson a nickname. The folks around Lacey came to know the boy as Otter, Otter Dumpkin.

"Hold her steady, Grandpa," Otter said, a little put out that the boat seemed to be drifting.

Dee emerged from his thoughts and quickly planted an oar into the soft boggy bottom of the lake to steady the boat. With the other hand he shined his flashlight into the cattails. The sleeve of the gig's steel tri-pronged fork glistened in the light just beneath the surface of the water.

The boy braced himself and lifted the pole slowly. Despite the fact that the ends of the fork were barbed, he wanted to be careful the frog didn't slip off. If the hit wasn't square, he could lose his catch. Finally, the pole was out of the water. Impaled on the gig was a large one-pound frog.

Otter picked up his flashlight and inspected the frog.

"This frog's a mess, Grandpa," he said, holding up the frog's mangled body. Otter shined the flashlight to the back of the boat, anticipating a response from his grandfather. Dee was grinning like he did when he was up to something. Otter pointed the light to the bottom of the boat. The beam fell on the brown muslin croaker sack used to keep the catch. The sack should have shown evidence of containing three large frogs. It was empty.

"Where're the other frogs, Grandpa?" Otter paused for a moment as he tried to solve the mystery in his head. He shined the light again on his grandfather's face. Dee squinted and put his hand up to block the light. "You've been pulling one over on me haven't you?" Otter said. Dee burst into a loud laugh that echoed across the lake. He had succeeded in playing the same old trick his father had played on him, as had his father before him. Another generation of Dumpkins had been successfully initiated.

It didn't take Otter long to figure out that after he had gigged his first frog earlier in the evening and passed it back to Dee for safekeeping in the croaker sack, Dee had taken the very same frog, and when Otter was not looking, heaved it a good ten yards in front of the boat. Hearing the splash, Otter had directed his grandfather to steer along the cattails toward the sound, hoping to find another frog. He was sure he had gigged three frogs. But when he saw the empty sack and heard Dee's mischievous laughter, he quickly came to the embarrassing realization that throughout the evening he had gigged the same frog—three times!

"Your time's comin'," Otter said to Dee, feeling a little hurt that he had not recognized sooner what was going on. Then he grinned a sly grin, and with a determination in his voice that made Dee feel a little uneasy, added, "I'll get you good one of these days!"

After another hour of gigging, with Otter examining each frog and keeping a close eye on the croaker sack, Dee started the electric kicker and the two left the cattails, setting out across the lake to return home. Otter folded his arms across his chest and sucked in a deep breath. The air out in the middle of the lake smelled clean compared to the slight smell of decay that hung over the cattail-lined shore. As the boat pushed toward the warm light flowing from the distant picture window, Otter felt a pang of hunger and imagined how good the fried frog legs would taste with mounds of hot steaming grits covered with butter.

Otter tied the boat securely to the dock, then helped Dee put away the life jackets and kicker in the shed behind the house. With a large butcher knife he got from the kitchen, Otter returned to the porch to de-legg the four frogs. He liked to imagine that he was a civil war surgeon in an Army field hospital. The back porch of the house was outfitted with an old industrial sink with large metal draining boards extending from each side, ideal for cleaning fish—or frogs. Dee had brought it home and installed it after his diner had been remodeled with a new kitchen.

After the surgery, Otter washed the amputated frog legs and took them into the kitchen. Dee had the skillet on the gas stove, and the cooking oil was already beginning to crackle. A large pot of boiling water was softening up the grits, and the corn meal batter sat ready to be spooned into the skillet to make the best hushpuppies ever tasted. Dee worked his wonders with recipes that earned him the reputation in central Florida as having a diner with some of the best home-cooking around. His specialty—catfish and hushpuppies. But tonight it was the catch-of-the-day.

The frog legs coated with Dee's special cornmeal and egg recipe followed the hushpuppies into the skillet. They were as big as chicken legs, and as far as Otter was concerned tasted a whole lot better. His stomach began to growl. In another smaller skillet, Otter noticed that Dee was working some fried okra. He could hardly stand it. He didn't like many vegetables, but fried okra was the exception. To distract his stomach, Otter hurried to set the table for the feast. When all was ready, they sat down to the table and looked at each other with tired but grateful eyes. The lake had provided once again. They dug in.

After supper, Otter helped Dee clear the dishes from the table.

"Got all your homework done?" Dee asked as he filled the sink with soapy water.

Otter hesitated. It was late and he thought Dee might be disappointed if he said no.

"There's this project I've been assigned, but I need your help to complete it."

"What kind of project?" Dee asked.

"A family tree. I have to make a family tree," Otter replied.

Dee stopped what he was doing and gave Otter a curious look. "A family tree, huh. Have you started it?"

"Yeah, but I didn't get very far," Otter confessed. "There's still a lot of blank spaces. I need you to help me fill them in."

"You gotta have it done for class tomorrow?" Dee asked. His question reflected the fact that he was bone-tired after working a full day at the diner and spending the evening gigging frogs with his grandson. He hoped for a reprieve. He didn't get it.

"Yessir. She wants us to turn it in tomorrow," Otter replied apologetically. He could tell Dee was tired.

Dee loaded the remainder of the dishes in the sink to soak, then wiped his hands on a dish towel he had slung over his shoulder. "We'd better get to it then."

Otter ran to his room to retrieve the worksheet from his backpack. Dee sat back down at the dining room table. On the sideboard next to the table was a framed photograph of the family he once had. His wife Ruth, and daughters Annie and Katie were all gone. Though it had been almost fifteen years, the litany of his loss was still very familiar. Ruth, diagnosed with breast cancer, had died within six months of the diagnosis. Then, before the first anniversary of her death, Annie, the older of their two teenage daughters, was killed in a car accident out on Highway 50 west of Orlando on her way home with friends from a high school football game. Dee remembered how debilitating his grief was, and how he had been of little help to Katie who was at least as devastated as he.

Dee imagined that Katie must have felt abandoned by him emotionally. When she couldn't take it any longer, she had left home and traded her old family for a new one, living among other homeless teenagers on the streets of downtown Orlando. Two days before her sixteenth birthday, she had returned home—pregnant. Dee closed his eyes and shook his head. Even after fifteen years, he still felt ashamed that when she needed him most, he had threatened to send her back out on the streets.

After the baby was born, things went from bad to worse between them. Crushed under the weight of being a parent at such a young age and living with a seemingly heartless father, Katie left the baby with Dee and disappeared. For months he searched for her but all his efforts, as well as those of the law enforcement agencies, were fruitless. She had simply disappeared. Was she still alive? That was the hard part—not knowing. If she was, she would be twenty-eight this November.

It was a nightmare. His family had been reduced from a wife and two teenage daughters to an infant boy in less than two years. Thanks to a few close friends, he survived the first few months with the baby. Several times he was tempted to give him up for adoption. But alone with the child on the first Christmas Eve after Katie had left, Dee had a kind of conversion experience. He dreamed he was drowning in the lake he loved so much, struggling hopelessly to get to the surface. He thought he had died, when someone pulled him from the water and breathed life back into him. It was a little boy. It was as if Dee had gone to sleep in one life and awakened in another. From that moment on he saw the child not as a burden, but as a gift, and it wasn't a matter of survival, but a chance to get it right, a second chance at being a parent. He felt he had been blessed and received the gift of his grandson with much gratitude. He wasn't going to squander the opportunity. He was determined to be a good grandfather to this little boy.

When Otter returned with the genealogy worksheet, Dee smiled affectionately at him and gave him a big hug. Together they sat down at the table and inspected Otter's progress. He was right. Lots of blanks.

With some anxiety, Dee began to anticipate the questions that Otter might ask, particularly regarding his absent father. Otter knew that his mother had run away. Since he was old enough to understand, Dee had done his best to explain to him that Katie had not been well, and that in no way was it his fault that she left. But it was a different matter with Otter's father. It would be the first time Dee would be asked to explain in any detail why his grandson didn't have a father.

"Your father was, as much as I've been able to gather," Dee said haltingly, "a young recruit from the Navy training center in Orlando. Your mother wouldn't divulge anything about him, I think she was afraid I'd kill 'im." Dee chuckled nervously, "In the condition I was in at the time, I probably would have. Anyway, after she left home, I had no way to trace him down. Her friends knew nothing about him, except to say that he was in the Navy."

"Should I write *Navy recruit* in the space?" Otter asked.

Dee smiled at his grandson's innocence. The question was sincere. It was important to Otter that the space not be left empty.

"That would be fine," Dee replied. He was surprised when Otter didn't ask any more questions about his father.

When Otter asked about the Dumpkin side of the family, Dee got up from the table and retrieved from his bedroom the Dumpkin family Bible. Otter looked with interest at the names and the dates of birth and death. For some of the family, dates of marriages were noted and children listed. He was surprised to see his name. Unlike most of the other names, which had faded over the years, Otter's name was written with a blue ballpoint pen and it stuck out from the others. It felt good to be a part of the Dumpkin family, he thought. With a satisfied smile on his face, he filled in the spaces.

Then there was the Fisher side of Otter's heritage. He looked down at the worksheet at his grandmother's name and beside it, the name he had printed in haste, *James Fisher.*

"Grandpa?" Otter said, "There's something I've been meaning to talk to you about, about this Uncle James of mine." Otter pointed to the name written on the worksheet. He hesitated, unsure where to begin. Suddenly the phone rang. Otter welcomed the distraction. "I'll get it!" He jumped from his chair and scrambled to pick up the receiver. "Hello." The familiar voice on the other end belonged to Vicky Koontz, longtime friend of the family and Dee's steady girl friend. "Hey, Vicky, how you feeling?" Otter inquired. Vicky was recovering from a bad case of the flu. Otter's brow wrinkled, betraying his confusion when Vicky skipped her usual playful banter and told him to turn on the TV. She then asked to speak to Dee. "Turn on the TV? What for? Grandpa, it's Vicky." Otter handed the phone to Dee. "She's sure upset about something. I hope she's okay." Otter ran to the living room. The remote control clicker was right where he had left it, for once. He turned on the TV. At the bottom of the screen were the words "Special Bulletin." The TV camera was panning an unfamiliar place to Otter, but he knew something was up—armored tanks, hundreds it seemed, were lined up side by side.

Otter knew from school, and from overhearing folks talking at the diner, that something was brewing somewhere. Dee had not said much about it, but Otter thought he seemed a little worried. At school his class had read in their *Weekly Reader* about the conflict among Croatians and Serbs, Muslims and Orthodox Christians. Still, it remained confusing to him. All he could figure was that they didn't like each other and hadn't liked each other for a long time. He also knew that there was talk of sending troops over there and this was especially worrisome to him—Dee was in the Army Reserves.

"Reserves aren't called up unless it's real bad," Otter reminded himself. Nevertheless, his full stomach began to feel a little nervous. Would Dee have to report? Would his reserve unit be called up as it had been seven years ago in Desert Storm? Otter was only five years old then. There wasn't much he could remember, just some feelings that were scary to him.

Otter didn't hear his grandfather hang up the phone. His eyes were fixed on the TV as he tried to make sense of what the commentator was saying. Dee stood in the doorway, his eyes also on the television. Otter looked up at him. His grandfather was silent. Then he spoke.

"Vicky says Glenn Sisson came by the diner just before closing. He's on his way over here." Glenn was a full "bird" colonel and the commander of Dee's reserve unit. They had grown up together and both had served in Vietnam as well as Desert Storm. "Vicky says Glenn said we're on alert. Dammit!" Dee exclaimed. Otter had seldom heard his grandfather swear, and he couldn't remember seeing such a worried expression on Dee's face. It scared him.

"Do you think you'll have to go over there, Grandpa?"

"I don't know Bud," Dee replied, staring blankly at the TV. "It doesn't look good. It doesn't look good at all."

Chapter Three

During the night it began to rain. The sound of its gentle patter on the roof usually relaxed Otter and put him right to sleep, but the news that the President was considering sending troops to a faraway place that Otter knew little about, left him with a stomach ache. He conjured up images of battles with tanks and jets and smart bombs and lots of dead people.

Dee seldom spoke of Desert Storm and even less of his experience in Vietnam. The few stories Otter remembered hearing him tell were frightening. The expression Otter saw on Dee's face as they watched the news that evening, was enough to convince him that his grandfather didn't want to go through another war. Dee had spent 29 years serving his country in the military, ten as a regular soldier and nineteen in the reserves. He was one year from retiring.

Otter was silent as Dee's old Chevy pickup truck splashed its way around the lake into town to school.

The rain was coming down hard, chopping the lake into a rough gray mass. Near the surface, it was hard to tell if the rain was rising or falling. It was all a blur.

"What's on your mind, Bud?" Dee asked. Otter knew that when Dee called him "Bud," things took on a more serious tone.

"I'm scared." Otter said. "Does Glenn think y'all will have to go over there, like in Desert Storm?" Glenn had stopped by the house as Vicky had said he would. While Otter was putting away his homework and getting ready for bed, he had heard the low murmur of the voices of the two men as they talked in the dining room.

"He's not sure yet," Dee replied, "but even if we do, you don't need to be worrying about that. If we go, it probably won't last any longer than Desert Storm did."

The truck turned away from the lake and made its way through the drizzle toward town. Otter felt the tears coming and turned away to avoid Dee's eyes. But he couldn't fool Dee.

"Come on now, it's gonna be okay," Dee said, patting Otter on the knee. "If I have to go, you'll stay with Vicky, and we'll treat it just like when I go off for reserve duty in the summer."

Otter winced. The idea of staying with Vicky didn't make him feel any better. Though he was fond of Vicky, he never really liked staying with her when Dee was away. To add to his anxiety, Otter was now aware that she was vulnerable. She seemed to be sick a lot lately. In fact, it was her recent bout with the flu that had precipitated the need for him to stay that ugly weekend with his Uncle James. Despite his curiosity to uncover more of his great-uncle's secret, he wasn't sure he was ready to welcome another overnight.

Dee drove around back to the cafeteria loading dock and parked the truck. It was a routine he had never performed with his daughters, but the memory of his own father dropping him off in the same spot on rainy days years before, surfaced when Otter started school. Like his father before him, Dee liked the spot because it was less crowded. Otter had not always appreciated the idea of being dropped off behind the school, but this year his class was in one of the several portable buildings located behind the school near the cafeteria.

The two sat quietly as the rain tapped on the metal roof of the truck cab.

"You got your homework?" Dee asked, changing the subject.

Otter nodded. He had done all he could. There were still plenty of things unanswered about his family, but it didn't seem to matter to him at the moment.

"Well, you'll be late if we sit much longer," Dee said. "We'll talk more about all this mess this evening."

Otter nodded his head in agreement. He unlocked his seatbelt and leaned over and hugged his grandfather. On seeing the tears on Otter's face, Dee felt his throat tighten. He placed his cheek on the boy's head and patted his shoulder. "It's gonna be okay, Bud. Hang in there."

Otter grabbed his book bag off the floorboard and opened the door.

"Walk over to the diner after school if it's not raining," Dee said. "Otherwise I'll pick you up here. Okay?"

"Okay." Otter slipped down off the seat and closed the door.

After a quick wave good-bye, he ran to the covered

walkway adjacent to the cafeteria and disappeared around the corner. Dee sat behind the wheel of the truck, staring into the cafeteria kitchen. The lunch ladies in their white aprons moved about carrying large pots, laughing and putting-on with each other. Dee turned to look out the side window, his breath fogging the glass. Would he really have to go? What if he was killed or wounded and couldn't take care of Otter? What then?

Dee did not hear the delivery truck pull up behind him. The honk of the horn startled him and brought him back to the present. He waved an acknowledgement to the driver then turned the key to start the engine. The rain was coming down harder now. He put the truck in gear and headed for the diner.

For the next three days CNN reported the escalating crisis. Tanks had crossed the border into Albania and fighting had begun. It was bad. The live pictures of bombing from the air and fighting on the ground were disturbing. Dee tried to limit what Otter was seeing, but it was on 24-hours a day and there was no way he was going to succeed.

Then the word came: Report to Fort Bragg to prepare for departure to Europe. Dee was going.

It all seemed to happen so fast. On the day Dee left, Otter stayed home from school. Vicky came over to help him get his things together to make the move to her house. Glenn came by to pick up Dee for the trip over to McCoy Air Force Base to board the big C-141 to Pope Air Force Base outside of Fayetteville, North Carolina. Pope is the base adjacent to Fort Bragg, home of the Army's 82nd Airborne. Otter had visited the Army post several times following Dee's summer reserve training. Often he and Vicky would make the trip north to pick him up, then travel over to the coast for a few days at Myrtle Beach. Dee had shown Otter around Fort Bragg, taking him to the 82nd Airborne Museum, the Special Forces Museum, and once he even saw a LAPES exercise out at Sicily drop zone. He learned that LAPES is an acronym for a Low Altitude Parachute Extraction of heavy equipment from an airplane. A big C-130, which looks like a flying eighteen-wheeler, swoops down to about four feet off the ground, then a parachute is released from the rear that pulls a tank or a cannon or some other piece of equipment out the back of the plane. The equipment slides across the ground to waiting troops. The plane then flies away without landing. Otter remembered how exciting it was to watch.

Dee's departure was hard for Otter. After hugs and promises to call and to write, Dee was in the truck and gone. Vicky and Otter gathered his things and headed to the diner for an early lunch before going on to her place to get Otter settled. Some comfort food will do us both good, she thought. She knew Otter's comfort food was a cheeseburger, fries, and a chocolate milkshake.

On hearing the jingle of the bell over the diner door, Flora Sanders peered through the order window separating the diner's counter from the kitchen. Flora was a big woman with fleshy arms, and a bright smile accented by her rich ebony skin. She loved to smother Otter with her hugs. When cooking at the diner she always smelled of onions and garlic. Otter liked the smell, but the hugs were a little embarrassing to him.

Flora already had the cheeseburger and fries prepared

and was working on the milkshake when Vicky and Otter arrived. Otter sat down on one of the several stools at the counter as Vicky made her way to the kitchen. Otter pushed off from the foot rest and began spinning on the stool. He enjoyed the sensation of spinning round and round, gripping the seat hard to keep from flying off. With each rotation, Otter noticed the blur of a lone figure in a booth at the far end of the diner, but he didn't pay any attention to who it was. Flora appeared through the swinging door and set the feast down in front of Otter.

"Here you go, sugar, you eat it all up now." Flora said. Otter came to a sudden halt and looked into her smiling eyes. He detected the sarcasm in her voice, and returned a sly grin. He knew she knew that the burger, fries and shake were not long for this world.

"Umm, umm, thanks Flora, this is great!" Otter said as he hurried to squirt some ketchup on his plate. Flora disappeared into the kitchen as Otter took a large bite out of his cheeseburger.

"Ain't you forget'n somethin', young man?" came a familiar voice.

Otter did not have to look over to the booth to realize that it was his Uncle James speaking to him. There was no mistaking that high twangy voice. He stopped chewing and put the burger down on his plate. A cold chill came over him, and the hair on his neck began to tingle.

"I know your granddaddy ain't taught you much about pray'n, but you are thankful for that food you're eat'n, ain't ya? It hurts me to see a boy like you ungrateful."

Otter resumed chewing slowly. Out of the corner of

his eye, he could see that the figure had moved from the booth and was approaching. He didn't turn to look. A bead of sweat formed on his right temple. He took in a slow deep breath. Where was Flora? he wondered.

Otter's Uncle James, who was known to the folks around Lacey as Little Jimmy Fisher, was a small, wiry, tough-as-nails sort, who had a reputation for being a scrappy fighter. In his younger years (he was fifty-one, the same age as Dee), comments about his high pitched voice usually led to a fight. He was little educated, having dropped out of school at sixteen to work full-time in Donnie Hager's auto shop. Donnie worked mostly on the big trucks that carried the citrus fruit from the groves of west Orange County to the packing houses. Little Jimmy worked there for 15 years until that fateful day when he "found the Lord."

Jimmy had traveled up to the University of Florida at Gainesville with Donnie who had tickets to a Gator football game. While wandering around campus after the game, he came upon a small crowd of students gathered on the Plaza of the Americas. They were being entertained by an itinerant preacher who went by the name, Harlan Strock. The preacher was jeered at by most of the students, but he did manage to convince Jimmy that indeed there was a burning hell reserved for the unrepentant and that he could be saved from the wrath of the Lord if he'd just give his life to Jesus. Little Jimmy gave his life to the Lord as well as his word that he would give up drinking. Dee said that something was troubling his brother-in-law and on that day, he had been ripe for the picking.

Little Jimmy Fisher became Brother James and traveled as Harlan Strock's disciple, learning to spout a gospel of fear on campuses around the South, and a few northern schools too. His first preaching experiences had been difficult for him, and often led to a fight when students made fun of his voice. Over time, he convinced himself that being ridiculed was the cost of keeping his promise to the Lord. But the other part of the promise, to stop drinking, James could not keep. This was a constant source of guilt for him, and made him an angry man.

James returned home to Lacey from time to time after his preaching tours. One day he returned to stay. There were rumors that he had killed the evangelist he traveled with. Some said he had seen the Lord face-to-face. Dee said James had not changed. There was still something eating him up inside. Eventually James returned to preaching, mostly at Holy Ghost tent revivals around Orange County. And he continued to drink.

Otter could feel his uncle's breath on his neck as James stood behind him, trying to intimidate him by standing beyond his peripheral vision. The smell of liquor increased Otter's anxiety. Keeping his eyes focused straight ahead, Otter tried to swallow the bite of burger he still had in his mouth, but his throat was too dry to get it down.

James leaned over to whisper something into the boy's ear when Flora busted through the kitchen door with an iron skillet. The sudden presence of her massive body frightened even Otter, causing him to tumble off the stool. James stumbled back and raised his arms to fend off a swipe of the skillet.

"Get out of here you scoundrel, and leave that boy alone. You're nothin' but no-good trash, Jimmy Fisher.

Get on out!" James was so startled that the utterances from his mouth sounded like no language Otter recognized. He stumbled against the glass door. For a moment he regained his balance, only to slip on a french fry flung from Otter's plate. This time James hit hard against the door, which opened with a little jingle, and he spilled out on the ground. He was livid. He feigned a movement to come back in, but Flora took a step toward the door with raised skillet, and he retreated. In an instant he was in his red Ford Escort wagon and gone.

"Lordy, that man is gonna make me a murderer someday, I declare!" Flora exclaimed. She put her arm around Otter. "You okay, sugar? I'm sorry I let that man get within a mile of you. I heard the bell jingle earlier but I didn't see no one come in. I shoulda made sure." She walked to the door and looked out in the direction James' car had disappeared. "Well, sugar, I promise you he won't set foot in here again while I'm here."

Otter picked up the french fries off the floor and set them on counter then returned to the stool. Flora walked over and wrapped her arms around him. Despite her warm embrace, he felt cold. He wished Dee was there.

For the first time, Otter admitted to himself that he feared his uncle. Until that moment he had never experienced him drunk. At no time during his recent stay with James, had Otter seen him inebriated. The time he spent observing his uncle only revealed a pathetic and lonely man. Otter had felt sorry for him. But seeing his uncle drunk like this was different and it was upsetting.

Otter sat quietly on the stool and reached into his

 pocket for the skeleton key. Immediately his thoughts returned to that weekend when he had been left in the care of his Uncle James and had discovered the troubling secret.

Chapter Four

That whole crazy weekend had begun with Dee preparing for his monthly Army Reserve duty at Camp Blanding, a small training facility just south of Jacksonville. Typically, when reserve weekends occurred, Otter would stay with Vicky. But on that Friday morning Vicky had awakened with a high fever and felt nauseous. She called Dee and he went right over. She looked bad. Dee wanted to take her to the hospital but she refused. Just a bout of the flu, she insisted. But Vicky would not be able to keep Otter for the weekend. Flora volunteered to come in and look after things at the diner and keep an eye on Vicky while Dee was away. That reassured Dee, but what about Otter?

Dee found himself in a bind. Normally he could skip out of weekend duty in cases of emergency, but this weekend a special military exercise had been planned and he was to play a crucial role conducting it.

It was as if some evil had fallen over Lacey that weekend, demanding that Otter stay with his Uncle

James. Dee had contacted numerous friends of the family as well as the families of Otter's school buddies, but no one could take him. Otter had suggested Flora, and at first it seemed like a good idea, but ultimately Dee decided against it, knowing she would be busy with the diner and Vicky. James, though kin, was a last resort. Dee didn't like it, but he was in a jam. As time drew near for his departure, Dee convinced himself that there was no other alternative. And after all, he rationalized, it was only for a weekend. Beyond this, Dee was sure James was aware what he would do to him if he didn't take the best care of Otter.

Otter resisted the idea of staying with James at first. But Dee came up with a satisfactory compromise to which he agreed. They decided that for the weekend James would stay at the Dumpkin home rather than Otter staying at James' house. Dee was in touch with James, and with a little persuasion his brother-in-law agreed.

The Friday night following Dee's departure was uneventful. At least it started that way. Dee had arranged for Otter to eat supper at the diner. James had agreed to pick up Otter at nine o'clock. He arrived on time. The diner was busy as usual on Friday evenings. Flora was busy back in the kitchen when the door jingled and James walked in. Finding Otter on one of the stools at the counter, James approached the boy and tapped him on the shoulder. Otter rotated around on the stool, looked up at his uncle and smiled. As if it was painful to see, James turned away.

James looked around the crowded diner then glanced back at Otter. For someone who speaks regularly before crowds, he seems awfully nervous, Otter thought. James was aware that on Friday nights Miss Flora Sanders stayed until closing. Imagining an encounter with her added to his anxiety level. There was something about the woman, herself a preacher, that made him want to flee whenever he was in her presence. It was as if she could see right through him to what was written on his heart. That made him extremely uncomfortable.

Otter went to the kitchen to tell Flora that James had arrived and they were about to leave. James was already in the car waiting for his great-nephew when Flora came through the kitchen door, wiping her hands on her apron. She followed Otter out the front door and held it open as she watched the young boy join his uncle in the car. James risked a glance at Flora. She was staring right at him. The message in her eyes was clear—be careful or else!

It didn't take long for James to reveal a change of plans. As if in defiance of Flora and Dee and anyone else who held a low opinion of him, James conducted the red Ford Escort wagon not to the Dumpkin home as agreed but to his own. Somehow this didn't surprise Otter. In his mind he had already imagined the eventuality and had prepared himself for it.

So when James pulled into the sandy driveway next to his house, Otter's lack of surprise and protest puzzled him. The small house was tucked away in the shadows of surrounding live oaks behind the drugstore off of Blount Street in downtown Lacey. It was a sparsely furnished two bedroom house painted an awful shade of institutional green. Inside, it seemed clean enough but had a peculiar smell that Otter was not immediately able to identify.

James had decided that Otter would sleep on the

tattered three-cushioned sofa in the living room. The sofa was stained from spills and years of body ash rubbed into the fabric. Otter breathed a prayer of thanks when James covered the cushions with a sheet. With little said between them except for directions to the bathroom, the two relatives retired for the evening. It had been a long, emotional day, and Otter was bone tired. Despite the unfamiliar surroundings, he fell quickly asleep.

Too early the next morning, Saturday, James took Otter out to breakfast at the drugstore around the corner from his house. The drugstore was a small locally-owned pharmacy with a sundries shop where James bought his regular morning coffee. This day he added a pack of miniature donuts to his meal along with a honey bun and a pint of milk for his great-nephew.

Outside on the sidewalk, James invited Otter to offer a prayer for the meal. Otter refused, to the irritation of his uncle. James then bellowed out a prayer so loud that one would have thought God was hard of hearing. Otter suspected that his uncle was only trying to embarrass him. After devouring the donuts in silence, James announced that he needed to buy some stamps and pay a bill. Before walking to the post office, James escorted Otter back to the house, where he turned on the TV and ordered Otter to watch cartoons while he ran his errands. Though irritated with his uncle's bossy tone, Otter cooperated—for a while.

Shortly after James left, Otter decided that exploring his uncle's abode would be a whole lot more interesting than watching Looney Tunes. He peeked out the front window and up the street to be sure James was not returning for something he might have forgotten. The coast was clear.

James was a frugal sort. From what Otter knew of his uncle and what he saw in his brief survey of the living room, James did not spend a lot of money on material things. That much was clear. Otter walked to the back of the living room to a hallway leading to rooms in the back of the house. The first door on the left was the bathroom that James had shown Otter the night before. It had seemed normal enough, even austere—a translucent shower curtain, a couple of white towels, one with Holiday Inn printed on it, a dirty bar of soap and a toothbrush in a glass. The medicine cabinet mirror had a small crack in the lower left side of it. Otter remembered that the black plastic toilet seat was also cracked and the porcelain toilet bowl was discolored with a rust stain from years of contact with the local hard water.

Bypassing the bathroom, he proceeded to the next door on the left, which opened into the kitchen.

"No wonder he eats breakfast at the drugstore," Otter said softly under his breath. "There aren't any clean dishes left to eat off of." The room smelled of rotting food, which Otter identified as the odor faintly permeating the rest of the house. This more intense concentration made him feel a little queasy.

He exited the kitchen and continued his exploration. On the right were two doors. He had seen James go in and out the second door and suspected that it was his bedroom. Passing the first door on the right, he proceeded to open the second one, expecting to see an unkempt room. To his surprise, the bed was neatly made and several trinkets on top of a dresser were arranged on a lace doily.

Otter closed the door to James' room and

backtracked to the other door on the same side of the hall. He turned the cut-glass handle. It was locked. The locking mechanism was the old system separate from the knob and built into the door itself, requiring a generic skeleton key to open it. It was a system Otter was familiar with from the doors in his own home. There was no key. He glanced back at the door to James' room. No key. From experience, Otter knew that one skeleton key could unlock most of the doors in these old houses. On a hunch, he quickly walked back and checked the lock on the inside of James' door. He found one.

Taking the key, he returned to the locked door and inserted it into the lock. He tried to turn it. It yielded slightly but not enough to unlock it. Otter had opened enough similar locks to know that it was probably frozen due to infrequent use. It was just a matter of loosening it up. After a few seconds working the key back and forth, the lock gave way. Otter turned the handle. With a slight creaking noise, sounding eerily like a prop out of a horror movie, the door opened. Inside, the room was cool and dark and smelled musty. Directly across the room from the door, a single window rested on three feet of wall before extending high to the nine-foot ceiling. It was covered by a thick drape. Next to it on the adjacent wall was what Otter guessed to be a closet door. A single bed with an iron head and foot board was shoved into one corner. Two simple paintings of flowers in oval frames hung on the wall above the bed. The wood floor, having no covering and painted a shiny chocolate brown, reflected the hall light. A dresser similar to the one in James' room clung to the wall next to the door.

Otter opened the door wide to get the full benefit of

the hall light. Some of the light reflected off the glass of a small picture frame. Despite being in the shadows, Otter recognized the photograph of his grandmother, Ruth. He found the light switch next to the door, and turned it on. Then he moved to the dresser to examine the picture. It was identical to the one Dee kept on his bedside table.

Otter carefully pulled open the top drawer of the dresser. Inside there was nothing save a few old newspapers. The faded papers he recognized as copies of the *Winter Grove Times.* On the front page of the issue on top, Otter thought he recognized another photograph. Though he had no memory of her, he recognized the picture from photos that Dee kept of her. It was his mother, Katie. Gently he picked up the paper and read the headline *Lacey Teen Missing.* The article began, "Katherine Sue Dumpkin, a student at West County High School was reported missing..."

Otter had begun to read the first paragraph of the article when he heard the sound of a car stop on the street in front of the house. He could hear two voices, one of which belonged to James. James thanked the driver for the ride and the car sped away. Otter quickly returned the paper to the drawer and shut it, then he ran to the door and turned off the light. Before stepping out into the hallway, he turned and looked back at the closet door. What is behind that door, he wondered? He wanted to look but his gut told him there was not enough time. He would have to look for an opportunity in the future to check it out. He closed the door and locked it just as the front door opened. James looked up to see Otter coming down the hall. Slowly he closed the door behind him, and glared at his great-nephew with suspicious eyes.

"Son, whachu doin' back there? You ain't got no cause to be back there. I told you to sit here and watch them cartoons."

"I had to go to the bathroom," Otter said. The words came without thinking. Impressed with his alibi, he felt a surge of self-assurance that he was confident would cover any guilty look he might exhibit. He plopped down on the sofa.

James took off his soiled baseball cap and tossed it on a small table next to the door. Slowly he walked around to the front of the sofa and looked down at Otter as if he were trying to see inside his head to determine what he was thinking. Otter stared at the TV the whole time, knowing that James' eyes were fixed on him. He wanted to ask his uncle about the newspapers in the drawer but decided against it, not wanting to invite his wrath. He continued to look straight ahead at the TV.

Having failed in his efforts to intimidate the boy, James gave in and retreated to the back of the house to his bedroom and shut the door. Otter realized that he had won the battle of wills this time. But the war was not over.

Lost in thought, Otter stared into the TV, unmoved that Wiley Coyote was about to be foiled again by the Roadrunner. Why did James have those old newspapers? he wondered. Did he know something about his mother and her disappearance? Somehow, he had to get back into that room. There must be more there. He felt for the key in his pocket, and pulled it out to look at it. Will I ever get a chance to use this? He wondered. He shrugged, then grabbed his backpack from beside the sofa and tossed in the key.

That all happened more than two weeks ago. Otter continued to fondle the skeleton key, unaware that Flora had returned to the kitchen.

Vicky managed to get off the phone and burst through the swinging door from the kitchen. “What on earth was that all about?” she asked worriedly. Flora followed her back out to the counter and offered her version of the story. “Ain’t nothin’but that no count Jimmy Fisher thinkin’ he could slip in here drunk and scare Otter here,” she said, as she took Otter’s plate and wiped the counter in front of him.

“You okay, Otter? You want something else to eat?” Vicky asked.

“No, I’m okay,” he said, looking up at her blankly. He had lost his appetite. He returned the key to his pocket, but his thoughts were still on the mystery that lay hidden in James’ house. He was determined to find out what James was hiding.

Chapter Five

Vicky spent the weekend trying to console Otter. It was a difficult task. By Saturday afternoon it had sunk in that his grandfather was really gone. Saturdays were often spent on the lake together swimming or fishing or gigging frogs. He already missed Dee and despite his skepticism promised himself he would pray each day that the conflict "over there" would be resolved and his grandfather would be sent home. Ever since Otter had been old enough to talk, Dee had encouraged him to pray. But Otter wondered if God really listened and if he really answered his prayers. Dee had told him that sometimes God's reply was "no." That didn't satisfy him. God was God, he ought to be able to step in and intervene once in a while.

Two weeks passed, then three. With the exception of a call from Dee to say he had arrived okay at Fort Bragg, there was no other communication. Had Dee departed for Europe? Otter sensed something was wrong but dismissed it as the same anxiety he felt when Dee was absent for summer reserve duty.

Otter was concerned about Vicky. She was obviously not well. Suspecting a relapse of the flu, she had stayed home from the diner on Monday following a very busy weekend. No one, least of all Vicky, had any idea that her appendix was about to explode. Likewise, no one suspected that her recent episode with what she thought was the flu had actually been a warning sign.

On Tuesday she was back at the diner, though still not well. Then, that evening after the diner had closed and she and Otter had returned to her home, Vicky began to feel nauseous. At 3:00 a.m. she woke Otter with her moans. She was in horrible pain. Otter called 911. Within minutes the rescue squad from the Lacey Fire Department arrived and took them both away to the hospital. She was in serious condition.

When Dee could not be reached at Fort Bragg, the hospital considered contacting James. A nurse who knew the family recalled that he and Dee were related.

On hearing that James might be called, Otter was initially upset. James must still be crazy with anger after the fiasco with Flora, he reasoned. And he probably blames me! Otter knew that he could have insisted on staying at the hospital or he could have called Flora or someone other than James. But after some reflection, he remembered that he had a good reason to want to risk being with his Uncle James. He agreed that James should be contacted.

James arrived at the hospital and took custody of Otter without saying a word to the boy. The paper work was signed and the two returned to James' home. It was warmer outside than Otter had remembered. The smell of approaching rain was in the air and there was lightning flashing in the east. A storm was brewing. By the time they pulled into James' driveway, the sky had let loose a gully washer. Through the pouring rain, James led the way to the front door with Otter close behind. He unlocked it and held the door for his great-nephew.

"Your sheets are over there in the corner where you left 'em," James said. "I gotta get up and go to work in two hours, so good night to you." And with that he disappeared down the dark hallway to his bedroom. Otter was a bit amused that after almost three weeks, the sheets he had used on his first stay were still where he had left them. James was a strange bird, he thought.

On most rainy nights in his own home, Otter would have dozed off easily to the sound of the falling rain. But James' house had a tin roof, and the rain pounding on it was deafening. The lightning was hitting close, with breath-robbing cracks of thunder coming on the heels of each flash. Otter dreaded the frightful two hours of darkness until daylight. He pulled the sheets over the soiled sofa, grabbed a blanket and pillow and turned out the lamp, then tried to get some sleep.

But he couldn't sleep. It wasn't the lightning and thunder that kept him awake, it was something more chilling. Is there some force that has put me back into James' house to discover the rest of the secret? Otter pondered. If so, is it a sinister force or a benevolent one? In the dark shadows created by the lightning flashes, Otter's creative imagination worked against him. All indications seemed to lean toward the sinister side. He kept his eyes open and the blanket pulled up tight under his chin. He half expected his uncle to appear from the back room to check on things, perhaps to be sure all the windows were closed or something like that. But there was no movement. James is probably sound asleep despite the storm, he thought.

Otter pitched and turned as his mind raced. He regretted that he had told no one, not even Dee, about what he had found the last time he was with James. I've gotta do something! When will I get a better chance to try it? he asked himself.

Otter had toyed with the idea that he could convince James that he needed to stay home from school the next day due to some made-up illness. He imagined that while James was at work, he would have plenty of time to return to the room for further exploring. But James would not fall for it, he had decided. Besides, when Flora got word that he was staying with James, and he was sure she would, the woman who was like his guardian angel would be over there in a flash. Sinister force or not, the time is now, Otter told himself. With the thunder, and the thunderous rain pounding on the tin roof, James will not hear a thing.

Otter sat up on the sofa. He stood up and dug the skeleton key from his pocket. Again his mind began to race. What would he find in the closet? What if it was so awful that he would yell and scream, waking James? There would be no way anyone would hear him cry for help if James decided to do him in. On and on his thoughts tormented him.

Finally he mustered up enough courage to do it. In his stocking feet, Otter tip-toed down the hall to the room, the periodic flashes of lightning helping him to see his way. Once in front of the door, he felt for the keyhole and inserted the key. Gripping the key tightly, he tried to turn it. As before, it would not turn. Again he strained to turn it. No good. Perhaps this time if I lean my weight on the door it might free the lock from wedging against the jamb, he thought. It worked. The key turned. He was in.

Carefully closing the door behind him, he stood in the darkness and caught his breath. He had not realized just how hard his heart was pounding and how hard he was breathing. Lightning flashed, followed by a clap of thunder.

The room was as he remembered it. But this time, in the flashes of lightning, the photograph of his grandmother seemed to be looking directly at him as if she was watching over him in the dark. He turned toward the closet door in the corner of the room next to the window and walked over to it. Slowly he opened it, bracing himself for the worst, expecting perhaps a skeleton to fall out. Nothing happened. Looking into the closet was like peering into a cave. It was pitch black. He could see nothing. He pulled back the drapes from the window to take full advantage of a lightning flash and waited. One came, followed by a jarring clap of thunder. He stared hard into the closet. It was like glimpsing at a photograph for a brief moment, then looking away and trying to remember what you saw. He thought he saw a few hangers and a lone suitcase on the floor. He stepped into the cave-like darkness and groped for the suitcase. Finding the handle, he dragged it into the open space of the room.

Its weight signaled it was not empty. There was definitely something in it. The lightning provided another snapshot. Something about it was familiar. Then it came to him. It was a piece of luggage of the style Dee owned, only a little smaller. The image of Dee's luggage was fresh in his mind. Otter had carried it out to Glenn

Sisson's truck the day Dee left for Fort Bragg.

Cautiously he picked up the suitcase with both hands and carried it across the room, setting it on the bed. He felt for the snaps on the ends and started to open it. Lightning flashed. This time the thunder did not immediately follow. The storm was moving on. Otter hesitated. He had seen something under the handle of the suitcase, something printed—initials? He waited. The lightning flashed again. No thunder. The light reflected again off the embossed initials under the handle—AFD. Otter felt his heartbeat increase once again and took a deep breath. Addison Foley Dumpkin. This was Dee's suitcase, he guessed. But why did his Uncle James have a suitcase belonging to Dee?

Otter squeezed the buttons on each of the two fasteners. They snapped open simultaneously. By the diminishing number of flashes, Otter could see that the assortment of clothes clearly belonged to a woman. Placed on top of the clothes was a heart-shaped pendant attached to a necklace. Otter recognized it as the kind that usually held a picture inside. He felt for the clip, holding it closed. With a little click it sprang open. Another flash of lightning revealed a tiny photograph of a baby. He walked to the window and waited for the lightning to flash again. It came. It definitely was a baby.

Otter set the necklace down next to the suitcase and searched through the clothing curious to see if there was anything else that might identify the belongings. He found a woman's wallet, the folded kind with the words "genuine leather" printed on the outside on the attached change-purse. He pushed the suitcase aside and sat down on the bed. Placing his thumb under the small leather strap that held the billfold closed, he popped it open. By the flashes of lightning he could see there were lots of pictures. Pictures of Dee and Ruth, and pictures of their two daughters. There were pictures of other teenagers that Otter did not recognize. There was a picture of a baby. It appeared to be the same baby as in the locket photograph, only larger. He pulled it from the clear vinyl pocket and turned it over. Nothing. He returned the picture to its place and opened the wallet to the back. There he recognized the familiar plastic-covered card—a driver's license. He noticed his hand shaking as he pulled it out. It belonged to Katherine Sue Dumpkin, his mother.

Otter reached down and felt for the necklace beside him on the bed and picked it up. As he opened the locket again, he felt his throat tighten and the tears coming. This is me in this picture, he realized. These are my mother's things. Otter began to feel dizzy as the thoughts crashed through his head. What did it all mean? Did his mother run away or not? If she did, then why did James have her belongings?

Otter felt anger beginning to creep up inside him. Why did James have these things? Suddenly his anger was interrupted by fear as the sound of coughing came from the hallway followed by the hawking of phlegm, then the spit. The toilet flushed.

Otter jumped up. He put the wallet back among the clothes along with the pendant and the driver's license. He tried to close the suitcase, but the clothes had begun to take on volume with their exposure to the air. Quickly he returned the open suitcase to the closet and set it down flat on the floor. He closed the closet door, taking care to be quiet but quick, and ran to the hall door and put his ear to it. Where was James now? Was he still in the bathroom? He felt the vibration of footsteps. Otter stepped away from the door, and looked down at the doorknob. Did he see it move? The lightening had all but ceased. Outside, dawn was breaking, but the new light was too poor to see clearly. It played tricks on his eyes.

Otter stood staring at the doorknob trying to decided if it was safe to open the door. He slowly turned the handle and stuck his head out into the hall. He could see no one. Stepping out of the room, he turned to close the door and lock it. He felt for the key beneath the knob. It wasn't there. Where was the key? He was sure he had left the key in the keyhole. He felt his pockets. No key. Where could it be? He must have dropped it on the bed or in the suitcase. Certainly if it had fallen on the floor he would have heard it.

Otter heard James moving in his room. He resolved that he would have to leave the door unlocked and hope that James would have no reason to enter. If he found the door unlocked, surely he would suspect that Otter had been there and discovered his secret. It was too late to return to the room to look for it. There was nothing he could do now.

Otter ran to the front room and jumped over the back of the sofa, coming to rest squarely on the sheet-covered cushions. With the blanket again tucked tightly beneath his chin, he listened to his uncle moving about in the back of the house, making little grunts and occasional sniffling sounds. He was proud of himself for discovering the secret and that his uncle was unaware of what he knew, at least for now. But what did he really know?—that in his great-uncle's house there was a suitcase belonging to his grandfather filled with his mother's belongings and a drawer containing an old newspaper with a headline about her missing? Was that all he knew? He frowned. Maybe he didn't know as much as he thought. After a moment of sorting it out, his frown turned into a smile. He was sure he had made an important discovery about his mother and that he would ultimately figure out what it all meant.

Chapter Six

James and Otter once again had their breakfast on the sidewalk in front of the drugstore. This time James did not feel the need to be so loud with his prayer. Otter looked for signs from James that he knew he had been in the room. He did not detect any.

Otter decided to go to school as he normally would, then, after school let out, stop at the diner and talk things over with Flora. It was time for him to talk to someone about his suspicions. But to his surprise, James was there to pick him up after school. They had not agreed that he would be there. Was he up to something? Now James *is* acting suspicious, Otter thought. But as it turned out James had taken the afternoon off to prepare for the opening of a tent-revival in Winter Grove that evening that would run Wednesday through Saturday. He thought it would be a good thing for Otter to attend. Otter was skeptical about the revival, but he was determined to find out more of what his uncle knew about his mother. He agreed to go.

 After an early supper at McDonald's on Highway 50 outside Lacey, James and Otter made their way to Winter Grove for the revival meeting. James said he would be "testifying" that evening. When Otter heard this, he pictured James swearing on the Bible, his hand in the air, promising to tell the truth, the whole truth, and nothing but the truth.

But when James got up later that evening during the revival and in his high piercing voice started shouting about the day he had been saved from a fiery hell and gave his life to Jesus, Otter knew that this was no courtroom, and that James' testimony stretched the definition of the truth. Otter had heard Dee speak of James' backsliding, his drinking and carousing around with unseemly women, women who somehow were convinced that this man of God had some kind of power to suspend God's judgement when it came to indulging in pleasures of the body.

It amazed Otter that the reserved little man he had come to know over the past few weeks could so quickly transform himself into such an emotional, verbose preacher. To most of the citizens of Lacey who knew him, James was not one to wear his feelings on his shirt sleeve. Yet when he preached at revivals, he was definitely a different man evidenced by the number of tears he shed. A standard part of his preaching was to recount how the burden of his guilt had one day become unbearable, then he would cry and act as if he could not thank Jesus enough for saving him. At revivals James tried desperately to wash himself clean of his past with a river of tears. But deep within his soul, he hated himself for clinging to a grace he peddled so cheaply. When he was in front of an unsuspecting audience, he lived in a different world, one where he and God were buddies, the mirror-image of each other. Many had been moved to come forward at his call to repentance and give their lives to Jesus Christ.

Otter listened for a while to James' testimony. But by the time James got around to recounting his trip to the University of Houston where the Lord had given him great success saving Cougar souls, Otter had had enough. Looking around the revival tent, he spotted another disinterested young boy who had slipped to the back of the tent and seemed to be having a good time with, of all things… a rabbit?

Otter glanced up at James, who was so caught up in his own story the entire congregation could have slipped away unnoticed. The self-proclaimed evangelist spoke tearfully into the stage lights positioned above the pulpit. As he spoke, he closed his eyes for dramatic affect, like an actor reciting a Shakespearean soliloquy. Otter shook his head in disgust then cut out by way of the side aisle, stepping on only a few toes as he scooted down the row to his freedom. He headed for the back of the tent.

He was right. It was a rabbit. Otter knelt down on a sawdust pile left over from making the walking path that formed the center aisle of the revival tent. The rabbit was held by what appeared to be a dog leash but was in fact just a plain piece of cord tied to a collar around the animal's neck.

"This your rabbit?" Otter asked, reaching out to pet the animal. It scurried away under a seat in the last row.

"Naw, it belongs to my sister. She raises rabbits," the boy replied. Otter guessed the boy was younger than him, probably in third grade. The idea that he was older gave him a sense of authority over the younger boy.

"What does she raise 'em for? To eat?" Otter thought he was being funny but the boy didn't seem to be amused.

"Speriments," the boy replied, tugging on the leash and looking seriously at Otter. The rabbit was about to get tangled around the leg of the chair. "She sells 'em to a lab over in Orlanda for seven-fifty each."

Otter had put together what the boy was saying when he mentioned the word lab. This rabbit was a guinea pig! Otter smiled again at his cleverness.

A woman with a bandage over her eye turned around and told the boys to hush up.

"She give you this one for a pet?" Otter whispered, looking up at the woman who had just shushed them, then down to the boy.

"Naw, she lets me take one out ever now and then just to play with. Daddy said I could bring it to meet'n tonight if I kept it tied up."

"What's going to happen to it when you take it back? Is it gonna go to the lab too?" Otter was beginning to imagine the rabbit's fate.

"Yeah, but it's okay. Daddy says these rabbits give their lives for us, just like Jesus."

Otter frowned. "Yeah, but they ain't gotta choice like Jesus did."

"Whataya mean?" This time the boy was frowning. "Daddy says Jehovah required a blood ransom and he gave Jesus up to be sacrificed so we wouldn't face a burn'n hell, and sister's rabbits give up their life so people don't get sick."

Otter was amazed. In the short time he had known his Uncle James, he had already become familiar with the blood ransom and the burning hell recitation. But comparing lab rabbits to Jesus? However, after mulling it over in his mind for a moment, Otter thought there might be some sense to it.

"Where's your daddy?" Otter asked.

The boy pointed to the front of the revival tent to a chair on stage. In it sat James' partner in evangelism, Brother Josiah Shelton. He was a slender man dressed in a modest black suit. His face was long and angular with high cheek bones, a pointed nose, and small puckered lips that made him look like he was tasting something bitter. Otter caught a gleam of the man's hair shining in the lights as he stood to announce the singing of a hymn. Then the blast of the Wurlitzer organ began and all the people stood up. The sudden loud music frightened the rabbit, and with a jerk on the cord, he was loose and on his way up the sawdust trail.

Otter watched as the rabbit scampered about halfway up the aisle, paused, then made a sharp left along a row of shoes, the cord dragging behind him. No one had noticed the escaped rabbit.

"You go down that side, and I'll walk up the middle aisle and try and scare him back your way," Otter said to the boy.

As he walked deliberately row by row searching for the rabbit, Otter wasn't aware of his uncle's teary invitation to the soul-sick sinners to come down front and give their life to Jesus and be saved. The crowd had just completed another verse of *Just As I Am Without One Plea* when Otter noticed the smiling faces of people looking at him. He stopped and looked to the front of the tent. James was waving him on down the aisle.

"Come on up here, son. The Lord is calling you

 home," James said enthusiastically.

Otter looked around. It appeared that every eye in the whole tent was looking in his direction. He bowed his head and tried to pretend that he was not aware of their gaze. Continuing the search, he glanced down another row. No rabbit. He stepped forward to the next row. No rabbit.

As Otter turned to backtrack a couple of rows, he ran smack into the woman with the patch over her eye.

"Go on, son, it's your time to get saved. Me, I'm gonna get healed." She gave Otter a little shove. He turned and walked again toward the front of the tent. He could feel the woman close on his heels, her hand lightly touching the middle of his back. An elderly woman with a cane stepped into the aisle from the left just ahead of them, then a sailor from the right side. The young man was twisting his cap into a tight spiral. Otter noticed the worried look on his face. The sailor hesitated as if to reconsider but then resumed his saving journey up the aisle.

Otter continued with the flow of souls inching along, bunched together as if they were joined by shackles. About the third row from the front, he glanced to his left. There in front of a shiny pair of cowboy boots sat the rabbit. Its nose twitched constantly, as if it was nibbling on something. Otter paused. The rabbit stood erect and the nibbling stopped. Caution! The rabbit sensed the approach of someone on hands and knees. Otter felt another nudge by the woman with the patch over her eye. Then he saw the little boy lunge for the leash. But the rabbit was off. It scurried right by Otter and headed again up the center aisle.

The procession of pilgrims froze dead still, each

having seen the scampering animal at about the same instant. The cord snagged briefly on the leg of one of the folding chairs, snapping the rabbit's head back. Otter crouched to grab the leash just as the procession resumed its march forward. He had it in his hand for only a second when he felt an enormous weight on his back, crushing him to the ground. The fleshy force shoved his face into the sawdust, and his right arm was caught under his body in a painful twisted position. The mass rolled off of him, and there before him lay the woman with the patch over her eye, staring at him face to face, not six inches away. The patch was gone from her eye, it was stuck on one of her very large breasts. Otter couldn't see that anything was wrong with the eye. Had the patch been over the left eye or the right one?

By now several in the crowd seated near the center aisle were aware of Otter's attempt to grab the rabbit, while others not as close to the action believed Otter and the large woman to be in such an emotional state that they were prostrating themselves before Almighty God in deepest humility, not an uncommon occurrence among revival regulars.

Otter had released the cord when the pain shot through his arm due to the woman's massive weight on it. The rabbit continued up the aisle. With a quick hop and a jump the rabbit found itself at center stage, ears cocked, eyes wide with terror, and still nervously twitching its nose. Otter looked up. Seeing the rabbit sitting there, the thought crossed his mind that it, too, might be seeking salvation. From the lab? Otter winced as the pain in his arm brought him back to his own predicament.

With the help of a man in a blue suit that looked much too small for him, Otter got to his feet. The man, a deacon assisting the evangelist, was one of several men escorting the about-to-be-saved to the stage. Otter looked up and his eyes caught the fiery glare of his Uncle James who stepped out from behind the pulpit to receive the throng of the sinful. James' shoe was on the cord. Did he know it? The rabbit made a quick bolt to escape but the leash jerked its neck again, causing it some momentary disorientation. Its legs quivered briefly, then it regained its footing and sat back on its haunches, still nibbling.

James motioned to one of the deacons to bring Otter up on the stage. Otter knew his uncle was not going to be made a fool of. James offered a fake chuckle and made a clicking noise with his tongue. "Seems we got a critter among us. Judg'n by the leash, it ain't a wild one. This rabbit belong to somebody here?" The owner of the rabbit tiptoed to the front of the stage. James' eyes turned to the shaking boy.

"This your rabbit, son?"

The boy nodded his head in acknowledgment then glanced over at his father, who had regained his place in the large padded chair at the side of the stage. His father's eyes were squinty now, matching his puckered lips.

"Come get 'im," James said, reaching down to grab the cord from under his foot. He picked up the cord and gave it a little jerk, just hard enough to be satisfied that the animal was aware of his anger, then he handed it to the boy.

The boy pulled the rabbit to him, gathered him up in his arms and vanished down the center aisle. Unnoticed were the several round rabbit droppings on the stage where the rabbit had sat.

The crowd was directed to be seated as the lights above them were turned down and the stage lights turned up. James moved toward Otter, who had been tempted to bolt with the boy and his rabbit but was frozen by his uncle's stare. James' eyes were fixed on Otter's and he could see in them the perverse glee he was taking in the moment. Suddenly James halted. The satisfied look on his face had turned to disgust. Otter glanced down and noticed the rabbit droppings next to James' shoe. He had stepped squarely onto the little pile. Otter could see on James' face that he knew what he had stepped in. Biting his lip, Otter bowed his head, feigning a prayerful pose and tried to keep from grinning. He knew that any hint of a snicker would only further enrage the man.

Otter looked up again just as his great-uncle's hand came to rest on his shoulder. Firmly but inconspicuously, James dug his bony thumb into the sunken place just above the boy's collar bone. To the audience it must have appeared that Otter was being gently led to center stage for the climactic confession of sins. Otter's face flashed a painful grimace, but his back was to the crowd and no one was in a position to notice.

James spoke in his high twangy voice.

"It does me proud that my great-nephew, my poor deceased sister's only grandchild, has come to give his life to the Lord Jesus Christ and be baptized, to be saved from Satan's fiery hell."

Otter was not ready for this. He felt like running, but his uncle's grip kept him fixed in place. For a skinny shrimp of a man, he sure has a strong grip, Otter thought to himself.

"Will brother Shelton allow me the honor of asking my great-nephew the question asked of all who seek to be saved by the blood of Jesus and who come to be baptized into his goodly salvation?" James looked over to the rabbit boy's father, who nodded his head and raised his hands to the sky.

"Hallelujah! Praise Jesus! Do it friend," came the enthusiastic reply.

Otter felt dizzy. Baptism? Did he hear the word baptism? He was beginning to sweat. He had heard of the strange rituals that some self-proclaimed revivalists put converts through. Not a few unsuspecting converts had endured a dunking almost to the point of drowning, in cow ponds where there was more than washed away sins floating on the water. In no way was Otter going to submit to that!

Otter felt his uncle's hand tighten again on his shoulder. James wheeled him around to face the gawking crowd anxious for something bizarre to happen. The pilgrims who had come forward were still waiting at center aisle in single file, a deacon standing next to each one jotting down juicy details of sins or sickness. The woman with the patch on her bosom had returned it to her eye. Wasn't it on the other side before?

By now, several older boys had left the tent to spread the word among the bored and unconvinced that a baptizing was imminent. Excitement was in the air.

The stage lights were blinding. Otter could see only the first two rows of the excited crowd. He was beginning to feel sick.

James closed his eyes and raised his free hand into the air, "O Lord Jesus, another young sinner has come to this holy tabernacle to be saved from eternal damnation.

He leaves his filthy ways behind, desiring to be washed in the blood of the Lamb!"

James paused, then cleared his throat. About to pop the saving question to his great-nephew, the wiry preacher realized he could not remember the boy's given name. He had always detested the fact that he had kin who went by the name of some squirrelly animal. He was not going to announce to God and everybody that "Otter" was about to be saved.

"What's your real name, boy?" James whispered, trying not to be conspicuous.

"Otter."

"You know what I mean," James shot back in a fierce whisper. Otter could feel the grip tightening.

"Otter Dumpkin." Otter knew what his uncle wanted, but he was determined not to give him his real name—Millard Fillmore Dumpkin.

James gave in, but didn't give up. He wasn't going to let the boy get the best of him. He looked beyond the lights out into the darkness of the tent.

"Do you, young man, believe on the Lord Jesus as your personal savior and by his blood, do you believe that you are saved from the eternal damnation of Satan's fiery hell?" The squeeze tightened. Otter refused to answer despite the mounting pain.

Finally, unable to stand it any longer, Otter issued a muffled "Yes sir."

"What was that, young man? Shout it out and let the whole world know that JEESUS lives in your heart!" The thumb dug in even deeper.

"Yes sir." The pain increased, but still Otter resisted any coercion to be enthusiastic.

"What's that you say?" James asked, applying more pressure.

The pain became too much.

"I said YES, goddammit!" Otter shouted.

The crowd let out a collective gasp.

Stunned, James loosened his grip on Otter just long enough to signal to the frightened boy that he had better get while the gett'n was good. He bolted.

James stood as if paralyzed, watching the boy disappear through a flap in the tent. He couldn't believe what had just happened. Finally, he shook his head, bringing himself out of his stupor.

"Brother Shelton, uh, while I go find the boy would you please direct the deacons to prepare the gathered for a baptism?"

The evangelist looked a little surprised at the request. The crowd had begun a confused murmur. Their shepherd was about to abandon them to pursue this one lost sheep.

"Where do you plan to do it, James?" the evangelist asked, "Can't we wait 'til tomorrow? I'm sure we can use the pool at the Baptist Church."

"We're doin' it now, right outside there in Keller's pond." James snorted. Then, not to be deterred, he was off and running in hot pursuit of his nephew.

The rabbit boy's father raised his hands and addressed the crowd.

"People! Brothers and sisters, please stay calm. The boy's just a little nervous about it all, but Brother Fisher will settle him down and we will proceed with the, uh, hmm, baptism." The crowd had quieted, but at the pronouncement of baptism, the murmur picked up again.

The rabbit boy pushed his way back to the front of the tent where his father stood. He couldn't believe what his father was saying. He felt bad for the boy who was only trying to help him get his rabbit back. How did all this happen? Where was the boy now?

The rabbit boy's father jumped from the stage and took one of the deacons by the arm.

"Tommy, you and the other deacons move the folks out to the pond, and bring those extra floodlights and extension cords we got back there behind the stage. We ain't never done a baptism at night here, but I think there's power in Keller's barn."

The deacon, sensing the urgency in the evangelist's voice, gave a little salute and headed off to carry out his assignment.

"Oh, and Tommy," the evangelist added, "when you're done there, get Burton and give Brother Fisher and me a hand rounding up the boy." After another quick salute, the deacon was off again.

Brother Josiah Shelton climbed back on the stage. Just below him at the front of the stage was the woman with the patch over her eye, the sailor, the woman with the cane and several others who had expected salvation and healing. In the disruption they had been abandoned. The evangelist looked at them sympathetically and gave a slight shrug as he shouted over the low roar of the exiting crowd, "Can y'all come back tomorrow?" Without waiting for a reply he stepped to the microphone and, as if he were the captain of a ship, bellowed out the words, "Now hear this, a baptism will take place over at Keller's pond in fifteen minutes. I repeat, a baptism will take place out at Keller's pond in fifteen minutes." He paused, then added, "Oh, and bring your hymn books." Then he disappeared beyond the stage lights into the darkness to help find a frightened boy that he wasn't sure was ready for baptizing.

Chapter Seven

The area immediately surrounding the revival tent was potentially dangerous. Heavy ropes holding the tent upright were attached to solid hardwood stakes pounded two-thirds their length into the ground. The exposed third could tear up a toe real quick. Josiah Shelton had kicked his share of stakes and nearly hung himself on the ropes enough times to know to proceed cautiously as he exited the tent to help James find the boy.

The large circus-style tent was situated in the middle of a makeshift baseball field between left-center and second base. John Keller, the owner of the property, had constructed his own "field of dreams," but the only thing people showed up for were these revival meetings. Being a sometime-member of First Baptist Church in Winter Grove, John saw it as his mission to provide space to the evangelists. He didn't mind the revivals. In fact, when the evangelists promised him a percentage of the offering collected on Fridays, the evening that attracted the biggest and most generous crowd, he began to attend some of the meetings himself. And he allowed them to use the pond for baptisms free of charge.

Most of the assorted automobiles belonging to those attending the revival were parked in several rows along the east side of the tent. The roofs of the shinier vehicles reflected the star-filled sky and the half moon rising in the eastern sky. Otter found himself crouching over as he moved through the maze of vehicles. Occasionally his head would bob up to see who might be coming his way. He wasn't sure where he was going. Then he spotted James, who had retrieved a flashlight from his own car and begun a search for the boy. The rabbit boy's father had joined him. After making a plan, the two headed in opposite directions.

Though it was unusually cool for the last night of spring, Otter found himself sweating profusely. He could feel his heart pumping and knew that his adrenaline had his body running in overdrive.

"Where do I go?" he asked himself. He sat down and leaned up against the back wheel of a dilapidated Chevy Impala. The slight scent of oil toyed with his sense of smell, reminding him of Dee and the times when they would change the oil in his truck. A lump began to rise in his throat. He felt like crying. But what good would that do him now? he chided himself.

The thought of Dee encouraged him. Then he heard footsteps. At first they appeared to be moving fast and coming from his left. Otter stiffened. Slowly he got to his feet, remaining crouched behind the old car. Something moved to his right. Was it the rabbit boy's father? Was he surrounded? Otter raised his head to get another look. His Uncle James was fast heading his way, shining his flashlight side to side as he walked. Otter knew he had to make a run for it. But where? And what about the rabbit boy's father? He raised up again. James was close.

Otter turned and scrambled quickly to the back of the car next to the Chevy. He had to get out of James' path. He inched up to have another look. James had moved passed him and now had his back to Otter. Turning to put more distance between himself and his uncle, Otter rounded the back of a minivan at full speed and ran smack into someone. His first thought was that he had run into the rabbit boy's father, but this person was too small. Otter had bowled over whoever it was and now found himself lying on top of the person.

The rabbit sniffed at Otter's nose as he lay on the ground wondering if he had been caught. He breathed a sigh of relief. It was the rabbit boy, not his father. Otter bounced up and helped the boy to his feet. The minivan was tall enough to permit Otter to stand upright without fear of being detected by his uncle.

"What are you doing out here?" Otter whispered.

"I thought maybe I could help you escape," the boy replied. Otter smiled at hearing the word escape. He imagined himself a spy fleeing the Nazi SS.

Suddenly a light flashed through the window of the minivan. Otter pulled the boy down to a crouched position. Again the footsteps. They were close.

"Quick, get under the van!" Otter whispered. He knew they had to act fast. The rabbit boy squirmed under the minivan with his rabbit under one arm. Otter quickly followed, rolling over on his back, then with another roll he was on his stomach again. He was pressed tightly against the boy, who was practically lying on top of his scared pet, embracing it with one arm and holding its head under his chin. Otter could smell the peculiar scent of rabbit fur.

"Do you see 'im?"

"Shhh." Otter put his hand over the rabbit boy's mouth.

Then the shoes appeared. Otter could see them—two cars over. The peculiar looking wingtipped shoes draped by cuffed trousers moved slowly from behind the Chevy toward the minivan. They stopped. James had heard the grunting sounds caused by Otter's collision with the rabbit boy and had backtracked. He was barely ten feet away. The two boys lay motionless. Could he hear their breathing, Otter wondered? His heart was racing but strangely he didn't feel scared. In his mind he was the righteous warrior still escaping from the Nazi SS. The light flashed to the ground. James took another step and stopped. The light disappeared. They were still undetected. Then Otter saw the cord. A portion of the homemade rabbit leash extended about a foot out from under the minivan.

The light appeared on the ground again, forming a bright ring in front of the shoes. The shoes resumed their step. James rounded the minivan. The ring of light moved forward and fell on the cord. The shoes stopped. A hand appeared not two feet away from Otter. It grasped the cord. Otter felt the first gentle tug of the cord under his body. The rabbit began to squirm. The second tug was more forceful. Feeling the tug, the rabbit boy held tighter to the rabbit. Otter's eyes were fixed on the shoes. The cord dropped to the ground. Then a hand touched the ground. Then a knee. Then a face. The light flashed bright into Otter's eyes, blinding him momentarily.

"Run!" Otter yelled to the rabbit boy. The hand lunged under the vehicle. To avoid his uncle's grasp, Otter made an attempt to roll away and banged his shoulder on the exhaust pipe. The light suddenly disappeared. The underside of the minivan was again dark. Otter guessed that James would circle to the other side of the minivan. He was right. Glancing to the rear of the vehicle, he saw the ring of light followed by James' shoes. The rabbit boy was already out from under the minivan and standing. Otter knew that he would not have time to make it out and quickly rolled back in the other direction. The light rounded the van.

"Come 'ere you little...," James made a grunting sound as he grabbed the rabbit boy.

"Leave me alone!" The rabbit boy started crying.

Scrambling to his feet, Otter could see James through the windows. The light flashed in his direction. Otter took off as fast as his feet could take him. James released the rabbit boy and pursued his nephew.

Otter noticed a stand of pines at the edge of center field. Leaving the security of the parked cars, he headed out in the open toward the trees. As he ran he could see the crowd gathered near the pond about 200 yards to his right. The pond was lit with two enormous spotlights that gave it the appearance of a crime scene.

Otter paused to catch his breath. He turned and saw James in pursuit, but he was still a good 50 yards back. James had slowed considerably and was limping. Unknown to Otter, the rabbit boy had bought him some time by tripping James up on the rabbit leash. James had fallen hard and injured his knee.

Out of the corner of his eye, Otter saw something moving. He turned to see that two young boys had broken from the crowd and were running toward him. Slowly, the crowd turned its attention to the action across the field. The rabbit boy's father followed the boys for a few steps, then halted.

"I've gotta get out of here," Otter thought to himself. In a flash he was off again, heading for the trees. As he ran, a voice from behind him began shouting. It sounded like James, but Otter could not make out what he was saying. Surprised that the voice sounded so close, Otter shot a quick glance over his shoulder. It was the wrong time to take his eye off his path. A gopher hole appeared out of nowhere. Fortunately he didn't step squarely into it, which would surely have broken his leg, but his foot did catch the edge of the hole, enough to upset his balance. His momentum carried him crashing to the ground with a thud.

Before Otter realized what had happened, he felt his uncle's hand on him. Gasping for breath, James held his nephew down and pushed his face hard into the grass. Two long shadows bounced across the ground, announcing the arrival of the boys. As they drew closer, they slowed and approached with caution, keeping a safe distance between them and the angry evangelist who held the young boy on the ground as if he were some wild animal that would bolt or strike if the man let him go.

"Go get Brother Shelton!" James shouted angrily. The boys froze. "D'you hear me! Get your little asses over there and get Josiah Shelton! Now!"

The boys took off like rockets back toward the lights. Still trying to catch his breath, James looked down at Otter.

"You're goin' in that water, boy, even if it kills you. And that wouldn't be no loss."

Otter tried to move, but his uncle had him pinned firmly to the ground, holding one arm cocked behind his back and the full weight of his skinny body bearing down.

"That'd be just like you, you murderer! Your soul's the one that needs saving!" Otter muttered, his jaw barely able to move.

"Shut up, boy. God doesn't listen to little bastards like you. You're his shame," James replied.

"You're a liar! And if there is a fiery hell, you'll be first in line!" Otter shot back.

James was really angry now. He leaned harder on the boy.

"I know you murdered my mother!" Otter blurted out. The words just popped out, a knee-jerk reaction in an attempt to return some of the hurt his uncle was causing him. For a moment Otter wondered if James would kill him right there.

"You don't know jack, boy, so shut up!" James said, pushing Otter's face harder into the ground. As much as Otter did not want to give his uncle the satisfaction of seeing him cry, the tears came.

Brother Shelton arrived with the two boys.

"Help me get him over to the pond," James said. "He's feeling the emotion of his sins. He'll feel better after he's passed through the waters."

The rabbit boy's father and the two boys helped James up. He let go of Otter's arm but kept a firm grip on his neck and shoulders.

The crowd grew silent as James and Brother Shelton approached with Otter. The powerful spotlights reflected off their faces. It was clear that Otter was crying. His tears washed away some the dirt that was caked on one side of his face, leaving little streaks that, from a distance, looked like scars.

"He's just fine," James announced to the crowd. "The Holy Ghost got in him and he's a little emotional from it, but he'll be fine. Turn in your hymn books to Hymn 123. Burton, lead them in a few verses of *Washed in the Blood*." The crowd began to sing.

"Hold the boy for a minute while I put on my waders," James whispered to Brother Shelton. Otter tried to squirm free but the evangelist's big hands were too strong.

The rubber fisherman waders had been brought down to the edge of the pond by one of the deacons. James stepped into the waders and pulled them up to just below his armpits and placed his arms through the suspenders. He was determined to step into the water without it touching him.

The crowd parted as James walked to the edge of the pond. At the the muddy shore, he turned and motioned Brother Shelton to bring the boy. Again Otter tried to resist but Brother Shelton tightened his grip.

"You're gonna be okay, son. It's only natural to be a little nervous, but you'll feel better when it's over," Brother Shelton said, trying his best to be sincere.

James took Otter by the arm and stepped down into the pond. Otter, shoes and all, followed his step. The still, brown water didn't feel quite as cool as Otter expected. It was warmer than the air temperature which, at nine o'clock, was nearing a pleasant seventy-two degrees.

James led Otter out into the water to a place where it

was just above the boy's waist. Otter had the feeling that he was about to be executed. But he was not afraid. To the contrary, a sense of confidence came over him as he stood in the familiar element.

James turned the boy around so that he was facing the crowd. From his position down in the water with the spotlights casting their light on the scene, Otter could see only the most anxious of on-lookers who had pressed their way to the shoreline. Off to the left he saw the small figure of the rabbit boy standing apart from the crowd. He was crying as he held tight to the rabbit. The boy looked at Otter and, choked by tears, shuddered. At that moment Otter saw the rabbit's lifeless body fall to the ground. The little boy gathered it up again in his arms and sobbed. Otter felt his anger returning.

James stopped his incantations and prepared for the dunking. He placed his hand in the small of Otter's back and braced himself to support the boy's weight. With a slight shove from his uncle, Otter slowly fell back into the embrace of the water. Any look of satisfaction showing on James' face was short-lived. Before he even had a chance to raise Otter from the water, the evangelist felt a foot slam hard into his belly. He gasped hard, making a painful grunting sound as the air was forced from his body. With another powerful kick, Otter easily slipped from his uncle's grasp and was gone.

Gasping for air and thrashing the water to regain his balance, James fought to keep from going under. Quickly, the waders began to fill with water. The weight became too much for James to hold up. He sank to the bottom.

Otter surfaced just long enough for another breath of air and to see his uncle go down like a ship bound for

Davy Jones' locker. Several bystanders had jumped into the pond to help the evangelist. Otter submerged again. His feet found the bottom and he pushed hard propelling his body away from the artificial light into the muddy darkness to the opposite shore some one hundred feet away. The smooth effortless motion of his arms pulling the water past him as his legs pushed off the bottom, felt good to Otter. He thought he could stay under forever.

Otter sensed a change in the pond's depth. He had been under for about half a minute and was confident that he was nearing the shore. He surfaced. Quickly, he turned to see who might be in pursuit. There was no one. Across the pond he could see that several deacons were dragging James to shore but were unable to lift anything but his head out of the water due to the enormous weight of his water-filled waders. The crowd seemed to be enjoying the spectacle, and few if any paid attention to the head that emerged from the dark water on the opposite shore.

Otter turned to pull himself out of the water and was startled to see a figure in the darkness. It was the rabbit boy. Through all the commotion, he had seen Otter make his escape to freedom just below the surface of the water.

"You'll most likely need this," the boy said, holding out his jacket to Otter. Otter took the jacket. He nodded his appreciation, but his eyes were fixed on the rabbit.

"What happened?" Otter asked.

The boy looked down at the rabbit. "That man kilt him when I tripped him up on the leash to keep him from gett'n you. He rung his neck and threw him on the ground." Tears flowed again from the rabbit boy's eyes.

Otter reached out and embraced the boy and the rabbit.

"Do you think rabbits go to heaven if they give their life for somebody?" the boy sobbed.

"I believe you already know the answer to that," Otter replied.

The boy looked up and managed a smile. "You better hurry and git 'fore they come," he said, looking back across the pond. Otter put on the light jacket and followed the rabbit boy's gaze to the other side. James was struggling to get to his feet, having slipped on some mud after being freed from the waders. Clearly angry and in pain, he pushed away a woman who approached to put a blanket around him.

Otter turned to the rabbit boy and gave him another hug.

"What's your name? I don't even know your name." Otter asked, as he stepped back to hear the boy's reply.

"Josiah, like my daddy, but people call me Josey."

Otter put his hand on the boy's shoulder. "Josey, if there is a God, I'm sure you're one of his favorites." Then he reached over and tenderly stroked the rabbit's fur. "And him too."

The rabbit boy smiled at Otter. "Where're you headed?" he asked.

"I don't know, but I'll think of something." Otter said. He smiled back at the boy then turned to leave. "You take care now, you hear?"

"I will." Josey replied.

Otter ran across right field of Keller's "field of dreams" toward the pine forest that had eluded him earlier. His water-soaked trousers felt cold on his legs as he moved through the night air. When he reached the stand of trees, he stopped to catch his breath. Holding on to a sapling to steady himself, he turned for one last look. One of the "crime scene lights" had been extinguished, and the crowd was dispersing. James was nowhere to be seen.

"He's probably in the revival tent rounding up a posse to come after me," Otter mused. He imagined himself on horseback, fleeing a posse led by James.

The last light went out, leaving the pond in darkness. Only a few lights near the revival tent remained lit. What now? Otter asked himself. Then all at once it came to him. He knew exactly where to go.

Chapter Eight

Otter made his way through the tall pines not quite sure where he would come out. Over the years dried pine needles had formed a spongy carpet around the trees that prevented the growth of underbrush. He was able to move quickly, and was glad of it.

It didn't take Otter long to get his bearings and to picture in his mind just where in Winter Grove Flora lived. There he would find a safe place, if he could find it before Uncle James found him.

Otter remembered two landmarks connected with Flora's neighborhood: the railroad tracks and Ninth Street. He knew that if he could locate the railroad tracks and follow them east toward Lacey, he would eventually come to Ninth Street, which intersected the tracks in what many in Lacey and Winter Grove still referred to as "nigger town." Otter hated that name and associating it with Flora, or anyone for that matter, made him angry.

His recollection was that Flora actually lived on Ninth

Street, and he figured that once he was in the general area, things would begin to look familiar. After all, as far back as he could remember he had accompanied Dee to Winter Grove to return Flora home from the diner after it closed on Friday evenings. Most days Flora drove her old Buick "deuce-and-a-quarter," as she called it, the six miles from her home in Winter Grove to the diner in Lacey. She was the breakfast cook at the diner and assisted Dee at lunch when business usually picked up. Only on Fridays when the diner served its crowd-pleasing catfish and hushpuppies special did she stay late into the evening to help close up.

As he continued to move through the woods, Otter recalled how horrified he had been when he learned why Flora didn't drive herself home on Fridays. He remembered vividly his conversation with Dee that night on the dark, lonely Lacey-Winter Grove road, as the old pickup sped them home after having dropped Flora off at her house. Why he had not inquired sooner he did not know.

"She's afraid to drive in Lacey after dark," Dee said, almost as if he expected Otter to know the answer.

The response confused Otter. He sat still for a moment, staring at the dashed centerline of the highway racing by in the headlights. Then he simply asked, "Why?"

"Black people have never been welcome in Lacey except as maids or cooks or gardeners and the such," he said. " Years ago, if a black was seen in Lacey after dark, he risked being found the next day strung up in some tree, or in a ditch somewhere shot through the head."

Otter swallowed hard. He had seen pictures of such atrocities on TV.

"Does that still happen?" he asked.

"Naw, a black person might get harassed every now and then, but nobody's been lynched around here for a long time."

"Then why is Flora still afraid to drive home after dark?" Otter was puzzled.

"Fear is a powerful thing. When you've suffered so much, it's hard to forget. I guess she's got her reasons."

"What reasons?" Otter asked.

"If I remember right, years ago, her granddaddy was lynched and some of her family killed in a riot. I asked my daddy about it after seeing some mention of it in a Florida history book when I was in college."

This is scary, Otter thought. He swallowed hard. "What did it say?"

"It said that back around 1920, a black man had tried to exercise his right to vote in Lacey and ended up being lynched. Evidently it caused such a stir that after it was over, several other black people had been killed and a number of their houses burned to the ground, including a church." Dee paused then shook his head and began to laugh.

"What's so funny about that?" Otter shouted, clearly hurt by his grandfather's response. The sudden anger and disappointment he felt toward Dee confused and frightened him.

"No, no, Bud!" The pain in Otter's voice caught Dee by surprise, and he reached out across the seat to console him and began gently rubbing his grandson's neck.

"I wasn't laughing at that. I just found it strange what my daddy said when I asked him about it." Dee paused and took in a deep breath. "I remember Daddy saying that the guy who wanted to vote was drunk. When I asked him more about it, he just sat there silent with a blank expression on his face." Dee's voice betrayed a sadness. The light from the dashboard illumined his face and Otter thought he detected tears beginning to glisten in his eyes. He waited for what seemed like a very long time for his grandfather to continue. Finally, Dee turned and looked at Otter. He reached down and patted his grandson on his knee.

"I suppose if a man's drunk and wants to vote, that's good enough reason to lynch 'im, kill a few of his friends, then burn down their houses and their church, don't you?" The sarcasm in Dee's voice was plenty thick for Otter to know how he really felt about it all. Dee shook his head. "Sometimes you gotta wonder what gets into people to make 'em act like that."

Otter sat quiet. He had not recognized how tense his body had become. Detecting Dee's sarcasm, he began to relax a little.

The stand of trees ended and in the clearing beyond, Otter could make out a road. It was a hard top—a paved road. As he moved toward it, he barely avoided getting his feet wet again when a small drainage ditch appeared out of the darkness next to the road. The reflection of the moon off the water that remained in the ditch from recent rains caught his eye in time. He sized up the drainage ditch that separated him from the pavement and readied himself to make the leap. With ease he cleared the stream of water and walked out to the middle of the road. He looked both ways. Not a car in sight.

The moon was just about straight over head. Otter

guessed it to be about ten o'clock. He reasoned that he had to walk north to intersect the railroad tracks, which he knew ran east and west between Lacey and Winter Grove.

"North would probably be that way," he whispered, turning right and pointing straight up the highway. To be sure, he found the Big Dipper high in the sky and projected up along an imaginary line that formed the front of the dipper. "Follow the drinking gourd," he recited, remembering the line from a story he had read at school about the Underground Railroad before the Civil War. For a moment he imagined what it must have been like to be a runaway slave looking for the route to freedom in the North. Locating the North Star, he congratulated himself that his instincts had been right and indeed he was headed north.

As he walked along, headlights appeared from a car that had turned onto the road in his direction about a mile ahead. As it approached Otter saw that the lights outlined the silhouette of a railroad crossing sign several hundred yards up the road. Otter jumped the ditch again and hid among the trees. He could hear the drone of the engine as it approached gaining more and more speed. Then the car slowed momentarily, and Otter heard the familiar bump-bump-bump-bump as the tires crossed the railroad tracks. The vehicle then sped past and out of sight.

Otter found the road again in the dark and made his way to the crossing. Turning right and following east along the tracks, he walked for what he guessed to be at least a mile. The steel rails, worn shiny by the regular schedule of freight trains carrying citrus fruit to processing plants outside Winter Grove, shone bright in the moonlight. Otter walked the rails for a while, his hands extended like a tightrope artist, until he grew tired keeping his balance. Then he walked on the ties, traversing every other one with long strides.

After about half an hour, he could see some lights ahead. Several cars passed over the tracks heading south. Soon Otter began to see the lights of houses shining through the large live oaks that now began to replace the pines growing near the tracks. He suspected that he was not far from Flora's house.

At the crossing Otter paused to check his bearings. Judging by the lights he could see through the trees, he surmised that most of the town was to the north of the tracks. He breathed easier and congratulated himself that again, his instincts had been correct. In his mind he pictured that Winter Grove would appear on his left.

As he approached the next crossing, another car appeared, this time from his right. Otter froze. The vehicle barely slowed as it crossed the track. The beams of light shot past his feet by inches. He stood in the dark and watched the car disappear around the next corner. Had it been broad daylight, he would easily have been seen.

Otter wondered if it had been James in that car? Did it resemble Uncle James' Ford Escort wagon? he asked himself. In the dark he had not been able to make out the color. Was it red like James'? He didn't think it was, but he wasn't sure.

"He wouldn't be going home this way," Otter thought to himself. "Unless, maybe, there's a search party out looking for me."

He moved onto the crossing and looked both ways. No cars. On his left in the next block, a streetlight revealed a side street intersection. He thought he could make out a street sign at the corner under the light. Otter left the rails and jogged up the road toward the light, slowing to a walk from time to time to check behind him for approaching cars. So far, so good. Nearing the corner, Otter could see street names on the signs. He smiled. "Third Street," he said out loud to himself. The cross street was Oak Street.

Otter predicted that Oak Street paralleled the railroad track and that the next street north would be Fourth Street, then Fifth, then Sixth, all the way to Ninth Street. Should I go up Oak or should I go back to the tracks, he wondered. Less chance of being seen if I stay on the tracks. Somebody might call the cops if they see a white kid walking around a black neighborhood, he thought. The thought struck Otter as odd.

He looked up Oak Street then back to the railroad tracks. Anxious to get to Flora's as soon as possible, he decided to stay in the shadows of Oak's canopy of trees and resumed his journey east.

Otter knew that in many ways, segregation of blacks and whites was still a way of life in many small towns in Florida and even some of the larger ones. Despite its dissolution in public institutions, segregation remained a reality in Winter Grove's society as well as Lacey's—its social clubs, its churches, its neighborhoods. As Otter walked past home after dilapidated home along Oak, he was reminded again of something Dee had said to him. " Everybody has their prejudices, whites and blacks. But not everyone has the power to enforce them. Racism is prejudice plus power." As on many other occasions when he had visited Flora's neighborhood, Otter felt embarrassed. It just isn't right, he thought to himself.

Why does she have to live here? Why can't she live next door to me?

As he approached Ninth Street, Otter's thoughts were interrupted, when a large dog ran out from under the porch of a nearby house, and announced with dreadful barking that he knew the boy was there and that he'd better not try anything. Otter stood still, trying not to appear afraid nor a threat as the dog approached. After a few sniffs, the dog lost interest and returned to his bed under the porch.

Otter recognized Flora's house, surrounded by huge live oaks. The bright porch light reflected off the front walls of the house, leaving the sides in dark shadows, and making it appear two-dimensional. It was a small wooden structure with a front porch that wrapped around one side of the house. At the end of the porch Otter could see the familiar wood swing suspended from the ceiling by chains. It swayed gently in the evening breeze. He recalled a time not so long ago when he and Dee had been invited to Flora's on her birthday and how much fun it was to swing on the swing with her. He remembered it made a comforting creaking sound as it moved back and forth.

The house was constructed on concrete block pilings that raised it almost three feet off the ground, high enough that an adult man could crawl easily around underneath without bumping his head. No grass covered the ground around the house, just hard packed sand and leaves. The towering live oaks which seldom lost their leaves provided such good shade that grass could not survive. Otter was careful not to trip over the tree roots that radiated out from the trunks for several feet along the ground before they dove deep to find water.

As he was about to climb the three wood steps to the porch, Otter heard a car coming up the street. He could see the lights approaching. Quickly, he moved up the steps and to his left along the porch, then around the corner out of the light, and into the shadows.

The car approached slowly. Otter peeked out around the corner, then lurched back. Dang it! I knew it! Just as he feared, it was James. Otter moved well back into the shadows. To be sure that he had a way to escape if he were detected by his uncle, he surveyed the surroundings. I can exit off the back of the porch if I have to, he thought.

The car stopped with a slight squeak of the brakes. The headlights went dark and the hum of the engine was silenced. Otter could hear the door of the car open, followed by the grunting sounds of his uncle as he struggled to get out. Was there anyone else with James? Perhaps there were others in another car parked up the street, he thought.

He chased from his mind images of being pursued by James' posse, and did his best to calm himself and steady his breathing. He thought of Dee and knew that he would approve of his decision to run from James and come to Flora's.

James was mumbling something as he rounded the car and moved slowly toward the house. He was clearly upset. Otter could hear the heavy breathing of his uncle as he made his way to the door, taking what seemed forever to ascend the steps. Once James was on the porch Otter could feel his uncle's weight as each step sent tiny vibrations through the wood structure. He pressed himself tight against the wall in the darkness. His uncle was so close Otter wondered if he might even be able to hear his breathing.

The screen door creaked as James opened it and knocked on the front door. The pounding of his fist was loud and rough and caused Otter's stomach to feel sick. He was afraid he might start crying. After taking in a slow deep breath and letting it out easy, he felt better.

There was no answer at the door. The pounding repeated. Then Otter heard the screen door close. James let out a deep sigh and again mumbled something unintelligible. The sound of footsteps made Otter think James had turned to leave. But the sound did not fade away down the steps to the car. Instead, he heard the slow limping rhythm of the footsteps coming straight toward him. Surely he doesn't know I'm hiding here, Otter thought to himself. Sweat formed on his forehead. Should I run? If he rounds the corner he's gonna run right into me!

Otter leaned backed into the shadow, pressing hard against the wall. The pained footsteps grew louder. Suddenly, James appeared. Otter stiffened. He was ready to bolt. But to his relief, James did not turn the corner. Instead, the tired-looking man headed for the swing.

Otter watched intently as James inched his way into the swing, each movement accompanied by a painful grunt or groan. With a deep sigh he unloaded his weight into the swing and began rubbing his knee. As it swayed, the swing seemed to issue a protesting squeak rather than the pleasant creak Otter remembered.

Otter was amazed that his uncle could not see him. But the contrast of light and darkness was stark and played tricks on the eyes. For a long time James stared straight ahead at the front door as if he could will someone to appear. At one point, he sucked in a deep nasal breath and caught up some phlegm. Collecting it on his tongue, he let go an enormous wad into the air off the front of the porch.

James fumbled around in his coat pocket for something. He produced a pack of cigarettes, took one out, and put it into his mouth. Otter again pressed against the house as if doing so would somehow make darker the shadow hiding him. He knew that the light from a match or a cigarette lighter would penetrate the shadow enough to expose him. Maybe the time to run is now, he thought. The element of surprise is still mine. James will certainly not catch me on foot with that limp.

It was a lighter, one of the small, cheap throwaway kind. James fumbled with it, rolling the little wheel with his thumb, creating tiny sparks off the flint. It wasn't catching. He mumbled his protest to the lighter, and the cigarette fell from his mouth onto floor. James reached down to recover his cigarette, grunting as he groped for it. He found it. Then, as if something had caught his eye, he looked into the darkness toward Otter. Suddenly, the front door opened, and a familiar but sleepy voice broke the tense silence.

"Who's there?" Flora's voice was firm, and there was no fear in it. If it had been a burglar, he had come to the wrong house. Flora shaded her eyes from the bright porch light. "Is that you, Jimmy Fisher?"

James inched off the porch swing and flicked his unlit cigarette into the darkness, hitting Otter on the chin. Had he seen him?

"Yes, ma'am. It's James Fisher, Miss Flora. I'm looking for little Millard." James paused. Otter knew that his uncle had surprised himself as he suddenly remembered the name that had eluded him at the revival.

"You better not've lost that boy, Jimmy Fisher! I'll have your hide if he's hurt!" Any sleepy tone in Flora's voice disappeared, giving way to its full booming capacity. Otter smiled at the obvious care she expressed for him. He felt like stepping out in the light and showing himself, knowing that Flora would protect him from his uncle.

"There ain't nothin' happened to the boy," James replied. "He just got scairt over at the revival meeting and run off."

"Do you blame him?" Flora boomed. James cringed at the sound of her voice. Down the street, the dog Otter had encountered earlier began barking. "The fool things you folks do over there! That ain't no Holy Ghost meetin'. You folks are full of the devil!"

"Now hold on, Flora," James said. That was a big mistake to address her in the familiar. James realized it too late.

"Don't you call me Flora!" she bellowed. "You don't know me. I ain't your nigger. I'm Miss Flora, or Miss Sanders, to you, young man."

James stood quietly for a moment then tried to muster a contrite voice.

"Miss Flora, all I'm askin' is have you seen the boy?" His voice was growing higher in tone. Otter knew this was a sign that James' anger was hovering close to the surface.

"No, I have not seen him. Now go on and git, 'fore I call the sheriff. In fact I'm gonna phone Sheriff Dave right now and report that you lost little Otter. Good gracious alive!" Flora feigned a step back into the house.

"Now hold on. There ain't no call to do that." James said. He was no friend of Sheriff Dave Vaughn and knew that the sheriff would do his best to make him remember not to be causing problems with Miss Flora Sanders in the middle of the night. James had been picked up a number of times in the past for drunkenness and disorderliness. And Dave Vaughn had never bought any story of religious conversion. He knew Jimmy Fisher and how wily he could be.

"Well, then, go on and git, you hear me?" Flora mustered up her most authoritative voice and gave the full extent to the little man.

"I'm goin', woman, don't get your bowels in an uproar!" James hobbled down the steps just quick enough to avoid the swipe of a broom. "Don't you hit me, or I'll be the one have'n the sheriff on you!" James' anger let loose, and like a scared child he bent down and picked up a stick and turned as if he were going to throw it at Flora. As he pointed the stick at her, his eyes narrowed, "I'll find the boy and when I do you can bet he'll wish he never run from James Fisher!" James turned and threw the stick down. As he turned, his foot caught on a root, causing him to stumble and fall to the ground. As his uncle struggled to get up, Otter could hear him muttering the familiar obscenities that poured forth when the Holy Ghost lost his grip on the evangelist. After considerable effort to get to his car, James climbed in and drove away.

Flora stood on the porch and watched, making sure the angry man didn't do anything foolish. After a moment, she shook her head, turned and pulled open the screen door to go back in the house.

Otter stepped around the corner into the light.

"Flora?" Otter said softly.

The big woman turned toward him in surprise. She

stepped from behind the screen door, stretched out her arms and with a mother's compassion and tenderness, beckoned him to her.

"Come here, baby." Otter felt the warmth of her arms wrap securely around him. "Baby, you're all wet!" Flora stepped back and looked down at Otter's pants and shoes.

"What did that man do to you?" Before Otter could answer, a sense of deep relief came over him. He felt as if the weight of the whole world had been on his shoulders and suddenly was lifted off. He began to sob. Flora's arms again held him. "It's all right, baby," she said tenderly. "You go ahead and cry, cry out all your heart's pain."

Chapter Nine

Otter woke the next morning to the smell of sausage cooking. He had slept well through the night in the security of Flora's home. Despite the shade of the tall oaks, he could tell the morning sun was shining bright and guessed it was probably close to eight o'clock.

He put on his pants and shirt and walked out to the kitchen expecting to be greeted by Flora's smile. But it wasn't Flora, it was her husband Rafe, a retired railroad man, tall and slender with a full head of gray hair, a little goatee, and a chuckle that he naturally offered before and after nearly everything he said.

"Good morning, young man. I was wondering if you was gonna sleep all day. You hungry?" Rafe asked, chuckling. Otter smiled and returned the greeting to his friend as he moved to the kitchen table and sat down.

"Where's Flora?" he asked.

Rafe chuckled again, then replied, "Oh, she's been gone to the diner for near three hours now. Her sista Salle comes to pick her up on Fridays. Salle works over in Orlanda and has to leave kinda early, so Flora usually catches a ride with her on Fridays, sure enough."

Otter felt a little embarrassed that he had forgotten her regular routine of rising early to cook breakfast at the diner for the early risers of Lacey and vicinity. The mention of her not driving on Fridays brought back his conversation with Dee.

"And I got to get you off to school, or she'll have my hide," Rafe said, still chuckling.

Otter smiled as he imagined Flora with her size and strength manhandling the slender Rafe. And school? He had forgotten about school.

Rafe set a stack of pancakes and three links of country sausage down in front of Otter. It appeared that Rafe had cooking skills as good as his wife's. Otter loaded up the pancakes with butter and syrup, and dug in.

"Have you heard anything from Vicky?" Otter asked, after taking a long swallow of milk.

"Yessir, she called last night about an hour before you showed up," Rafe replied. "We had done gone to bed when the phone rang. Flora talked to her a minute or so. I could tell she wasn't appreciating that you got stuck with that fool uncle of yours." Rafe shook his head and chuckled as he pulled another plate from the drainer to dry.

"So I guess she's doing okay?" Otter asked. He figured that if she could talk on the phone surely she must be okay.

"Yeah, she oughta be going home tomorrow is what the doctor say. She said somethin' to Flora about ol' Glenn Sisson calling, though." Otter stopped eating and looked up at Rafe.

"What'd he say?"

"I don't know." Rafe turned and faced Otter; there was no chuckle. "You gonna have to ask Flora that, but it sounds like there's been some trouble up there at Fort Bragg."

"What kind of trouble?" Otter felt his appetite suddenly disappear.

"I can't say for sure, you'd do better to wait and talk to Flora. I got to stop by the diner to pick up her paycheck on the way to gett'n you to school so you can ask her yourself." Rafe finished wiping the plate and turned to put it away. He knew more than he was letting on, but it was disturbing news, and he didn't want to be the first to break it to the boy.

Otter was not able to finish the pancakes and asked to be excused. He went to the back bedroom where he had slept to put on his shoes. Soon Rafe knocked at the door and said they needed to hurry along. Otter grabbed the rabbit boy's jacket and was heading to the door when he noticed a rifle leaning against the wall in the corner. He moved closer to inspect it. It was longer than most rifles he had seen. The stock was a dark wood of some kind, and its color blended in with the wall paneling. It had some rust on the barrel and looked very old. Otter stuck his finger in the barrel. It's probably a smooth bore, he guessed, but definitely an old flintlock musket.

Rafe was already out the front door and on his way down the front porch steps. Otter made a mental note to ask him about the musket later. He ran quickly across the living room and out the door, pulling it closed tightly behind him. Then he turned and jumped from the porch to the ground without touching a step. The old man and the young boy climbed into the Electra 225, Flora's deuce-and-a-quarter, and were on their way to the diner.

The stop at the diner was brief, long enough for Rafe to pick up the paycheck and for Otter to get the few details there were about Dee. The long and short of it, according to Flora's recollection of the conversation with Vicky, was that Dee was missing and suspected of being AWOL. Otter knew the acronym AWOL meant Absent Without Leave, a designation often given to cowards in the military who desert when the going gets tough. Otter didn't take it seriously. Dee would never desert. Something else was going on. He was sure of it.

On the short drive to the school from the diner, Otter was quiet. Rafe let him off at school at the front circle drive where most of the kids were delivered by their parents. Otter didn't think to direct Rafe around back to the spot where Dee dropped him off on rainy days. In fact, when the old deuce-and-a-quarter came to a halt, he was still deep in thought, unaware that they were already at the school.

The heavy door of the car was hard to open, and Rafe reached over to help give it a little push. Otter thanked him for the ride and for being a good friend. Rafe simply smiled and said good-bye and with his usual chuckle reassured Otter that everything would work out. He then admonished him to learn something good.

The door slammed shut with only a little effort. Otter waved to Rafe, and the car moved on as another pulled forward in its place. A boy and a girl, probably first or second graders, Otter thought, exited the vehicle and ran past him. He watched the old Electra 225 as it turned onto the main road from the parking circle. The old gentleman waved another good-bye, then sped on out of sight.

Otter stood still for what seemed a very long time, watching the children file past him to their classes. He felt a numbness in his body, and his usual ease of coming up with solutions to predicaments seemed strangely absent. Dee was accused of being a deserter in a place miles away. Otter felt his teeth begin to grind as his jaw tightened.

"No! Dee did not desert!" he announced out loud to no one in particular, scaring a third grader enough to break into a run as he passed Otter. He tried to chase the doubts from his mind. They kept coming back.

The first bell rang, shaking Otter from his melancholy stupor like an alarm clock. With a deep revitalizing breath, he ran toward his class. The route to class took him by the main office. As he passed the large plate-glass window of the office, Otter froze. He couldn't believe his eyes. His Uncle James stood in front of the receptionist's desk. Betty Lou Reed nodded her head as she listened to the small, lean man. By chance or by some charitable act of providence, she glanced past James and caught Otter's eye. Otter quickly jumped out of view just as James turned to follow the receptionist's gaze. Otter felt his body begin to tense. There was no way he was going back to stay with his uncle, he thought. Not after the incident last night.

Ms. Reed knew of James Fisher's reputation and was quietly disgusted with the man's presence in the office inquiring after "little Millard Dumpkin." She quickly steered his attention away from the window, offering a believable excuse for her glance away.

Otter hurried on to his class, looking over his shoulder every few steps to be sure he was not about to be clutched by his uncle's bony hand. All along the way he was thinking hard—What do I do? Vicky is in the hospital; Dee is suspected of being AWOL; and Uncle James is after me, certainly more for revenge than for honoring his responsibility to take care of me.

Outside the portable classroom, Otter paused. The appearance of his Uncle James had suddenly forced a solution. He knew what he had to do. Looking around, he saw only a few students milling about, each having calculated to the second the time remaining before the tardy bell would ring. As it rang, several students scampered past Otter. Richard Griffin, a good friend who lived up the hill from the Dumpkin home, offered the usual adolescent quips, including what Ms. Newberg would do to Otter's testicles if he were late. Otter didn't hear it. The door to the portable building shut, and in an instant the campus took on a peaceful quiet.

He stood for a moment feeling invisible, like a director sitting in a darkened theater watching his own film. "I know how it's going to turn out," he whispered to himself, " Grandpa is not a deserter. Something tells me he needs me to help him prove it."

Otter turned and walked quickly toward the cafeteria, retracing the route he would take on rainy days. As he rounded the corner of the cafeteria, he heard the familiar clanking of pots and pans and the gleeful banter of the lunch ladies over the hum of the kitchen exhaust fan. He crossed the staff parking area and headed down Blount Street. The narrow red brick street descended the hill toward the lake and the road home. Once there, the determined young man would gather the necessary things for the journey.

"Dee has always been there for me," he thought to himself as he hurried along. "Now it's my turn to be there for him." It was uncanny. After all the doubt and confusion and inability to decide what to do, it was clear there was no other solution. Otter was going to Fort Bragg.

Chapter Ten

Sergeant Joel Gage opened the insulated aluminum case, raised the monitor screen and flipped the on-switch. The computer prompt flashed and an army of pixels scrambled to form an image of the rocket it controlled. The words SR 70—Class C Surface-to-Air Missile (SAM) READY FOR COMMAND faded into view beneath the image. Sergeant Gage hit the ENTER key. The command ENTER LAUNCH ACTIVATION CODE began its intermittent flash.

"Private Gallworth!" barked the sergeant. "Give me the LAC. And don't screw it up this time."

"Yes sir!" Private Jeremy Gallworth's reply was quick and crisp, but he was nervous. The previous launch had been delayed when he misread the code, costing the unit precious time in completing the exercise. They were being judged on every aspect of their performance. And time was crucial. If Company B was to be selected to participate in the Fourth of July Capabilities Exercise, they had to score a hit in record time on this try.

Clipboard in hand, Private Gallworth pointed to each number of the code with his finger as he read deliberately, "Alpha6772Charlie, *sir*!" Gage typed in the code. WEAPON READY FOR LAUNCH appeared on the screen. "Hallelujah! Okay, Jamison! You got CP on the line?"

"Yes, sir! Command Post on the line, sir!" Private Justin Jamison, Bravo Company's radio operator, held the receiver to his ear and waited for instructions.

"Tell 'em we're ready, they can release the drone," Gage said. Jamison passed on the information and within thirty seconds the drone, a dummy self-propelled aircraft, appeared from behind the pines.

"Altitude?" Gage requested.

"Thirty-seven hundred feet, sir!" Jamison began to feel the nervous perspiration on his forehead as he replied to the commands of the sergeant. Sergeant Gage was tough and sometimes, Jamison thought, a little crazy. Anything short of an excellent rating, meant a hike in full gear along every inch of road on Fort Bragg. After the last hike, several guys were hospitalized with heat stroke. One grunt (the name used by soldiers to refer to each other), a female, Gage hounded particularly hard. She requested to be transferred to another unit.

Gage's view on women in the military was no secret. They didn't belong in the military. Period. He could hardly talk to the few women in his outfit without the hair on the back of his neck bristling. What he kept a tighter leash on were his racist tendencies. He knew the Army would not tolerate any discriminatory behavior on his part, so he learned to be subtle. But now, for the first time since his arrival at Fort Bragg, Sergeant Gage was surrounded by recruits who found in him a kindred racist spirit. Six new grunts to be exact, four of them from out-of-the-way places around the country. Of the remaining two, one was from Detroit, the other from Los Angeles. They all idolized him. His hatred of African-Americans, Hispanics, Asian-Americans, Jews, homosexuals, and women (military women, especially officers) served only to inspire these young recruits. Consequently, his bigotry needed less disguise.

"Clear for launch!" Sergeant Gage raised his arm, then pressed the launch switch and covered his ears. The rocket shot straight up from the ground, then seemed to hesitate for a moment. Jamison's heart jumped. But in the next instant, like a bloodhound catching the scent of a raccoon, the rocket directed itself with full force toward the drone. Within seconds the drone had been hit and exploded into pieces. A cheer went up from B Company and Sergeant Gage breathed a sigh of relief.

In two weeks Sergeant Gage was counting on the same exercise to be repeated at the annual Fourth of July Capabilities Exercise, called Capex for short. Only then, if all worked according to his plan, B Company would not be shooting the SAM at a drone, but into a crowd of dignitaries on hand to watch the show. Among the observers would be the Vice President of the United States.

Gage knew that this Capex was the best Fourth of July fireworks display in the country. The "Million Dollar Minute," as it was called by its detractors, was so named because in the space of one minute examples of all US Army firepower, firing simultaneously, could expend $1million of ordinance—everything from M-16s to

SAMs. It would be the perfect opportunity to make a statement, a very powerful statement, he thought. The Vice President was now running for President. Where he went, so went the news cameras. Gage knew that on that day the nation would be watching.

The press was predicting that in the upcoming elections, the Vice President was sure to win. To Gage that meant four more years of a misguided, immoral administration whose policies permitted homosexuals to serve in the military and expanded military service opportunities to other minorities. He was fed up with it all. Things were going in the wrong direction. As a patriot, he felt the time to act was now. What happened to him was not an issue. He was prepared to make the ultimate sacrifice, even if it meant taking some of his grunts and a couple hundred innocent civilians with him. Gage never said it openly, but to him, Timothy McVeigh was a hero for blowing up the Federal Building in Oklahoma City. But Gage believed that McVeigh could have made a much greater statement as an active soldier. Had he remained in the Army, there would have been repercussions that would have led to a full congressional investigation. The nation would have learned what I know, Gage thought, that there are others, plenty of others, wearing the uniform, who believe the United States of America has lost it's way. Only then would things begin to get back to the way they were meant to be.

As a civilian, Gage had always felt powerless. Frustrated that majority rule would never get him what he wanted, he had joined the Army when he was twenty-six. He ascended quickly to the rank of sergeant and enjoyed the power of command. Army life fit him like a glove. It fed his need to control the way people thought. But Gage was approaching his twentieth year of service, and word had it that he would not be encouraged to re-enlist. He was good, but not that good, and the occasional reprimands for poor conduct resulting from what were undeniably racist attitudes, made some of his superiors anxious to see him go. The time to act was now. He would never have the same opportunity to exert his influence "out there" as a civilian as he would at the present moment. In Sergeant Gage's mind, fate had taken over. His plan had the mandate of something beyond himself. He was ready to die to persuade a nation to see things as he saw them. If he could pull it off, he would get to be all he wanted to be.

But then there was the problem of the reservist—Dumpkin the "nigger-lover"—as Gage called him in private, and Private Terry Warren, the cocky black man who knew too much. To the sergeant, "the old man and the nigger" were in the wrong place at the wrong time and stuck their heads into the wrong business—his business.

Dee Dumpkin didn't agree that he was in the wrong place at the wrong time, nor that what Gage did was not his business. In Dee's mind, he had simply come to the aid of another human being who was being harassed and roughed up by a bunch of hoodlums disguised as American military.

Terry Warren had been Gage's token black grunt in B Company. Until recently there had been three young African American recruits in B Company. But two had requested transfers, along with a young Puerto Rican woman. After a bitter confrontation between Gage and the company commander, the transfers were granted. However, Sergeant Gage was told in no uncertain terms that B Company would not have within it even the slightest hint of racism, and that new recruits of varying ethnic backgrounds would, without hesitation, be assigned to B Company.

Dee first met Terry and his wife Janine at a post chapel service. Despite the difference in rank, Terry and Dee became fast friends, enjoying many of the same outdoor activities. However, it was Janine who had the most in common with Dee. She was from Orlando and was familiar with West Orange County, having relatives in Clarkton outside Lacey.

When Terry was assigned to Bravo Company, he initially found Gage to be a skillful and fair company sergeant. During his years in the Army, Gage had become very good at covering his prejudices. But he would slip up occasionally, and more than once when Terry was present. It wasn't long before he was on to Gage.

Terry discovered the Capex plot while filling in for the one of the company computer technicians who was sick. Gage was out of town on leave, and there was no one to block the temporary reassignment. Terry was a genius on computers, but it wasn't his computer wizardry that uncovered the plot it was dumb luck. Given a routine computer assignment by the duty officer, Terry checked the delete bin for a segment of a weapons manual that was missing. He found a message referring to the plot, a message that should have been permanently deleted or saved in a secure file. Someone had been careless. And now for good or ill, Terry knew what was going on.

Dee's age and experience in the military made him

Terry's first choice for counsel about what to do. Dee immediately called the post military police. The dispatcher, a Private Hall, was uncooperative and put Dee on hold. After several minutes, Dee hung up. The inefficiency surprised him. It wasn't characteristic of the Army. He decided they should report directly to the Corps Commander about the discovery.

En route to Corps Headquarters, another surprise: They were abducted by Gage's cronies. That Terry was privy to the plot had somehow been found out by Gage. It wasn't just coincidence that the abduction came so soon after the call to MP headquarters. Gage had inside help—Private Hall. Hall contacted Gage. The sergeant immediately had Terry and Dee picked up by grunts disguised as MPs.

In a wooded area off one of the many back roads on the military post, Terry and Dee were made to strip and change into civilian clothes. They were blindfolded, bound, and gagged, then put into a civilian van and transported to a mini-storage facility located in the little town of Raeford, just west of Fayetteville until Gage could decide their fate.

Gage had a big problem. He would have to use all his powers of deception if his Capex plot was to go forward as planned. As soon as Private Warren turns up missing, he thought, Company Command would be on me like "white on rice," especially given his recent citation.

Gage's diabolical mind didn't take long to come up with a plan. If he could make it look like someone else was responsible for Warren's disappearance, someone with no connection at all to B Company, then he could buy enough time to pull off the bombing before anyone was the wiser. I can pin it on the old man, Dumpkin,

Gage schemed. His mind was made up. "I'll see that Dumpkin, the nigger-lover, turns out to be Dumpkin, the nigger-killer," he whispered under his breath. He smiled, pleased with yet his newest twist of deception. The big show at the Capex was still on track.

Chapter Eleven

Otter wasn't sure just how he was going to get to Fort Bragg. He had some cash he had put aside from mowing lawns and doing some work at the diner, but was it enough for a bus ticket? "Could a kid even buy a bus ticket?" he wondered. Otter knew he needed to think things through. He could do it. Somehow he would get there.

He packed his backpack in the same manner he packed for a camping trip, figuring it would likely turn out to be just that. In the pack went a change of clothes, towel, toiletries, two extra pairs of socks, and food—MREs (Meals-Ready-to-Eat) left over from one of Dee's reserve exercises at Camp Blanding enough for a week. He packed it neatly and tightly, just as Dee had taught him.

After closing the pack, he attached his sleeping bag with the nylon straps made for that purpose. Then he tried it on to check the balance. It was a good fit. He cinched up his waist belt and headed for the door. From the small table by the door he picked up an envelope addressed to Vicky. It was stamped and ready to go. Inside was a simple message:

Don't worry. I will be all right. Will call soon. Love, Otter

Closing the door hard behind him, he checked to see if it was secure and locked. Then he walked down to the end of the driveway, deposited the letter in the mailbox, and raised the little red flag.

Despite the fact that it was a small town and Vicky's house was less than two miles away, Otter knew that she would not get the note for at least two days. For some strange reason, at his address, the mail was picked up and taken to Orlando for processing, then returned to Lacey, even if you were just wanting to send a get-well card to the neighbor down the street. This inefficiency was part of his plan. Otter figured he would have at least a two-day start before anyone got seriously suspicious of his whereabouts. This would certainly be the case given that Vicky's stay in the hospital was indefinite.

He headed up the hill along the road leading away from the lake and away from town. The weight of the pack rested on Otter's hips. He reassured himself that he could handle it for as long as it would take to get to North Carolina.

Passing Butch Dowling's house, he again pictured in his mind West County High School's star athlete. Many times Otter had imagined himself a star quarterback like Butch. Perhaps someday he would get the chance, he thought. He picked up his step and hurried on.

Just over the hill, east toward Orlando, was a bus stop. It was a small shelter used by kids while waiting for their school bus on rainy days. It was originally built by the Greyhound Bus Line Company for the passengers that, at one time years ago, regularly took the bus into Orlando. Otter had observed while at home during the summer that a bus passed by once a day around noon. On occasion, he had seen it stop to pick up a lone rider. He was counting on the bus to follow its regular schedule. It was 10:45 a.m. He had plenty of time.

When he arrived at the shelter, he was surprised to see the familiar face of Mrs. Clark, a neighbor who lived on the east side of the lake. She was sitting quietly on the shelter bench next to a canvas shopping bag attached by bungee cords to a small collapsible cart. Otter didn't really know Mrs. Clark except to say hello when he passed her in town or on the street. Dee knew her much better. Her son, Leonard, had joined the Army in 1968, the same time as Dee. They did basic training together at Fort Benning. Leonard served his four-year stint and married a girl from Frankfurt, Germany, where he was stationed the last year of his service. Leonard and his wife returned to the States for a while, then decided to move back to Germany where, as far as Otter knew, they still were.

"Good morning, Mrs. Clark," he said, trying to make his sudden appearance seem as normal as possible. Mrs. Clark nodded and continued to sit in silence. Otter suspected that she was a quiet woman and that was okay with him. But he felt a little nervous that he had been seen. Mrs. Clark looked down at Otter's pack as he set it on the ground and leaned it against the inside wall of the shelter. He continued standing.

"Aren't you suppose to be in school, young man?" she asked.

Otter had anticipated that someone might ask him that question soon enough. He just didn't think it would be Mrs. Clark. He was caught off guard. "Uh, yes, ma'am. I'm to meet my class in Orlando, and we're going on an overnight field trip down to Lake Okeechobee. It's to do some research on a science project we're doing about the Kissimmee River." He had it all planned out, even to the point of anticipating the follow-up question.

"Don't you usually take a school bus for something like that?" she asked.

"Yes ma'am, but you see, I missed my ride to school this morning. With my Grandpa gone and all, I got up late. So I didn't even try to catch up to my class there. They were leaving at 8:30 a.m. But I remembered that they were making a stop at Evans High School in Orlando to pick up some equipment, so I thought I could catch up with 'em there. It's only a couple of blocks from the Greyhound station." Otter was impressed with his story. There was no way she could help but believe it, he thought.

"That's ridiculous," she said. "Evans High School is a good five miles from the bus station. I oughta know. I attended Maynard Evans High School for three years." She straightened her posture, as if to exude an air of pride in her alma mater. But the response stunned Otter. He knew Evans High School was somewhere in Orlando. He hadn't counted on Mrs. Clark being a graduate from there. His story was constructed for someone less concerned with details.

"But isn't there a school near the Greyhound station?

Maybe I've got it mixed up with some other one." Now Otter was counting on Mrs. Clark's knowledge of the area surrounding the bus station to get him off the hook. There must be some school close to it.

"Central Junior High School is about ten blocks from there, but that's still a long way to tote a sack like yours." Otter was saved. Mrs. Clark came through.

"Yeah, that's got to be it. Mrs. Newburg said it was the one near the bus station, and ten blocks is nothing. I've hiked ten miles before with this pack." Otter relaxed for a moment, but Mrs. Clark's next response was again unexpected.

"Well, that surprises me. Ida Newburg was a classmate of mine at Evans until she moved to Lacey. She should know better."

"Well, she's getting kind of old," Otter responded. "I imagine she's forgotten a few things."

Mrs. Clark tightened her lips and shot a stern glance at Otter but continued to sit quietly. The boy turned his head and rolled his eyes.

How could I be so dumb, he thought to himself. Calling Mrs. Newburg old is like calling Mrs. Clark an old fogey. Otter walked out to the road, hoping to get a glimpse of the bus coming around the lake and to avoid having to add any more strands to the tangled web he was weaving. He looked back toward the lake—no bus. From his vantage point on the hill, the road seemed to disappear into Spring Lake. Across the lake he could see a car, clearly not the bus, slowly making its way along the perimeter road.

The sun was out and it was beginning to warm up. Otter started back toward the shelter when he heard the sound of the bus straining up the hill. Mrs. Clark stood and made her way to the edge of the road with her shopping cart as Otter threw his pack over his shoulder. Would the driver be suspicious?

Mrs. Clark paid her fare and moved toward the back of the bus. Otter reached in his pocket and pulled out a wad of cash and sorted out a twenty-dollar bill. He thought he saw Mrs. Clark give the driver ten dollars and return to her two dollars change.

"Where to?" The driver asked.

"Fort..." Otter caught himself. "Orlando."

The driver smiled. "Never heard of Fort Orlando. Is that in Disney World?"

Otter knew the driver was pulling his leg, and he tried to laugh as sincerely as he could. But it did sound a little forced. The driver gave Otter twelve dollars change and a ticket. The door closed, the air brakes released, and the bus moved back out onto the highway as Otter sat down.

The Greyhound Cruiseliner was not crowded, so he was able to set his pack on the seat next to him. After taking a moment to gather himself, Otter looked around. Mrs. Clark was sitting two rows back on the opposite side with her eyes closed. She opened them and caught the boy's gaze. Otter turned away. Does she think I'm running away? he wondered. Would she call Mrs. Newburg? Otter glanced back toward the elderly woman. Again her eyes were shut. He leaned back in his seat and watched as endless rows of orange trees rushed by.

The Orlando bus terminal was crowded. The smell of diesel fuel and exhaust from idling engines hung heavy in the air. Otter stepped into the waiting area and approached the ticket counter. An elderly gentleman was requesting a ticket to Macon, Georgia. He looked to be about the same age as Rafe, Otter thought, but did not stand straight and tall like Rafe. He was slightly bent over and carried a cane. He was dressed in a suit and wore a derby hat that matched.

When the gentleman received his ticket and turned to move away from the counter, he paused, looked at Otter and smiled. Otter returned the gesture, and felt himself relax a little.

Otter stepped up to the counter and quickly reviewed in his mind what he had rehearsed on the bus. He had counted his money and had just shy of two hundred dollars. To be safe, he had figured, he would ask for a one-way ticket, insuring that he would have enough money. To be caught short would look like he didn't know what he was doing.

With as much confidence as he could muster, he asked for a one-way ticket to Fayetteville.

"Fayetteville, where?" the agent asked.

"Uh...North Carolina." It had not crossed Otter's mind that there were other Fayettevilles in other states.

"Can't do it."

Otter caught his breath and paused as if waiting for the agent to laugh out loud, slap his knee and say, "just kidding," or "I'm pulling your leg," something that Dee might say as a practical joke. It didn't come. Instead, the agent began to pry.

"You traveling alone, young man?" It wasn't an accusing voice so Otter didn't feel defensive.

"Yes, sir. Do I need an adult with me?"

"Technically, no," the agent replied, "but usually an adult buys the ticket and puts the child on the bus.

There're some restrictions." The agent stopped abruptly. "You're not running away somewhere are you?" His voice changed from a matter-of-fact business tone to one of genuine concern. Otter looked up at the man. He could see that the concern being expressed was not just in the agent's voice but also in his eyes as they looked down at him over his half-eye spectacles.

"No, sir. I'm running *to* some place." Otter was surprised by his own answer but thought it was sincere and a pretty good one to boot.

"Well, I can sell you a ticket, but, like I say, there are some restrictions." The transaction was becoming more complicated than Otter had expected.

"What restrictions?" The boy took a deep breath and awaited the explanation.

"Well, son, you look to me to be a minor. How old are you?

"Twelve." Otter responded. The agent shook his head.

"Nope, can't do it. Company rules restrict travel by a minor to destinations no more than five hours away. Fayetteville arrival time is..." The agent turned and looked at the clock above the large silver greyhound mounted on the wall. "Well, if you left on the 1:20 this afternoon, it would be 4:30 a.m. tomorrow morning. That's fifteen hours." The agent turned and peered again at Otter over the half-eyes, waiting for his reply.

"What's five hours away? Toward Fayetteville?" Otter asked, his voice wavering somewhere between hope and disappointment.

"The bus stops in Jacksonville at about 7:30 p.m. But you would still need an adult to meet you there."

Otter's creative mind kicked into high gear. He could

 buy another ticket in Jacksonville to the next town within five hours away, then another to the next town, then another, until he was in Fayetteville.

"If you want a ticket to Jacksonville, I need some ID and the name of the adult meeting you at the other end. Is there someone you know in Jacksonville?" Otter had the suspicion that the agent knew what he was planning.

"As a matter of fact my Aunt Delores lives there." Otter did not have an Aunt Delores. "Delores Dumpkin," he continued as he pulled his school identification card from his wallet and laid it on the counter. "She's my grand…uh, my father's sister."

The agent looked at the card. "You're... Millard Fillmore Dumpkin?"

"Yes, sir, my mother named me that when I was a baby. I don't think she was feeling too good."

"You go by Millard Dumpkin?"

No, sir. My name is Otter, Otter Dumpkin.

The agent smiled and handed the identification card back to Otter, then typed something into the computer.

"One way to Jacksonville is fifty-nine dollars," the agent said. "The bus boards in stall seven in twenty minutes."

Otter paid the agent and took the ticket. He thanked him, then turned away and examined it.

"It's good that you're running *to* something and not away from something, son."

Otter turned back to the agent to see him looking past the next customer, a young woman who seemed a little irritated that she could not get the agent's attention. The agent's sympathetic eyes again peered over his half-eye spectacles. Otter acknowledged the concern and tried to show his appreciation with a smile and a nod of his head. It felt a little awkward.

Otter turned and walked through the crowded waiting area. As he made his way across the room, he narrowly escaped a collision with a toddler who had broken free from her mother's hand. After excusing himself, he continued on toward the sign that pointed to the bus stalls. Through the glass door he could see several buses parked, each ready to embark on a journey to towns and cities near and far. Otter watched as the bus in stall seven was being made ready to go. He thought about Dee and longed to see him, to hold him.

Otter looked up at the clock over the silver greyhound. It was already a quarter to one. He found a vacant seat next to the woman and the little girl with whom he had almost collided earlier. Holding his backpack on his knees in front of him, he recalled the stories he had concocted thus far to get where he was: The field trip to Lake Okeechobee; the missed bus story he had told Mrs. Clark; and now the one yet-to-be-concluded he just told the ticket agent. He shook his head and let out a little laugh. Soon he would be on his way to Jacksonville to be met by an aunt that didn't exist. What next?

Chapter Twelve

Otter's Uncle James woke with a start to the sound of someone pounding on the roof of his car. A Florida Highway Patrolman had spotted the car parked alongside the road and stopped to investigate. He found James asleep in the front seat, leaning against the driver-side window. To the officer's surprise, the motor was still running.

James ran his hand through his matted hair and fumbled to collect himself, then rolled down the window.

"You'll need to move on, sir. You're creating a hazard parked here on the shoulder. There's a rest area about five miles up the road," the deputy said. He shined his flashlight into the backseat of the vehicle. A styrofoam takeout plate containing a neatly stacked pile of chicken bones lay on the vinyl seat. A Bible lay next to the plate. The deputy had no reason to be suspicious. He had pulled up the license number and registration on his computer, and the car had not been reported stolen.

“You James Fisher?” the deputy asked. “James Fisher of Lacey, Florida?”

“Yessir, I am.” James reached for his wallet, anticipating the request to see his driver’s license.

“Put your hands on the steering wheel, sir.” The deputy’s voice was curt but calm.

“What?” James continued to reach for his wallet.

“Put your hands on the steering wheel! Now, sir!” Now the deputy’s voice was urgent.

James froze. He turned and looked up into the officer’s face, lit red, then blue, then red again by the patrol car’s oscillating emergency lights. James noticed the deputy had unsnapped the buckle on his revolver and his hand was resting on the handle. He slowly put his hands on the steering wheel.

“I was just goin’ for my wallet, sir.” James was clearly irritated but wanted to demonstrate respect for the officer’s authority and made sure to address him as “sir”. He could remember too many times in the past when his quick temper and disrespectful attitude had landed him handcuffed in the back seat of a patrol car.

“Please turn off the vehicle and step outside, sir,” the officer said. Both men were tense but polite.

James had not noticed that the car’s engine was still running. Embarrassed, he quickly turned it off.

“I ain’t done nothin’ wrong, sir,” James said, trying not to sound guilty.

“Please, step from the car, sir.” The officer’s voice was firm but still controlled.

James slid his feet around and strained to get out of the red Ford Escort wagon. He was stiff from sleeping sitting up.

“Place your hands on the roof of the vehicle, sir, and

spread your feet apart, shoulder width."

James could feel the warmth from the car interior mixing with the cool evening air. While he was asleep it had rained, and the temperature dropped several degrees. The officer frisked the thin, wiry man, then asked him to slowly turn around and show him his driver's license. Now that he was standing, James pulled out his wallet with little trouble. He handed the license to the officer. The officer checked it, shining his flashlight, first to the license then to James' face, making sure the photograph was of the same man standing before him. The officer returned the license and reiterated his concern that James find the rest area up ahead and avoid a possible accident.

The patrolman returned to his car. James resumed his place behind the steering wheel. His hands were shaking. He turned the ignition key, then glanced in his rearview mirror at the patrolman's car. He could see little save the lights of the patrol car. He buckled his seat belt and shifted the car into drive. The patrolman sat waiting for the nervous man to leave. James slowly conducted the car off of the shoulder and back onto the highway. The patrol car followed. After a mile or so, the patrol car sped past the slow-moving Escort and disappeared beyond the lights of the few cars ahead. James breathed a sigh of relief, then silently cursed the officer. Then he cursed the boy who nearly drowned him and who he was sure had learned his dark secret.

Of the last 24 hours, James had slept less than three. The debacle at the pond was bad enough, but what had caused him more concern was Otter calling him a murderer. Unsure how much he knew, James was worried about what the boy might do with any information he had. Throughout much of the night, he had searched all over Winter Grove and Lacey for the boy, but found no sign of him. That morning he had tried to intercept the boy at his school. Otter didn't show up. But James' luck soon changed. During the afternoon, while searching the Dumpkin home, he had checked the mailbox and discovered Otter's letter to Vicky. Suspecting that Otter might try to join his grandfather in North Carolina, he had headed straight for the bus depot in Orlando. His hunch was correct. Otter had boarded the bus shortly after 1:00 p.m. The kindly ticket agent had confirmed James' theory that the boy was headed for Fayetteville, but added that he was stopping to visit an aunt along the way. James racked his brain to figure out who this Aunt Delores in Jacksonville was, and grew more and more furious with his great-nephew.

Though exhausted, James was determined to make it to Jacksonville to meet the bus and apprehend his nephew before this so-called Aunt Delores entered the picture and complicated matters even further. But his intended fifteen minute nap had stretched out to almost two hours. It was already 6:45 p.m. and getting dark. The bus was scheduled to arrive at 7:30 p.m. Could he make it in forty-five minutes? The little car sped along.

At Starke, just ten miles to the north, the Greyhound bus en route to Jacksonville was about to depart the depot after a fifteen minute delay to replace a worn wiper blade on the bus' windshield. It had rained off and on since the bus left Orlando. At dusk, just outside Ocala, the rain had come down hard for about fifteen minutes, then settled into a drizzle. The driver managed for a while, but when darkness fell, he decided the repair had to be made. Starke was the next stop on the route.

The bus was parked alongside US 301 in front of a travel agency that doubled as the bus depot. Otter decided to use the time to get something to eat. On the bus he had munched on some crackers from one of the MREs, but seeing a convenience market across the street from the depot, he decided to buy a hot dog rather than use any more of his food supply. It was expensive for a hot dog—two dollars. He vowed not to frequent such places again for food. He'd be broke fast at those rates.

As he sat down to eat on the porch attached to the travel agency, Otter noticed a middle-aged woman sitting nearby in an old padded recliner. The woman smiled a friendly smile, one that kind people usually project to anyone who will receive it. Otter smiled at people that way, so he was receptive.

As he ate his hot dog, he watched the woman doing a very strange thing. On the ground next to her she had a large canvas sack that appeared to be full of women's hose—stockings as Dee called them. But these stockings were of a variety of bright colors: there were red ones and pink ones, and purple, yellow, and orange ones. Stranger still, they didn't have any feet in them! They were cut off at the ankle.

Otter watched as she pulled a stocking up over the length of her arm. Then she began at the shoulder and rolled the stocking down to her wrist, creating a kind of nylon donut. Otter watched a while, amazed that the woman could make at least one and sometimes two nylon rings in the space of a minute. His curiosity got the best of him and he decided to inquire about the purpose of this bizarre undertaking. He walked over to the woman to introduce himself.

"Hi." he said.

The woman looked up and smiled.

"I couldn't help but notice what you were doing with those, uh...stockings. My name is Otter, Otter Dumpkin." Otter extended his hand, repeating to perfection everything his grandfather had taught him about politeness and introducing himself.

"Hello, Otter Dumpkin, a pleasure to meet you. I'm Margie, Margie Downs." The friendly woman finished another donut, tossed it into the bag and pulled out a bright yellow stocking. " It does look a little weird, doesn't it?" She giggled as she pulled the stocking up on her arm. "Wanna try one?"

"Sure, but what's it for?" Otter took off his jacket and reached in the sack for a stocking. He pulled out a red one.

"Well, it's for a lot of things but mostly fun things that kids like to do. You can create some great toys for almost nothing." She reached into the sack and pulled out six nylon donuts, each a different color, tied together to form a kind of snowflake-looking doily.

"What's that?" Otter asked.

"It's a frisbee. An indoor frisbee. See." She flung the flat object across the porch toward a plate glass window, hitting it with a light thud but doing no damage. Otter was not too impressed. He got up and retrieved the donut frisbee.

"Cool." He said with as much sincerity as he could muster. "What else can you do with them?"

Margie reached into the sack and produced a thick, braided rope about six feet in length and made of alternating red, white, and blue nylon donuts.

"I'm making this for the Fourth of July celebration next week. See, you just link them together like you do rubber bands." Margie demonstrated how to add another donut to increase the rope's length.

"Do these stocking come in all these colors?" Otter asked, holding up a bright orange one.

"No, hon, they come just plain white, I have to dye them the different colors. Fortunately I don't have to buy them. I get them for free where I work. They're waste hose."

"They're what?" Otter asked, puzzled by the name.

"Waste hose. The company I work for makes pantyhose for women. In production some of the hose don't meet the quality standards, but rather than throw them away, we've come up with a way to recycle them."

"That's a great idea!" Otter said enthusiastically. The Dumpkin family had recycled things even before it was popular to do so. The toys looked a little less boring to him now that they served a larger purpose. " Anything else you can do with them?" Otter asked.

"Oh there's a bunch of neat things you can do with them. You just have to... "

Margie was interrupted by the bus driver announcing that the bus to Jacksonville was ready for reboarding.

"You going to Jacksonville?" Otter inquired.

"No, hon. I'm heading home to Florence," Margie replied, packing up her hose.

"That's in South Carolina, right?"

"Sure is. You been there before?"

"I see the signs on I-95 when we drive up to Fayetteville. That's in North Carolina."

"I know, I've been to Fayetteville many times. I have a good friend who used to live there."

"Was your friend in the Army?" Otter asked.

"How'd you know that, sweetie?"

Otter felt a little strange being called "sweetie," but he could detect the care in her voice.

"My grandfather is in the Army Reserves, and he goes up to Fort Bragg at least once a year for training. He's there right now and I'm on my way to see him."

"I see. I suppose he's there now because of this thing in Albania?" Margie picked up her bag of stockings and a small suitcase beside her. "Listen, sweetie, we'd better get on the bus before we get left behind. Would you mind sitting with me? I've enjoyed our conversation and we can talk some more on the bus. I can show you how to make some more stocking toys," Margie said, looking down at Otter.

The talking was fine with Otter. The woman seemed pleasant enough. But he wasn't sure about the stocking toys. He stood and helped Margie with her bag.

"Yeah, that'd be good," he replied, as they walked together to the bus. "Are you just getting on here at Starke?"

"Um hmm," Margie replied. "I've been visiting my mother. She lives here with my Aunt Lois. I try to get down to see them a couple of times a year."

"Do you usually come on the bus?"

"No, sweetie, usually I drive, but my car broke down just before I was about to leave, so I took the bus this time. "

"Do you live alone in Florence?" Otter was curious.

"Yep." Margie smiled, amused at her new friend's questions.

"Are you married?" Otter was a little unsure why the question popped out. It suddenly crossed his mind that she might think he was being too forward. Certainly she would detect that he was genuinely interested. No, the question was quite appropriate, he thought.

"I used to be married, but it didn't work out."

"Where's your husband?" Otter paused. "I mean ex-husband, now?"

"Oh, he's still in Florence. He's a mechanic at a truck stop out near the interstate. He's a nice enough guy and we're still good friends. We just, well, we weren't right for each other."

Otter walked on toward the bus with Margie. He was comfortable with the silence. Margie glanced over at him. She sensed that she had made a good friend. This young man was mature beyond his years.

Relationships with women had always been fascinating to Otter. Not having known his mother nor his grandmother, he had never experienced a personal relationship up close. He wondered what it would be like to live with a woman in the house. He and Dee had lived alone for as long as he could remember. He had watched Dee and Vicky and even Flora and Rafe, but always from somewhat of a distance. He had friends whose parents were divorced. In fact, he was at Jimmy Webb's house the very day his mother threw his father out along with all his belongings. With clothes scattered all over the yard, it looked like a hurricane had blown through. And lots of screaming. Otter was amazed, even a little bit amused, yet not frightened. He had no sense of the injury and pain taking place inside the Webb home that had led to the relationship being ripped apart. He saw only the dramatic release, the final cry to be free from it all. His only hint of the pain came from the look on Jimmy's face. It was a kind of terror, as if he was being confronted by a mean dog. Otter was unaware that the repercussions would affect people he did not even know, family and friends of Jimmy. But he was smart enough to recognize that it couldn't be easy to live day in and day out with someone of the opposite sex. Even he and Dee stepped on each other's toes from time to time.

Otter broke the long silence. "Did you say you live alone?"

"Yes, sweetie. Does that surprise you?"

"It's just hard to imagine, I guess," Otter replied. "I think I'd have a hard time with it."

"I like living by myself," Margie offered. "It's the first time I've been completely on my own. I really do like it. I wasn't sure I would, but I do." After a brief pause, she continued. "I do have two cats though. Do they count?"

Otter shook his head. "No. Pets aren't the same, especially cats. They're too independent. What are their names?"

"Stripey and Blackie," Margie replied. "Can you guess how they got their names?" She smiled at Otter. "You probably think I'm strange, don't you?"

"No, no," Otter replied reassuringly. "I like strange people." Otter rolled his eyes and then apologized. "Sorry, I didn't mean that like it sounded. What I meant to say is that I like different kinds of people that aren't..." Otter hesitated, searching for the right word. "Well, boring. You're not boring." Otter felt like he had said the right thing. Margie laughed again and patted Otter on the head.

"I like you, Otter Dumpkin. By the way, you're gonna have to tell me how you got the name Otter."

"I'll tell you how I got the name Otter if you tell me

 why you're called Margie," Otter said with a grin.

Margie smiled back. "Deal."

The new friends mounted the steps of the bus and claimed two seats together halfway down the aisle on the left. Margie placed her small suitcase along with Otter's backpack in the overhead bin and they settled in for the short ride to Jacksonville.

The two shared the stories of the origin of their names. Otter recounted his naming by his grandfather and revealed with a little embarrassment that his real name was Millard. Margie was of the Roman Catholic faith and spoke of Sister Mary Margaret, a dear childhood friend of her mother and for whom she was named. Margie was short for Mary Margaret.

As the bus turned east onto Interstate 10, Otter suddenly recalled that, once at the terminal in Jacksonville, the driver would be expecting to deliver him to the adult he had designated when he purchased his ticket in Orlando. The thought caused him to break into a cold sweat. He had to think of something or he would soon be in a real fix.

What was her name? he asked himself. Was it Denise? No. That wasn't it. It started with a D. That much he could remember. "Delores!" The name was no longer just a thought. The sudden recollection produced a verbal utterance that caused Margie to pause from her donut-making and give Otter a puzzled look.

"Who's Delores?" she asked, resuming a donut.

"Uh, she's my aunt who's meeting me at the bus station. My Aunt Delores…uh, who doesn't exist." One again, Margie stopped her donut-making, but this time she looked at Otter with sympathetic eyes. It was the response he was hoping for. It was enough to convince him he could trust her.

Over the next ten minutes, the floodgates opened and Otter's story poured forth. Margie heard about Dee's disappearance, Vicky's appendicitis attack, Uncle James' secret, Flora's rescue, and the fictitious Aunt Delores, all in an attempt to explain how a runaway boy ended up beside her on a Greyhound bus to Jacksonville. Otter had indeed woven a tangled web to get to where he was. That was certain. But to Margie, it seemed justified. She imagined herself doing the same thing if she were Otter. But the problem now was how to get Otter off the bus after arriving in Jacksonville.

The two thought hard for a solution. Margie hesitated to create another lie, but Otter had no problem. "The end justifies the means" was his motto at the moment, though he had heard time and again from his grandfather that this was not usually the case as far as he was concerned.

Earlier, Otter noticed that Margie carried a cellular phone. Perhaps she could call someone in Jacksonville to meet them at the station, posing as the awaiting Aunt Delores, he thought. If he could be convincing and make the driver believe that he really knew this person, give her a big hug and call her Aunt Delores, then perhaps the driver might not ask for any identification. He shared the idea with Margie. As it turned out, she did have a friend, Claudia, who was an attorney and lived in Arlington, a suburb of Jacksonville. But Arlington was across the St. John's River, east of the city. It would take at least twenty minutes for her to drive from there to the station downtown.

Before they knew it, the bus had exited I-10 and was not far from the Jacksonville terminal. Margie could see the frightened look on Otter's face. A gentleman across the aisle from Otter got up and headed toward the back of the bus. Otter watched the man enter the small closet containing a toilet and sink. The door shut with a click.

There were no passengers on the back row, and the other seats surrounding the small restroom were also vacant. Otter had an idea.

"Give me one of your stockings," Otter whispered. "These are strong aren't they?"

"What? Why yes, they're as strong as any rope," Margie replied. "What are you up to?"

As Margie looked on, Otter took a bright green stocking and quickly made his way to the back of the bus. As fast as he could, he tied one end of the stocking around the closet door handle and stretched the other end tightly around an adjacent seat and tied it to the metal leg that secured the seat to the floor. The door can probably be opened a little, he thought, but hardly enough for a grown man to exit. At best, the trapped gentleman would have to squeeze under the tightened nylon material that traversed the opening.

Otter returned to his seat. Margie tried to hold in her giggle, which resulted in a snorting sound. Then her face grew pale. It suddenly dawned on her that she had no reason to be on the run. I don't need to escape, she thought. Otter was the one who needed to get off without being caught. But the stocking tied to the door would implicate her as an accomplice. Besides, enough people on the bus, including the driver, had seen her with the stockings, making her donuts. And the boy? It was certainly clear to anyone sitting near them that they were friends. She was stuck.

"You're sure it'll hold?" Otter asked nervously.

Margie awoke from her convicting thoughts. "What?

Yes. Yes, it will hold. If your knots are good enough, he'll never get out of there without help. Gosh, I'm going to have to come with you. The driver will know I helped you and I could get into serious trouble."

Otter was in his own kind of trance.

"Will it hold?" He stared straight ahead. Through the windshield of the bus he could see the neon sign on the Greyhound bus station ahead.

"It will hold!" Margie's voice was hushed but emphatic. "Shoot, I have a rope at home made of these things that I used to pull a car out of a ditch once," Margie said, holding up one of her nylon donuts. Otter remembered the red, white, and blue rope she had shown him back in Starke. He turned and looked at the nylon stocking still stretched tightly from the handle of the cabinet door to the seat. A sudden whooshing noise came from inside the restroom.

The bus had just turned into the station parking area when the pounding from inside the restroom began. Then came the yelling. Otter could see the driver's face in the rearview mirror as he looked up to see what was going on. The pounding persisted and the yelling became vulgar. The bus halted in the stall. The driver got up and walked quickly to the rear of the bus, muttering something that Otter could not interpret. He had not opened the bus door.

"Get ready. We're going to have to move fast," Otter whispered, slipping on his backpack as he watched the driver move past them to the back of the bus.

"I sure hope you know what you're doing." Margie whispered. Holding her stocking bag tightly in hand, she squirmed past Otter to get to the aisle. "Oh shoot!" she said with a start, covering her mouth with her hand to muffle her voice. “My suitcase. Can you reach my suitcase?” Otter grabbed the suitcase from the overhead rack and scooted up the aisle to the door.

The trapped man continued to protest.

“Hold your horses!” the driver called out, irritated at the man’s impatience. He surveyed the curious situation. Recognizing immediately the bright green stocking tied to the door, he turned to the front of the bus to see what the woman with the stockings might know about it. She and the boy were no longer in their seats but had moved to the front and were struggling to open the exit door.

“Hey! Don’t open that door until I say so!” The driver took a step back toward the front of the bus, but the pounding and yelling resumed, halting his step. Reaching in his pocket, he pulled out a pocket knife, opened it, and sawed through the tough green stocking, freeing the frantic passenger.

The driver shouted at a couple of passengers who were reaching for luggage overhead to clear the aisle. He shoved his way through to the front of the bus. Otter could not figure out how to open the door. It was not like the mechanical system he had seen on the buses at school. The lever that he thought would open the door did not budge. Margie was frantically pushing buttons and pulling any knob that looked like it would result in some action. Window wipers were whooshing back and forth and lights were flashing before the door finally opened. In a single leap, Otter jumped to the asphalt quay below, skipping the three steps. Margie was on the second step when she felt a sudden tug.

“No you don’t, sister. You’re not going anywhere!” The driver had hold of the shoulder strap of her stocking bag.

“Let go of her!” Otter shouted. At the same time, Margie let the bag slip from her arm, and she darted out of the bus on the heels of her very fast friend. The bus driver’s attempt to follow the two riders was cut off by a crowd of passengers disembarking from another bus. Shaking his head in resignation, the driver opened the canvas bag to check for identification. It was filled with women’s stockings of a variety of colors and little donut-like things. He turned to see the other passengers exiting from his bus.

“Anyone know that woman or that boy?” he asked the passengers who filed past. They paid no attention to him.

“What boy are you talking about, mister?”

The driver turned to see the angry eyes of a small, weary man looking up at him.

“That boy,” The driver responded. His outstretched arm pointed in the direction of the lit boulevard to a boy and a woman hurriedly dodging traffic to get across.

James Fisher turned in the direction indicated by the driver. Through the drizzle he strained to get a good look at the smaller of the two fleeing figures.

Chapter Thirteen

The Capabilities Exercise was set for Saturday of the July Fourth weekend. B Company had received high marks in the qualifying competition and was one of three companies chosen to participate. Sergeant Gage was ecstatic. The final piece to his plan was in place. The US Government would finally sit up and take notice of just how far it had slipped from its original mission. Redemption day was at hand.

For a week both Dee and Terry were listed as AWOL. There were reports that the two had been seen together before their disappearance. To Gage's delight, these were sightings he did not have to concoct.

Terry's wife Janine was frantic. She began to suspect the worst. She even began to suspect Dee. Their encounters at the post chapel and the occasional social gathering gave her no reason to think he would do anything to hurt Terry. He seemed to be a kind man. But as time wore on, in her frustration she could not help recalling that Dee was from Lacey, and she was all too aware of the awful stories her grandmother had told her of the racist violence associated with that part of Orange County. She didn't want to implicate Dee, but she was desperate. She decided to share this history with the military police. Local and state law enforcement had been assisting with the investigation. With Janine's newest revelation, it became a potential civil rights case. The FBI was called in.

The whole thing was baffling. Dee's friend and commander, Glenn Sisson, could not understand it. The MPs had questioned him twice. He had no clue what was going on. Having no luck in his search for Dee in Fayetteville and Cumberland County, Glenn called the diner back in Lacey and managed to get Vicky on the phone. She was still recovering from her surgery.

"I haven't heard a thing, Glenn," she said, her voice still weak. "I've been worried sick about Otter, and now this. I don't know what's going on." Vicky explained that Otter had disappeared, too. That information made Glenn even more suspicious.

"Something's up," Glenn replied. "This is not like Dee at all. And for Otter to be missing at the same time… something's not right. Listen, let me know if you hear from Dee. I suspect, assuming he's alright, he'll be contacting you. And if he shows up there, tell him to get his ass back here on the double!" Glenn paused to regain his composure, said goodbye to Vicky, and hung up the phone. He was angry but not sure at whom. He was responsible for all his men. Their behavior reflected on him. But Dee had never been a problem. In fact, he was the model reservist to whom Glenn pointed as an example for the younger guys. Certainly Dee was not the impetuous type, and that's what really worried him. Something was wrong. Very wrong.

Dee felt the cold grainy concrete pressed against his cheek when he woke. He was lying on his side stretched out with his ankles tied together and his hands tied behind his back. His head was throbbing and his body ached. He tried to sit up but the pain was too intense. Then he remembered Terry.

"Tehrwee." The gag in his mouth allowed only a muffled sound. He tried again, "Tehrwee." There was no response. Dee was blindfolded, so he could not see if his friend was near. He managed to roll over on his stomach and then to his other side. When he did, he bumped into what felt like a body. He was sure of it.

"Hehh, Tehrwee! Woowokay? Tehrwee?" There was no response. Dee pressed his body against the silent heap beside him, trying to sense its warmth. "Is he still alive?" he wondered. "Is it even Terry?" Dee could not sense any heat radiating from the body. He lay still, straining to hear a hint of breathing. He feared the worse.

Dee lay silent in the darkness on the cold slab. He slipped in and out of consciousness for a time, then was startled awake by the chilling sound of metal scraping on concrete. Through the blindfold he could detect the beam of a flashlight.

"Yeah, Sergeant. He's still alive. I don't know about the other one. He ain't movin' any." The voice was not familiar to Dee.

Then a second voice. It was Gage.

"Okay. Put the old man in back of the van and stick Warren in the Hummer. And be sure and clean up any blood," Gage ordered. "I don't want any evidence they were here."

Dee felt sharp pains in his shoulders as he was lifted

off the floor by at least two persons, one at his arms and one at his legs. He tried to mount some resistance but was quickly reminded how little strength he had. Quickly, he was heaved into the back of a van and covered with a tarpaulin. Terry did not follow. He must have been put in the other vehicle, Dee speculated. Is Terry okay? he wondered. Is he even still alive? Dee was livid. What were these guys up to?

The van's motor started. The Humvee remained silent. Dee could hear a few words of a muffled conversation but not enough to understand what was being said. Then the van slowly moved forward and traveled for what seemed like several miles along a bumpy dirt road. Dee could hear nothing of the other vehicle. Finally, the van slowed, then inched onto a paved road. It felt to Dee like it turned left. Still, no sign of the other vehicle.

For what seemed like an eternity, the van sped along at a high rate of speed. The whining sound of the engine was deafening. Dee strained to hear anything familiar that might help him locate where he was. For a long time no oncoming traffic passed the van.

Finally an occasional car could be heard. Dee was sure they were entering a populated area. Not a lot of traffic, but some. Where were they? Fort Bragg? Fayetteville? They could be as far away as Raleigh, he judged.

The van made several turns before coming to a stop. Dee heard gears grinding beneath him and felt the vehicle back up. It stopped. Two doors opened, then slammed shut. Dee braced himself, expecting to be pulled out of the back, possibly executed. But the footsteps faded. Then silence. For a long time Dee heard nothing but the sound of his own breathing. After a futile attempt to stay awake, straining for some hint of what was going on around him, Dee fell asleep.

To their surprise, Gage ordered Gallworth and Jamison to steal a car from downtown Fayetteville. They couldn't figure out what he was up to. Why couldn't they just get rid of both men and be done with it. Their buried bodies wouldn't be discovered for weeks, maybe even months. By then their plot would have been carried out and they would be reaping the rewards. But Gage didn't see it that way. Something about the old man and his self-righteous ways irritated him. It was too easy to just do away with him. He was determined set Dee up to take a hard fall and willing to go to great lengths to do it.

The two men came back with a '72 Cadillac. Initially Gage was upset. He was expecting a newer model vehicle. Later that evening, Gage instructed the two grunts to drive to Dee's apartment located in off-post housing designated for visiting reserve officers. Under the cover of dark, the two soldiers entered the apartment with Dee's key and planted racist propaganda tying its occupant to a known white-supremacist organization. It was material that Gage had also begun to distribute secretly in strategic places around Fort Bragg.

Before leaving the scene, a pistol encased in a plastic sack, was set aside. It was a military-issue 45 caliber Smith and Wesson, the weapon Gage used to shoot Terry in the back of the head shortly after he was taken from the storage shed. The pistol was carefully removed from the sack and placed in a kitchen drawer. On the weapon's handle Gage had arranged for a clear set of fingerprints—the finger prints of its owner—Major Addison Dumpkin.

Terry's body was taken to a wooded area not far from post, and dumped. Gage didn't want it buried, he was counting on someone finding it, part of the trail of evidence that would lead to Dee.

The final piece of Sergeant Gage's plot to frame Major Dumpkin was about to be put into place. Gage's grunts moved Dee from the van to an abandoned building. There, they were given strict orders to keep Dee under guard, cuffed and blindfolded for the next five days, feeding him only beer and baloney sandwiches twice a day. The elaborate plan continued to confound Gage's accomplices. They were beginning to wonder if he was losing his mind.

Dee was awakened by the noise of what sounded like two vehicles approaching. They stopped just outside the building. Then came the familiar sound of footsteps on the gravel. A door rattled, then opened. Dee could see nothing, but he could hear boots on the concrete floor moving quickly in his direction.

He was hoisted by his arms and legs and carried out of the building. The warm fresh air engulfed him as he exited the building. It felt good. Through the blindfold he could detect no light. He had lost all track of time. It was his only clue that, once again, he was being transported at night.

Dee was not aware that he had been put into the trunk of the '72 Cadillac that had been used to transport Terry's body. His only sensation was the vehicle moving slowly through stop-and-go traffic before speeding swiftly onto a freeway or interstate highway.

Private Jamison drove the Caddy and was followed by Private Gallworth and Sergeant Gage in Gage's '97 Pontiac Firebird. To avoid detection on the highway, the

 North Carolina license plates on the Cadillac had been replaced with Georgia plates stolen off the car of a soldier who had shipped out to Germany. The two vehicles traveled the speed limit south on Interstate 95 careful not to attract attention. But to Gage's irritation, the Caddy, after less than two hours on the road, began to overheat. Gage kept his cool. It was another skill gleaned from the Army—be prepared for the unexpected. It will surely happen.

The two vehicles exited the interstate in search of a mechanic. Despite the setback, Gage's luck was still working for him. They were in Florence, South Carolina. The intersection of I-95 and I– 20 at Florence was home to at least six gas stations.

Chapter Fourteen

Margie was able to locate her friend, Claudia, in Arlington. Claudia and Margie had been close friends and roommates while attending the University of South Carolina in Spartanburg in the early '70s.

Claudia was glad to offer sanctuary to her old roommate and her new friend and, after hearing Otter's tale, was even willing to drive the two as far as Florence. Not wanting to impose, Margie insisted that she and Otter could take the bus, confident there was little chance they would encounter the same driver. However, Claudia, using her skills as an attorney, was more persuasive. She was planning to be in Columbia in a few days to take a deposition in a case she was working on. She insisted that she could drive them up to Florence, spend a couple of days, then drive over to Columbia in plenty of time for the deposition. Otter liked the plan. Margie reluctantly gave in.

The next day around noon, they headed north up Interstate 95 to Florence. Otter enjoyed having the back seat of Claudia's Lexus to himself. The plush sedan still smelled new. At first he hesitated to stretch out on the seat, not wanting to appear disrespectful. But finally, dulled by the chitchat of the women in the front seat swapping stories and getting caught up, he stretched out and fell asleep.

At the Georgia-South Carolina border, Claudia and Margie decided to stop at the welcome station for a bathroom break. Sensing the car slow down, Otter awoke and sat up, rubbing his eyes and looking around to see what was going on.

After parking the car, the two women made their way around one side of the facility and Otter headed in the opposite direction. Though this sort of stop was routine to him from the several trips he had made with Dee and Vicky up I-95 to Fort Bragg, Otter didn't remember stopping at this particular rest area.

The restroom was not crowded. An elderly gentleman was at the first of four urinals. Otter instinctively moved to the urinal the furthest away from the old man. Peeing in urinals always made him feel self-conscious, and he moved as close to the porcelain fixture as he could possibly get without brushing up against it.

The old man had already finished washing his hands and was drying them with a paper towel when Otter zipped up and prepared to flush. He searched for the handle but there was none. A little red light at the top of the fixture stared back at him in his perplexity. Otter turned to see the old man smiling at him. When he did, the urinal flushed itself. Otter smiled sheepishly and moved to wash his hands. The faucets had no handles. Suspicious, Otter glanced around for another little red light. There was none. By accident he waved his hand under the faucet and the water came on. He was impressed and moved to turn on each of the four faucets.

As Otter reached the last faucet, which was adjacent to one of the several commode stalls, he heard someone stirring on the other side of the petition. He was a little surprised at the realization that he was not alone in the restroom. His playfulness ceased, and he made his way to the paper towel dispenser to dry his hands. Turning in the direction of the stalls, he could see the shoes of the occupant barely exposed from beneath his trousers crumpled on the floor. Otter stepped forward to get a better look. There was something familiar about the wingtipped shoes. A sudden surge of fear shot through Otter's body. Like a rocket, he flew out the door of the restroom. As he rounded the corner, he bumped into Claudia who was drinking a Pepsi and eating cheese crackers.

"Whoa there, Otter! What's your hurry?" she asked, holding tight to her crackers. Otter ignored her words and gestures. Frantic, he ran to the curb and searched both directions. At the north end of the parking area he saw it—the red Ford Escort wagon.

Otter turned back toward Claudia and ran smack into her. She had followed him to the curb.

"Hey, what's the matter? You look like you've seen a ghost!"

"I've got to hide," Otter said, his eyes glued to the men's room exit. "Can you open the car so I can hide? Please, hurry. It's him."

"It's who?" Claudia asked.

"You remember the story I told you about my uncle? He's in there," Otter said, pointing to the restroom entrance.

At that moment they heard the faint sound of a toilet flushing. Otter turned and ran toward the car with Claudia following behind, foraging in her purse for her keys.

As Otter approached the Lexus, he was greeted with a flash of headlights as if the car was excited to see him. Claudia pushed the remote once again, and the door locks jumped to attention.

Otter quickly opened the back door and scrambled onto the seat. Just as he did, he glimpsed James exiting the restroom. Claudia shut the door behind him and moved quickly back onto the sidewalk.

The small, skinny man standing on the walkway, blowing his nose into a handkerchief, had to be the notorious Uncle James, she figured. Claudia recognized the volatility of the situation and hurried to alert Margie before she came out of the women's room. She halted at the entrance and waited, not wanting to lose sight of James and Otter. James looked up at her and caught her eye. She looked away. He folded his handkerchief and returned it to the breast pocket of his coat.

James moved slowly toward the parking lot. Claudia noted that he would have to pass her car on the way to his own. Her heart jumped when Otter's head briefly bobbed above the front seat of the Lexus as he tried to survey the situation. Otter saw his uncle and immediately crawled as close to the floor of the car as he could get. Margie emerged from the women's room.

"Where's Otter?" she asked, thinking surely he must have finished in the restroom by now.

Claudia turned and put her hand to Margie's lips. "Shhh." Looking back toward the car, she saw that James had halted. Had he heard anything? Margie had blurted out Otter's name loud enough that it could have been heard from that distance, she figured. But had he heard?

James stood by a garbage can peeling an orange. He didn't seem to be acting suspicious. Claudia motioned Margie to follow her to the vending machines.

"That's Otter's uncle, that man over there." Claudia motioned with a brief glance in James' direction.

"Are you sure?"

"Otter is sure. He recognized him in the men's room."

"Did his uncle see him?" Margie's voice revealed her amazement. She even seemed amused. Claudia frowned.

"This is serious stuff, Margie, and no, I don't think he saw him. If that guy discovers we have Otter and calls the police, we could be in serious trouble. He's a relative and probably has some custody rights."

The two women looked toward James. He was staring at them. They turned away and pretended to study the vending machines.

"Do you have any change?" Margie whispered.

"No. I used my last for the Pepsi and crackers." Claudia searched her wallet and produced a one-dollar bill.

"Here use this." As she handed the dollar to Margie, Claudia glanced up to see James' reflection in the vending machine.

"Oh, no! He's coming this way!" Claudia's loud whisper startled a young couple on their way to the restrooms. They laughed and hurried on.

James approached the vending machines and fumbled for some change in his pocket. After staring at the change in his hand for a few seconds, he turned to the two women.

"You ladies wouldn't happen to have change for a dollar would yuh?"

Claudia turned to look at James. His smile was mocking. She looked down at his open hand full of change. He had plenty.

"No, sorry. We've used all of ours."

"Do I know you ladies? There's somethin' familiar about that 'un there," he said, pointing to Margie as if she were on display.

She looked up at him and stared hard into his eyes.

"Don't I know you, Miss?" James asked. His voice sent a chill up her back.

"No, sir, I don't think so. Please excuse us." Margie took Claudia by the arm and pulled her toward the car.

"I'm looking for my nephew," came the shrill voice again. The women slowed, trying to appear polite but in a hurry. "He's 'bout this tall, kinda sandy blond hair. You haven't seen 'im, have yuh?"

Claudia looked over her shoulder at the man who was now following them. She spoke as she continued to walk. "No, sir, haven't seen anyone of that description." With a squeeze of the remote, Claudia's Lexus greeted the two women with a flash of the headlights.

The women moved quickly to open the doors and get in the car. They fastened themselves in and with a turn of the ignition, the Lexus was ready to go. James followed them to the car, still eating a section of orange. He stepped down off the curb and motioned Claudia to roll down her window. She hesitated just long enough for Margie to whisper to Otter to stay down. Then she pushed the button, lowering the window halfway.

When Otter heard the familiar voice, he gasped. At the same time, Margie's jacket, which she had taken off before getting into the car, came flying over the seat on top of him. He lay perfectly still. He was afraid his heart might betray him with its loud thumping.

James leaned close to Claudia, closer than she felt comfortable with. His fruity breath invaded her space. She leaned back slightly.

"His name is Millard, Millard Dumpkin. He's my dead sister's grandson. Some call him Otter, ya know, like that squirrelly animal. He might be travelin' with a lady about your age. The man at the bus station told me they was headed for Florence, South Carolina. Where're you ladies headed."?

"Well, that's none of your business, mister," Claudia said sternly. But if you must know, we're on our way to Spartanburg."

James cast a quick glance to the back seat as he straightened up and moved back from the car. "You ladies have a good day."

Claudia backed out of the parking space and resumed her northerly direction. In the rearview mirror she watched James watching them as they regained I-95. The car merged into traffic and the two front-seat passengers sat in silence. After a few moments Otter poked his head up and looked back toward the distant rest stop. Relieved, he sat back and closed his eyes. The Lexus sped on to Florence.

Chapter Fifteen

Most of the gas stations closest to the interstate off ramps were convenience markets with gas pumps. The only one with a mechanic on duty was Howard's Truck Stop. Gage signaled to the driver of the Caddy to pull in. The large parking area was full of eighteen-wheelers. The Cadillac pulled up behind a Peterbilt that was being serviced in one of the garage bays. Gage's Firebird swung in next to the Caddy. He jumped out in search of a mechanic. A middle-aged man appeared, wiping his hands on a rag.

"Howdy," Gage greeted the man.

"Evenin'. What can I do for you?" the man replied. He stuffed the rag in his back pocket.

"I've got a vehicle that's overheating and was hoping you could take a look at it."

The mechanic eyed the column of steam spewing from the hood of the Cadillac. "Looks like you blew a hose."

"Yessir. Think you could fix it?" Gage's voice had a

slight sense of urgency about it.

The mechanic walked over to the vehicle. "Let's take a look at 'er."

As he moved to the front of the car, he motioned the driver to pop the hood. Gallworth fumbled for the lever under the dash by his left leg, then pulled it. Nothing happened. Gage's sudden sprint to the rear of the car startled Gallworth. His arm pressed against the steering wheel, causing the horn to blast. Then he turned to see what the sergeant was up to and realized what he had done. The lever he pulled had opened the trunk! His heart jumped. "Shit!" he exclaimed under his breath. Gage quickly shut the trunk as the mechanic laughed and shouted to Gallworth, "No, the other one!"

Gage moved back to the front of the vehicle, casting dagger eyes at Gallworth as he passed. Catastrophe averted—narrowly.

Gallworth opened the driver-side door and the interior light came on. He leaned down and found the proper lever and popped the hood.

"Yeah. It's a busted water hose. Look here. See it?" Gage pretended to be interested as his eyes followed the mechanic's finger.

"Can you fix it?" Gage asked.

"Shoot, I love working on these babies—lots of room. There's enough space under this hood to hide a body."

Gage glanced up at the mechanic. A coincidence, only a coincidence, he reassured himself.

"If I've got the right size hose, I can knock it out in about fifteen minutes, give or take a few." The mechanic wiped his hands on the rag and returned it again to his back pocket.

"Great," Gage replied. "The sooner the better for us.

We're in kind of a hurry to get back on the road. I don't like driving too late. I start seeing things in the road that aren't there." Gage was doing his best to make small talk and relieve any tension in the air. Gallworth was still agitated with his blunder.

"I hear you," the mechanic said. "I don't like driving late at night myself. If I can't see what's going on around me, I go stir crazy. You guys can go in and get a cup of coffee or something to eat while I finish this, if you like. I'll call you when it's ready."

At first Gage thought they should all stay with the cars but decided he needed the caffeine pickup.

"Gallworth, you stay here. Get some sleep. You look tired." Gallworth could read Gage's eyes. They made it clear—keep an eye on things and don't screw up, or else.

Gage and Jamison headed for the truck stop diner. Gallworth sat in the Caddy listening to the radio. He could see the mechanic through the narrow space between the raised hood and the dashboard, working methodically to replace the busted hose.

Gage and Jamison had been gone only a few minutes when car lights signaled the approach of another vehicle. Gallworth looked into the rearview mirror in time to see the approach of a Lexus with three occupants pull up behind the Caddy. Gallworth sat up straight and turned to get a better look at who it was getting out of the car.

Margie was the first out. The mechanic paused and looked around the hood.

"Well, hey Babe! Where've you been?" he asked. He didn't wait for an answer. "I thought you were coming back yesterday. Your mother's called me twice. She's worried sick. She thought somethin' happened to you." He wiped his hands on the red rag then leaned over and kissed Margie on the cheek. "I fixed your car, Babe. You had a bad fuel pump. It's parked out back behind the diner. What'd you say kept you?"

"Something came up. I ended up staying over with Claudia in Jacksonville last night," Margie replied. At the same instant Claudia and Otter appeared.

"Well, look who's here! My favorite lawyer," the mechanic quipped.

"Hey, Tim, good to see ya. How long's it been?" Claudia's voice seemed distant to Tim. She was usually more jovial. He enjoyed the banter and kidding that flowed easily when the two were together. She was too serious. Something was up.

Tim looked at her for a moment in wonder, then turned his attention to Otter who had moved around to stand next to Margie.

"Who's this? A new boyfriend?" Tim joked.

"This is Otter Dumpkin from Lacey, Florida." Margie put her arm around Otter and moved him in front of her. Otter could feel her hands on his shoulders. It was an act of affection that he welcomed. "Otter, this is my ex, Tim Patterson." Tim extended his hand to the boy.

"Well, hello, Otter Dumpkin from Lacey, Florida. Where the heck is Lacey?" Tim asked playfully.

"West of Orlando." Otter replied. "It's just a little place."

Gallworth, who had relaxed when it appeared that the new arrivals were harmless, suddenly leaned forward. *Dumpkin? Otter Dumpkin?* Did he hear right? Dumpkin was an unusual name, but what really caught his attention was the name Otter. Gallworth had taken his turn guarding Dee back in Fayetteville and had the occasion when the prisoner was eating to talk to him.

He spoke of Lacey and his grandson—Otter.

Gallworth continued to listen to the conversation. The boy was heading to Fayetteville to find his grandfather. Gallworth strained to collect as many details as he could gather. Then he decided he needed to get Gage.

When Gallworth exited the Caddy, Claudia jumped and let out a little squeal. She had not noticed the young man sitting in the driver's seat of the car.

"Excuse me, ma'am. I didn't mean to scare you." Gallworth shut the door softly as if he didn't want to wake someone. "I'm going to step inside for a moment and use the restroom. I'll be right back," he announced to no one in particular.

"You can use the one right around the corner there if you want," Tim said, pointing in the opposite direction.

"Naw. I think I'll get me a cup of coffee while I'm inside." Without waiting for a response, Gallworth turned and headed for the diner.

Inside, the nervous soldier relayed to Gage what he had heard. Initially Gage was upset with him for leaving his post, but the news of Dumpkin's grandson being just outside the door cooled his anger quickly. He sat for a moment thinking hard about what to do.

Jamison nudged Gage. "Hey, we've got more company."

Gage looked out the window across the parking lot to the garage bay. "Who the hell is that?" Gage almost laughed. Someone with a red stocking pulled over his head was holding a gun on the two women, the boy, and the mechanic. "Shit, we gotta get out there before this fiasco gets any worse." Gage threw down a twenty dollar bill on the table and the three men headed out.

"Jamison, circle around to the back of the bay and try to get behind him," Gage said. Jamison headed for the back exit.

Gage and Gallworth approached the Caddy and what appeared to be a holdup in progress.

"What's going on here?" Gage asked. He was cool as a cucumber.

The small figure in the stocking mask was startled. In a sudden move he turned to face Gage. Gallworth ducked, avoiding the haphazard aim of the pistol. Gage stood still with his hands up. Regaining his composure, Gallworth joined Gage with his hands in the air. The gunman was shaking. He turned back and forth between Gage and Gallworth and the four others. The gunman motioned the two new arrivals to join the other four in front of the Cadillac.

Gage began a calm inquiry. He had some training in hostage situations and it showed. "If it's money you want, these folks don't look like they've got a lot. I've got a little cash, you can take it and leave them alone."

"I ain't interested in your money. I want the boy," the masked man said. The voice was unmistakable. In the security of his friends, Otter felt the impulse to laugh.

"Uncle James, you look like a fool with that thing on your head," Otter said. He took a step toward his uncle.

James pointed the gun at him. "Stay back over there, boy! I don't wanna hurt you or nobody else. But I will if I have to."

Gage spoke up. "What's your interest in the boy? he asked, again exuding cool.

"He's my sister's grandson." James replied. "He's the only blood kin that I have and he's my responsibility."

"So why the gun?" Gage asked. "It doesn't look to

 me like you're his favorite uncle."

"I got rights and responsibilities. He's my kin and he needs to be with me. The authorities gave him to me." James was beginning to exhibit some of the bulldog characteristics that he was known for when he got angry.

Claudia spoke up. "They didn't give him to you, sir," she said to James. "If anything, he was placed in your care and protection by a social worker, not a judge, and from what I have seen here and heard from Otter, not much care has been exhibited." Despite her attempt to persuade James, she knew that if it were left up to the courts, he would most likely be awarded custody. A judge would rule for kinship every time unless there was clear evidence of negligence. In this case, she was confident she could convince a judge that Otter's safety would be compromised if he were released to his uncle.

Gage saw the opportunity to resolve his new problem.

"Well, if he's your kin, I guess he ought to be with you," he said.

"I'm not going with him. He's a ..." Otter stopped short. Out of the corner of his eye, he caught a glimpse of a figure in the shadows. James turned to follow Otter's eyes. Gage seized the opportunity and lunged at James seizing him around the neck with one arm and grabbing his wrist with the other. James was no match for the sergeant. Gage twisted the wrist back on itself causing James to scream in pain, dropping the gun to the ground. Jamison moved out of the shadow and picked it up. It was made of plastic.

Otter caught everyone off guard when he stepped quickly toward his uncle, grabbed the end of the red stocking and yanked it off the little man's head.

"Damn you, boy! You 'bout burnt my nose off!" James snorted.

Margie reached out and pulled Otter back close to her, keeping him out of James' reach. Then she spoke to Gage, "Thank you, sir. Thanks a lot."

Gage held tight to James, who wanted desperately to make his nephew pay for his sore nose.

Tim echoed Margie's sentiment, then asked, "Who are you guys? Are you the FBI or something?"

Gage smiled. "No, just some B Company grunts from Fort Bragg headed to Charleston for some R & R before being shipped out. Private Gallworth here saw what was happening from the window and alerted us. Y'all looked like you were in some serious trouble. Of course, the important thing was I didn't want to risk this guy stealing our car and ruining my vacation." Gage laughed at his attempt at sarcasm. No one seemed to get it.

Otter squirmed out of Margie's grasp. "You wouldn't happen to know my grandfather, Dee Dumpkin? He's at Fort Bragg getting ready to go overseas to that war over there too."

"You're Dumpkin's grandson? Well I'll be… Yeah, we know about Dumpkin. Everybody on post knows about him. Never met him, though," Gage said, appearing to be sympathetic. "Son, I don't mean to upset you, but my advice would be for you to go with your friends here. Your granddaddy has got himself in some deep trouble with the murder of that …" Gage caught himself before he revealed his racist slur. "…that guy, what was his name?" He turned to Jamison.

"Warren, Private Warren," Jamison replied.

"Yeah, Warren. Damn good soldier, Warren."

Tears formed in Otter's eyes. "My grandfather wouldn't murder anyone," he said, fighting back the tears. "He's a good man!"

"That's not what they're saying around Fayetteville. It seems they've found a lot of evidence to convict your grandfather as some kind of racist fanatic."

"It's not true! It's not true! He's not like that!" Otter sobbed. He turned and held tight to Margie.

At that moment, a loud banging came from the back of the Cadillac. But the sound was soon drowned out, as an eighteen-wheeler roared by on its way back to the interstate. Gage glanced at Jamison, then at Gallworth. They knew it was time to leave, and fast, before the noise from their captive created suspicion and a new set of problems.

Gage did not hesitate to create a diversion. He pushed James in the direction of the diner, kicking him in the seat of his pants. "It doesn't appear that the boy is going with you, little man, so you'd better be on your way."

James was rounding the back of the Cadillac when the loud banging noise started again. He paused and looked down at the trunk of the car, then at Gage. Gage ignored the noise and growled at James.

"Get going, mister, or I'll have the police on you like stink on sh..." Gage hesitated, looked apologetically at Claudia and Margie, then again at James. "Now git!"

Gage opened the door of the Caddy and started the engine. The 500 cubic inches of controlled explosion roared. Any noise from the trunk now would be barely audible, if heard at all. Gage stepped from the car, pulled his wallet from his back pocket and approached Tim.

"Well, I guess she's ready. What do we owe you?"

Tim was puzzled. What just happened? He looked at Margie and Otter. Both had the same look of confusion on their faces.

"Uh, that'll be twelve dollars for the hose and twenty

dollars labor," Tim said, looking at the Caddy then up at Gage. The big sergeant produced two twenty dollar bills and handed them to the mechanic.

"Keep the change. Appreciate your service." Gage looked at Otter. "Sorry about your granddaddy, son. Too bad." He looked at Margie and Claudia and tipped an imaginary hat. " Ladies, a pleasure coming to your rescue." Then, in a burst of energy, he turned and barked orders to the other two men. "Gallworth, you drive the Caddy. Jamison, you and I will follow in my car."

The four stood alone, silent, watching the Cadillac and the Firebird move out of the parking lot to I-95 south. Then, moments later, a small red station wagon appeared from around the corner of the diner, headed in the same direction.

Chapter Sixteen

James followed the two cars south on I-95 as close as he could without arousing suspicion. His reasons for following the three men were muddled in his mind. The embarrassment he felt at the hands of the thugs made him angry, but perhaps more than that he was determined to know what was in the trunk of Sergeant Gage's Cadillac. Being a sly character himself, it was easy for him to spot kindred minds. He suspected kidnapping. Someone, he convinced himself, was in the trunk of the car.

After crossing the long Lake Marion bridge, the two cars took the next exit and headed west on a rural South Carolina road. James followed. About half a mile down the road, a convenience mart appeared on the left. The Firebird and the Caddy slowed and pulled in. Gage got out and went inside. James pulled off the side of the road, well back from the store, and watched. After only a couple of minutes Gage exited carrying something. Curious, James leaned forward over the steering wheel, trying see what it was. Beer? It's two six-packs of something, he thought to himself.

The cars backed away from the convenience mart, and continued west down the two-lane highway. After waiting a moment to let the two cars get well under way, James steered the Escort back onto the road and followed, keeping well back, almost a half-mile, he figured. After several minutes, the tail lights of the two vehicles suddenly went dark. He slowed and leaned forward with both hands on the wheel, trying to make sense of it. Had they turned off the road? Turned off their lights? Were they suspicious that they were being followed? In any case, just like that, they were gone.

James approached cautiously. His guess was that Gage and company, suspecting they were being followed, had pulled over and turned off their lights. He flashed his high beams. No vehicles on the shoulders of the road. He sped up. Then, off to the left, something caught his eye through the trees—brake lights. The two cars had turned off onto a dirt road, driving several hundred yards into a densely wooded area. James slowed and extinguished his lights as he pulled off onto the shoulder.

He sat and watched. What the heck are they up to? he wondered. With their lights still on, the cars remained parked in the woods among the pines. James could see figures milling about, casting long shadows. Suddenly, the headlights were extinguished. Only the faint glow of the interior lights could be seen.

James reclined his seat just enough to rest his head and still be able to see the distant light of the cars. Fearing he might doze off, he turned on the radio. The only station he could pick up was a rock station out of Charlotte.

At 11:00 p.m. the news came on. Among the reports was one that prompted James to turn up the volume—the murder investigation of a young Fort Bragg soldier. The principal suspect, Major Addison Dumpkin.

James' attention to the story was suddenly interrupted by the sound of a car engine starting, followed by the flash of headlights through the trees. The car made a U-turn and headed out to the road. The headlights flashed high into the trees, then low to the ground as the car bounced its way back to the pavement and resumed its journey west.

James waited a few minutes to see if the other vehicle would appear. He was sure he had seen two vehicles go into the woods. He started his car and slowly directed it back onto the road, keeping well back from the car ahead. Several minutes passed when a pair of headlights appeared in his rearview mirror about a mile back. James' first thought was that he had fallen into a trap.

The mystery car quickly caught up and for a moment was only feet behind the Escort. Sweat began forming on James' forehead. He tried to increase his speed but the little car had given all it had. A sign appeared—Ellerbee 3 miles. James' mind raced. Can I make it to the next town before the fool runs me off the road? Is it even Gage? he wondered. And if it is him, is he coming after me?

James was breathing hard. With the accelerator floored, the car struggled to maintain its speed. Suddenly the little Escort wagon jerked, sputtered and coughed. Fear shot through the little man's body. He glanced at the fuel gage—empty! Now panic gripped him. In all the confusion back at the truck stop he had not remembered to gas-up. On I-95 with his eyes glued to the tail lights of the Caddy and the Firebird, he had not noticed that he was riding on empty. The car sputtered again. James slowed. His heart pounded wildly when the high whine of the Firebird's motor announced its presence and moved past the little red car. The tail lights of the Firebird quickly moved away as the wagon slurped the last of the gas in the tank. James put the gearshift in neutral and coasted as far as he could, then pulled off onto the shoulder of the road.

For a few moments he sat in the dark thinking about what to do. With the lights out he could see very little.

"Sweet Jesus, I need a miracle," he whispered. He reached over to the glove compartment and took out a flashlight. When he opened the door to get out, the interior light came on. The light reflected off something across the road that caught his attention. Pointing the flashlight into the woods, he saw two John Deere tractors with attached mowers in a clearing just off the side of the road, implements belonging to the South Carolina Department of Transportation. Positioned far enough off the road so as not to be a traffic hazard, the machines were left there by a work crew who would return the next day to continue mowing the roadside.

James was an expert at siphoning gas. On more than one occasion, while on the road with the evangelist preaching in college towns, they had received offerings of gas in lieu of cash. Even after parting company with the evangelist and returning to Lacey for good, he maintained the practice of carrying a hose and a plastic gas container in his car. He wanted to be ready in case he ever ran across a penniless convert who might have little money but plenty of gas.

James retrieved the hose and gas container and made

 his way in the dark to the tractors. In no time, he was on the road again, headed toward Ellerbee in search of Sergeant Gage.

James could see the lights of the town in the distance. He slowed, not knowing what to expect. Gage was clever and James didn't want to walk into a trap. The road curved to the right, revealing the first of the streetlights of the small town. As he approached, the tall maples and stately houses lining the quiet street betrayed a well-to-do but older residential neighborhood. The two-story frame houses with their red brick steps and wrap-around porches reminded him of some of the finer homes of Lacey.

Sidewalks appeared, separating the road from the neatly manicured lawns of the homes, many of which were lined with white picket or cast-iron fences. Nothing moved along the concrete trails or the streets.

James pulled over to the side of the road. Ahead on the right a streetlight was out, resulting in an expanse of darkness stretching for two city blocks before another house was illuminated by the next streetlight. A single blinking light flashed at the edge of the darkness. He took his flashlight and got out of the car, then walked cautiously toward the blinking light. It was coming from a car that leaned slightly to its right side as if it had been jacked up to replace a flat tire. James looked around. The closest houses were dark. Maybe it was later than he thought. He shined the light at his watch. It was almost midnight.

Inspecting the scene, James could see that the wood pole supporting the darkened street light had been sheared in two. The power lines were not broken but were swaying dangerously close to the car.

It was Gage's Cadillac. The collision with the power pole had smashed in its front and shattered the windshield. The car was resting on the remaining stub of the pole which caused it to sit at such a strange angle. James noticed that the trunk of the vehicle was slightly open. He raised the hood and breathed a sigh of relief when he saw that it was unoccupied. Maybe I was hearing things back at the truck stop, he thought to himself. Maybe there was never anyone inside.

James checked for approaching traffic. None. It's scary, he thought. This town is too quiet. He was confounded that no one was standing at a door or a window, or out on the porch of even the closest houses. There was no sound of approaching emergency vehicles or police. Certainly a crash like this would have made a heck of a noise!

James stepped cautiously towards the front of the car taking care not to get too close to the power lines. He sniffed the air. The smell of beer floated from the interior of the car. He shined his light on a lone occupant slumped against the steering wheel of the car. You drunk SOB, James thought. Which one of you done kilt yourself? He hoped it was Gage.

As he moved to get a closer look, James pointed his flashlight into the darkness in the direction of what he had guessed to be a park or some large vacant lot. He froze. It was a cemetery. Though he never liked to admit it, James was a little superstitious. The realization that he was so close to a cemetery made his already trembling hands tremble even more. Quickly he turned his attention back to the body.

The smell of beer grew stronger as he approached the

driver. He stopped and looked around, checking again to see if there were onlookers. Still nobody in sight. The silence was eerie and now the idea of touching a dead body caused him to shudder. He took a deep breath, and through the broken windshield he whispered to the body, "You sure did it right, fella. You ain't got but fifty foot to get to the graveyard." James chuckled at his little joke.

Emboldened by his humor, he reached past the shattered glass into the Caddy and pushed on the shoulder of the man leaning against the steering wheel. The body fell back. At the sound of a moan, James jumped back. He gasped and stumbled away from the vehicle as if he had been pushed. Collecting himself, he approached the car again. "He sure enough ain't dead!" he whispered to himself. Trying to steady his shaking hand, he shined his flashlight into the dark front seat of the car. The light fell on a familiar face, but it wasn't the face of Gage or one of his cronies. It was the face of his brother-in-law, Dee Dumpkin.

Chapter Seventeen

Dee woke to the sound of rushing wind and music. He was lying flat on his back, his head turned to one side. He had the sensation that he was moving. The vibrations were familiar, yet there was something different about his surroundings. Suddenly it occurred to him that he was not blindfolded and his hands and feet were no longer bound. He was not in the pitch-black darkness of the trunk of a car

His vision was blurred. For a moment he thought he must be dreaming. He lay still, trying to take inventory of his condition while giving his eyes a chance to focus. He felt nauseous. He tried to move but he ached badly. Finally his eyes cleared, and he recognized that he was staring at the interior door of a car of some kind. Occasionally lights illuminated the space and the sound of a passing car would follow.

After a while he managed to turn his head slightly toward the ceiling of the car's interior. A station wagon, he thought, with its back seat folded down. Though his legs were stiff, he could almost stretch out the length of his body. He pushed against the back of the car to extend his legs as far as they would go. It felt good. Then he closed his eyes and again he slept.

When Dee awoke again, it was to the light of day. He had wondered if he would ever see it again. He felt better and a little stronger despite his aches and stiffness. The driver of the car had the windows rolled down and the radio turned up, and did not hear Dee stirring behind him. In an attempt to get the driver's attention, Dee managed to raise his arm, hoping whoever was driving would see it in the rearview mirror. It worked. As if the gesture controlled the car's velocity, it slowed.

"You awake back there?" The voice was strangely familiar, though the radio and the wind rushing through the windows muffled it. "We'll pull over in a minute, soon as I can find a decent place." The voice sounded more familiar to Dee. He tried to roll over to see who it was speaking to him, but the pain stopped him.

After a few moments Dee sensed the car slowing down again. It continued its slow pace for a while then stopped. The driver exited and opened the back-seat door. Dee rolled over and shielded his eyes from the light in an attempt to see who the person was. He closed his eyes and smiled.

"I don't believe it," Dee said, as he laid back down. "Jimmy Fisher is my savior."

"Watch out now," James replied. "There's only one Savior. I mighta rescued you. Fact is, I did rescue you, but that's all I did. You a lucky man." James paused for a moment.

Dee opened his eyes and looked at him. "I guess so. At least I'm still alive."

Dee slowly raised his legs to his chest and pivoted around toward the open door.

"Here, let me help you out," James said. He took Dee's arm and pulled him forward taking care that his head did not bump on the roof. Dee made a pathetic attempt to stand and fell into the arms of his brother-in-law.

"Pewee, you need a bath! You smell like you been on a drunk-and-a-half!" James said, steadying himself to support Dee's weight. "Come on and let me sit you down over here at this picnic table."

Dee leaned heavily on James and managed the few steps to the table. James eased him down on the bench. Dee closed his eyes, took a slow, deep breath then opened them again. He was staring into James' smiling face. It was an expression Dee could not remember ever seeing on the man. Dee shook his head and returned the smile.

"You gonna be okay?" James asked, as he walked to the back of the car.

"I think I'll make it. You got anything to drink? Anything but beer." Dee grinned, knowing that he reeked of the stuff. He hoped his brother-in-law would catch his humor.

James raised the rear hatch and removed a grocery sack. He had stopped at a little country store along the way and picked up some food, taking care to park his car where it would not be seen.

"You know me better than that," he replied.

Dee looked down at the ground, shook his head and smiled. "Yeah, I know you," he thought to himself.

Dee slowly swung around to put his legs under the picnic table and awaited James' return with whatever was in the bag. He felt dizzy and laid his head on the table, using his arms for a pillow. His cockeyed view revealed a roadside picnic area secluded among tall pines. James had found a table exposed to the morning light. In the slightly chilly morning breeze, the sun felt good.

James set the bag on the table and pulled from it a bottle of ginger ale and some saltine crackers.

"I figured your stomach would be in none too gooda shape after layin' in the back of that Cadillac for so long, so here's what momma would give us kids when we was feeling sick at our stomachs," James said.

Dee sat up again. The ginger ale and saltines immediately brought back memories of his wife, Ruth. Her brother James' recollection reminded him that ginger ale and saltines were served at the Dumpkin home when stomachs were on the mend.

Dee sipped the beverage. The sweet taste was welcome relief from all the bitter beer he had been forced to drink. Gage had provided nothing else. It was beer or die of thirst.

Dee nibbled on the crackers. It was all he could ingest. He put his head back down on the table.

"Tell me what's happened, Jimmy. What's happened since I've been gone. And why in tarnation are you here?" Dee asked in a whisper. Before James could begin to answer his questions, Dee was once again asleep.

As Dee slept, James sat in the car and resumed the conversation he had begun with himself the moment he discovered Dee half-dead in the Cadillac. "What the heck is this all about?" he whispered to himself. " And why am I gett'n myself mixed up in it all?"

Rather than flee the scene of the accident back in Ellerbee, James had decided to put Dee in his car and take him back to Florence to his grandson. He wasn't sure why, but it was the only thing he could think to do short of taking him all the way back to Lacey. Besides, Dee needed to be with his grandson. The least I can do is take him to the boy, he had reasoned.

James felt for his handkerchief in his coat pocket. He wiped his brow and sighed deeply.

He was tired, just plain tired. Tired of running, tired of hiding from his past. It was a deep sense of fatigue, emotional as well as physical. Just thinking about his past sapped his strength. Everyday for most of twelve years he had walked past the bedroom door in his house behind which lay evidence of his crime. He thought he had been successful in ignoring it. His drinking had helped his denial. Bad memories were easily washed away, for a while at least. On the outside James had learned to control what people saw. But on the inside, and he knew it, he was being eaten alive.

James reached under his seat and found a half-empty bottle of liquor. For a moment he looked at the golden-brown liquid, silently cursing its power over him. Then he screwed off the top and poured it out on the ground, a ritual he had ceremoniously performed a hundred other times. But somehow this time seemed different. He was doing it out of resignation rather than some false hope.

James walked over to a trash barrel made from an old 55-gallon oil drum, and deposited the bottle. Returning to the car, the canvas sack on the passenger-side floorboard caught his eye. He sat in the car and reached over to pick it up. Inside were the colorful stockings, little nylon rings and some kind of braided rope that appeared to be made from the rings. The stockings reminded him of the incident back at the truckstop. He shuddered and tossed the sack back on the floor. He glanced into the rearview mirror at his tired, scruffy face, and shook his head. So what, if the boy tells my secret, he thought. It could only lead to a prison sentence. James leaned back in the seat and closed his eyes. Somehow the idea of lying on a bed in the solitude of a prison cell seemed appealing.

As he rested, James thought about other things. He thought about Gage. Where is he now? he wondered. He recalled again with renewed anxiety what had happened in Ellerbee and tried to piece together how Dee could be involved. It didn't make sense. Why would Gage and his buddies from Fort Bragg carry around a reserve officer accused of murder in the trunk of their car? What gives? James wondered. Did Dee escape and lose control of the car while trying to flee, resulting in the crash? There must be more to it than that, he thought. James suspected that the scene of the accident had been staged. For some reason Gage wanted to make it look like Dee was drunk and on the run. But why?

James looked at his watch. It was 10:30 a.m. They'd better be moving along, he thought. He got out of the car and walked over to the picnic table and sat down next to Dee.

He had always known his brother-in-law to be a strong man. It was strange to see him so beat down. He inspected the back of Dee's head. A scab covered a wound. It seemed to healing well enough, no infection that he could see.

James nudged Dee awake. As the tired man raised up,

he began to fall over. James caught him.

"Hold on there, now. Take it easy. You don't want any more gashes in that head of yours," James said, holding Dee steady. Dee recovered his balance, and looked around.

"Where am I?" he asked, rubbing his eyes.

"You're with me, and we gotta go." James replied, as he stood up.

"Where're we going?"

"To Florence, to find that grandson of yours."

"Grandson?" Dee looked up at James. "You mean Otter?"

"You got any other grandson?" James asked, smiling back at Dee.

"What's he doing in Florence?" Dee shot a puzzled look at James and shook his head. He was still having difficulty thinking clearly and wondered if he was hearing James correctly.

James wasn't sure just how much to reveal to Dee. He knew he shared some of the blame for Otter running away in the first place. But then there was also the matter of the secret he had been hiding all these years. If Otter knows something, he determined, Dee will be hearing about it soon enough. James picked up the bottle of ginger ale from the table and took a swig, then he looked again at Dee, who still seemed dazed.

"Come on and get in the car. I'll tell you what I know," James said, not sure what exactly that would be.

James helped Dee into the passenger seat and in a few minutes the two men were on their way again. He continued north on US 301, taking care to maintain the speed limit. The radio blasted out the sounds of a local country music station loud enough to be heard over the rush of air coming in the windows.

At eleven o'clock, James scrolled the radio channels for some news and found a CBS affiliate out of Columbia. This time the Fort Bragg murder took top billing. The fugitive murder suspect had fled the scene of an accident in Ellerbee in Clarence County. A statewide manhunt was underway for Major Addison Dumpkin. Dumpkin was being sought by state and federal law enforcement agencies for the murder of Private Terry Warren. Could be armed and dangerous.

James looked over at Dee who was asleep. A murderer? Armed and dangerous? I don't think so.

Sergeant Gage took the last drag of his cigarette and flicked the remaining butt out the window of the Firebird, waiting for the traffic light to change. It had been a four hour drive back to Fayetteville. It was 3:00 a.m. and he was tired. At 6:00 a.m. he was scheduled to be at the parade grounds for PT (physical training) with his men.

The light turned green, and the Firebird's tires squealed slightly as it turned left onto the All-American Freeway leading to Fort Bragg. The cool night air felt good. He had insisted that they travel with the windows down so that Jamison wouldn't doze off at the wheel.

Ten minutes later the three men were parked outside the barracks that housed B Company soldiers. Gage ordered Jamison and Gallworth to get some rest. He expected to see them at 0600 hours sharp.

Leaving the door open to take advantage of the night air, Gage went into his office and sat down behind his standard government issue desk. The chair creaked as he sat down. He lit up another cigarette and inhaled deeply.

As he sat in the dark, the only hint of his presence was the orange glow at his fingers. He thought about his plan to frame Dee. Liberal SOBs like Dumpkin are as much a problem to this country as the idiots in Congress, he thought. He wasn't sure exactly why he let himself get hooked by Dee. He had dealt with his kind before. But there was something about the way he stood up for Private Warren, like they were brothers or something. The memory relit Gage's anger. He shook his head and exhaled a column of smoke. No black man will ever be my brother, Gage reassured himself. As for Dumpkin, before the end of the week, he will regret he ever knew Warren.

Gage felt his energy return. It was time to address the big picture. The Capex was less than a week away. On that sacred day, Gage thought, the cries of my patriot brothers will be heard. Their dreams of an America purified white in fires set by courageous men like me, will become a reality! He felt exhilarated at the thought of his participation in changing the course of history. He would be a hero. Maybe not immediately, but in due time his nation would recognize its error and thank him for correcting it.

Gage got up and turned on the light, then made a pot of coffee. Taking a sip of the hot drink, he sat back down and turned on the radio on the corner of his desk. His favorite country station played an old Merle Haggard tune, *Okie from Muskogie*. Gage hummed along.

At 5:00 a.m. the news at the top of the hour caught his attention. It was breaking news concerning the search for Major Addison Dumpkin.

"Search!" Gage shouted, looking up at the radio as if he expected the newscaster to recant and admit he had made a mistake. Gage was expecting to hear that Dumpkin had been apprehended when the stolen Cadillac he was driving crashed into a light pole in the small town of Ellerbee, South Carolina.

There had been no arrest. The abandoned car had been traced back to Fayetteville as a stolen vehicle. There was good evidence at the scene to indicate that Major Dumpkin had been at the wheel, but he was still at large.

Gage got up from his desk and reached for the pot of coffee. The last of the drippings hissed on the hot plate. As he poured another cup, he questioned how Dee could have gotten away. If Dumpkin is loose somewhere, that poses a problem, he speculated. Would Dumpkin turn himself in? Possible but not likely, Gage thought. Warren's body had been found and all the evidence pointed to Dumpkin as the killer. Would he try to make his way back to Bragg? The answer to that question puzzled Gage. He didn't think Dumpkin could even get close to Fort Bragg or Fayetteville without someone recognizing him. His picture had been splashed across the front page of the *Fayetteville Observer* for a solid week. But the thought of him snooping around concerned Gage, though not one that would mean a change in his plans. He sipped his coffee and looked out the window at the first light of morning. He was sure Dumpkin would not be a problem.

Chapter Eighteen

Claudia stayed on for another day before leaving to take the deposition in Columbia. Margie and Otter were both a little nervous about the possibility that James might be up to something—perhaps plotting again to kidnap Otter—and they hated to see her go. Despite the fact that she was not a police officer, being an officer of the court gave them the illusion of being protected by some higher authority, and that was comforting.

To help Otter find his grandfather, Margie decided to seek the counsel of a close friend with ties to Fort Bragg. The two left Florence and drove the 25 miles north to Dillon, South Carolina to see Kirk Rossi, a retired Army chaplain. Margie had met Kirk while he was serving at Fort Bragg. As a chaplain, Kirk had been an advocate of children's ministries for families on post. He had read about a textile company down in Florence that specialized in women's panty hose. The company had created an innovative program that promoted the recycling of defective panty hose to make toys for kids, thus helping to combat rampant materialism. He liked the idea and drove down from Fayetteville to learn more about it. That's when he met Margie, waste hose guru, and the program's administrator.

During his career as a soldier, Captain Kirkland Rossi (known to the troops as Captain Kirk) was very popular among the grunts and the chaplains. He served two tours in Vietnam where he had jumped into battle right along with his 82nd Airborne parishioners. He was a pastor to three generations of soldiers, marrying some, burying too many. He was a good preacher and was often requested by Corps Command to offer public prayers and to be the guest speaker on special occasions. He loved the Army. The Army seemed to love him.

Kirk was on schedule to become Major Kirkland Rossi when his alcoholism began to drag him under. Kirk had successfully hidden his problem for years. He thought he could control it long enough to retire after twenty years with full benefits. But when his wife of eighteen years had finally had enough of his deceit and left him, he suddenly found himself on a slippery slope.

The support he received from his fellow chaplains made the Army bearable for a while. But in the end depression took over and he started to gain weight. That was a problem the Army wouldn't tolerate—no fat soldiers. This included chaplains. He tried to prove he could keep up, despite his size, by continuing physical training with the troops, as well as participating in training jumps. He even had an extra large parachute made in order to slow his decent and keep his back and knees from blowing out when he hit the ground.

Finally, word came down from Corps Command that Kirk was finished. He left the Army quietly, not sure what he was going to do next. The chief of chaplaincy thought he would make a successful parish minister and encouraged him to try it. But Kirk had convinced himself that no congregation would want an alcoholic for a minister. He decided that he didn't want to lie anymore.

Kirk became the owner of a wedding chapel in Dillon, wedding mill of the South. Not long after he arrived, he began to wonder if he had made a mistake. The wedding business in Dillon was more competitive than he had imagined. In order to make a living at it he had to come up with an innovative angle. One evening while watching a rerun of *The Adams Family* it occurred to him to add a funeral parlor to the business. It worked. With only one funeral home in Dillon, Kirk had plenty of business. The drawback was that young brides didn't take too kindly to being married in a place that doubled as a funeral home. Nevertheless, the idea of a macabre wedding chapel intrigued Kirk. Soon he introduced and promoted the concept of the Halloween wedding. It wasn't long before young couples from all over the county began flocking to Dillon for spooky weddings—and not just at Halloween!

Margie was slow getting used to it all. In her mind, the addition of the funeral parlor made the lovely house creepy. It was a while before she ever agreed to stay overnight in it. The idea of sleeping in a house with dead bodies downstairs made her shutter. Of course it didn't bother Kirk. In fact, he saw the cadavers as guests: friends weary of this world who needed to be dressed and packaged for the next.

Not long after they had become friends, Margie discovered an even deeper connection she shared with the retired chaplain. They were both alcoholics. She had been in recovery for almost five years. Kirk was yet to start. With Margie's help, he found his way to AA—Alcoholics Anonymous—what some have called the truest expression of Christian faith in America. The group met in the basement of the First Methodist Church in Dillon every Tuesday at seven o'clock. It was Margie and AA that helped Kirk begin a new chapter in his life as an officiant at weddings, director of funerals and friend to himself. He rediscovered that life was good.

Kirk was excited when Margie called to ask about spending a few days with him in Dillon. Margie had not explained in detail why they were coming, only something about hiding from an uncle and trying to find a grandfather. It didn't make sense to him, but that didn't matter. He loved Margie's company. Before she hung up, Kirk took the opportunity to request some more hose. He was always finding new ways to use it in weddings and funerals, and to entertain the kids of Dillon.

After a brief stop at the factory, Margie and Otter made their way north. Along the way Otter saw the billboards that he had always found so amusing on trips up I-95. The Pedro signs, he called them. They publicized Pedro's South of the Border, a kind of weird tourist attraction that included a shopping center and hotel complex with a Mexican theme—and fireworks, plenty of fireworks. Anyone who could advertise like Pedro, using giant three dimensional hotdogs on billboards with slogans like, "You never *sausage* a place" and "You're always a *weiner* at Pedros," was someone

Otter could appreciate. It wasn't long before Otter spied Pedro's observation tower shaped like a sombrero, at the North and South Carolina border. Unfortunately, the turnoff to Dillon came first. Margie promised Otter that they would make a trip over to see Pedro's while they visited Kirk. Though he was disappointed, Otter reluctantly agreed.

The sky was dark with thunderheads most of the way north to Dillon. By the time they exited the interstate, the bottom fell out. The rain came down in buckets. Margie double-checked to make sure her headlights were on. She drove slowly but not too slow, fearing someone might run into the back of her. She strained her eyes trying to see well enough to keep the car moving straight ahead and in the correct lane. A car approached from the opposite direction, traveling much too fast. It sprayed a deluge of water onto her windshield overwhelming the wipers for a moment and shaking the car.

Soon a few homes began to appear. Then lights from downtown Dillon flashed in the rain like beacons guiding her safely through the storm. The first intersection was Main Street. Margie inched through the intersection and headed up Main to Oak.

A few blocks down on the right, she pointed out to Otter a large stately white house with a picket fence. Next to the house was a vacant lot where several cars were parked. Oddly, they all sat with their headlights on. In front of the house on Oak Street were two cars—a long black, older model hearse and an older model Mercedes. Along an adjacent side street were still more parked cars with their lights on.

"That's Kirk's car, that Mercedes up there," Margie

 said, pointing to the car in front of the hearse. "He didn't say anything about a funeral today."

Otter leaned forward to take in all that was going on. He was a little nervous and wary at the prospect of meeting yet another preacher-type. If this guy was anything like his Uncle James, he would have nothing to do with him. On the other hand, Margie's description of Kirk made him sound pretty cool. At the very least, different.

Margie pulled up alongside of the Mercedes and saw that Kirk was in the car. Kirk recognized her car and rolled down his window. Margie instructed Otter to do the same.

"Park up ahead there and come go with me!" Kirk bellowed over the noise of the pounding rain.

Margie followed his instructions and pulled in front of the Mercedes. She turned off the motor, looked at Otter, and smiled. Everytime she was with Kirk it was an adventure, she thought to herself. She was excited that Otter would get to know him.

"Ready? On the count of three, let's run for it. You get up front with Kirk, I'll sit in the back," Margie said.

"No, that's alright, you can sit up front," Otter replied, thinking the back seat would be a safer place from which to evaluate the new acquaintance.

"Okay. I'll sit up front." Margie took in a deep breath. "One, two, three!" The two jumped from Margie's car and ran back and got into the Mercedes. In the few seconds it took to make the trip, the two were soaked.

"Ain't this a heckuva mess! How you doing, shug?" Kirk laughed and reached out and squeezed Margie's hand. "I'll hug you when you're not so wet." Margie smiled. Kirk struggled to turn and offer his hand to

Otter in the back seat. He was still overweight, and he seemed to be stuck tightly behind the steering wheel. "Hello, young man! Kirk Rossi, pleased to make your acquaintance."

Otter shook hands with the man but remained quiet.

"This is Otter Dumpkin, Kirk. A finer young man you won't find!" Margie turned and smiled at Otter.

"No doubt in my mind, no sir," Kirk replied. He looked in the rearview mirror and winked at Otter.

Otter was still not sure what his first impression was. The guy seemed friendly enough, but then Uncle James was capable of being pleasant and glad-handed. He reserved judgment as Margie and Kirk exchanged pleasantries.

"You didn't say you had a funeral today, Kirk. Was this unexpected?" Margie asked.

"I plum forgot about it until I hung up the phone, then I thought that it'd probably be over by the time y'all arrived. The rain slowed us down." Kirk paused, then asked, "You gotta umbrella in your car?"

"No, I didn't think to bring it. Shoot!" Margie replied, snapping her fingers.

"No problem, we can run over to the IGA and pick up a couple." Kirk reached down to the floorboard and produced an umbrella. "This one's a big one, but it still wouldn't be enough to cover my load and yours too." He winked at Otter again from the rear view mirror. "Well, we gotta get Charles in the ground. The hole's dug and everything's ready and my diggers are getting paid by the hour. Charley doesn't have a lick of kin. All these cars you see around here are his buddies, and they're wanting to get on with it. Let me go tell Rod to head on out to the cemetery, and we'll catch up to him in a few minutes." Kirk grabbed the umbrella and opened the door. The rain poured in as he struggled to get out from behind the steering wheel. Frustrated, he sat back, and shut the door.

"Otter Dumpkin, how about doing me a favor?" Kirk asked. "You could save me from getting drenched and embarrassing myself before God and everybody." Otter sat back for a moment, then decided he was interested and leaned forward. "Would you take my umbrella and run back to that hearse there and tell Rod to lead the procession on over to the cemetery? Tell 'im that we'll catch up in a few minutes. I'd be much obliged if you would."

"I'll do it, Kirk," Margie interjected.

"No, no, I can do it!" Otter said enthusiastically.

Kirk smiled appreciatively and passed the umbrella back to Otter. Then he looked at Margie. "Hold on just a minute! How would you like to ride in the hearse with Rod?" he asked, talking to Otter's reflection in the mirror. "Just thought you might be one of the curious types."

Otter didn't hesitate. "Cool! Is that okay with you, Margie?"

"Well, I guess so." She looked at Kirk then back at Otter. "You'd never get me in one of those things, at least not while I'm still breathing," she laughed. "Go on, we'll see you over at the graveyard."

Before Kirk could hand him the umbrella, Otter had darted out the door.

"Remember to tell Rod what I said." Kirk said, his words dissolving into a laugh. It was too late. Otter was already gone.

"He's got a good memory. Don't worry," Margie said

reassuringly. "That was sweet of you to offer to let him do that."

Kirk watched Otter through the rearview mirror as he got into the hearse. Rod waved his approval.

"Okay," Kirk said out loud to himself. "Let's get those umbrellas and get Charles in the ground." The Mercedes pulled away from the curb and headed for the IGA.

Chapter Nineteen

"Como estas amigo? I'm Rodrigo Arias Riviera, but you can call me Rod." The man smiled and extended his hand out to Otter.

As Otter shook Rod's hand, he was distracted by a small cassette tape recorder on the seat between them. It was playing some kind of Latino music.

"Uh, hi, I'm Otter, uh, Otter Dumpkin," he replied, looking down at the recorder.

"Ohhter. Is that like the animal that swims in the rivers?" Rod asked with interest, in only slightly broken English.

Otter looked up. "Yessir, my grandfather named me that 'cause I can swim real good."

Otter smiled back at Rod, studying his face. His smile immediately put Otter at ease. His intuition about people had always served him well. This man was not hiding anything, he thought. He was real, and he seemed to be genuinely happy.

Rod was not a big man but he was fit. Otter noticed

the muscles of his forearms extending from his shirt sleeves as his hands rested on the steering wheel of the hearse. They were the arms of someone who used them a lot, someone who stayed in shape, perhaps even worked out with weights. Rod looked to be about Dee's age, Otter thought, probably just over fifty or so.

"You a friend of Miss Margie?" Rod asked. Boy he had nice teeth! Otter thought, looking at Rod's beaming smile.

"Yessir, I've known her for just a short time, but she's been really good to me." Otter looked ahead, then suddenly felt the lurch of the hearse as Rod's right arm dropped down, thrusting the gearshift into drive and pulling out into the street to follow Kirk's car. "Oh, by the way, Kirk asked me to tell you not to follow him. He said for you to go on over to the uh… the cemetery." Otter looked out his window and watched as other vehicles began slowly moving to fall in behind the hearse.

"He said what?" Rod slowed but did not stop.

"He and Margie are going to stop by the IGA to pick up a couple of umbrellas."

"Ohmbrellas? Okay, Rod replied, shaking his head and looking a little puzzled. "He must mean we go to Parker's. We always go to Parker's."

Otter, too, was puzzled. Was the cemetery called Parker's? It seemed like a funny name for a cemetery.

"All I know is he said we should meet him at the cemetery," Otter reiterated. He looked at Rod who stared straight ahead past the long windshield wipers waving back and forth, doing their best to keep the rain off the glass.

"I better make sure," Rod said. "Perhaps he changed

 his mind about Parker's. But I can't believe it. We go to Parker's after all the funerals."

Otter wondered what Rod meant by "making sure." Perhaps he had a cell phone or a radio of some kind to contact Kirk. But Otter saw no indication that this was the case.

Surely this guy knows what he's doing, Otter thought. He sat back to take in the experience of riding in a hearse. The sleek Cadillac wagon continued through the rain. At one point Otter turned to look at the casket. It was no more than a simple pine box draped with an American flag. The flag on a coffin usually means whoever is inside was in the military, Otter remembered. He was curious.

"That's an interesting coffin," Otter said, turning back to look at Rod.

"Yeah, it's what Charley requested. He showed me exactly what he wanted, and even tried it on for size."

Otter's jaw dropped. The man spoke of making a coffin as if he was a tailor making a suit.

"You really made it?" Otter asked, a little amused.

Rod turned and smiled at Otter, "I make all our coffins. Each one custom made to fit perfecto!"

Otter thought it all sounded a little bizarre. He rolled his eyes and looked out the window at the rain.

The hearse stopped at a four-way stop then turned left. Otter looked over his shoulder again, this time past the coffin and out the rear window. He could see the lights of the procession of cars and trucks as each paused to make the turn then fell in line once again. There must be at least twenty, he thought to himself.

For about five minutes, the procession continued through the rain on a well-traveled highway headed north. Just ahead on the right, the IGA sign appeared. As they pulled into the parking lot, Otter pointed out Kirk's Mercedes. With great care, Rod navigated the hearse through the lot, followed by the funeral procession. In order to make room for all the cars behind him, he turned up one aisle of parked cars then down another, creating a serpentine formation of vehicles.

Kirk had just dislodged himself from his car and was almost to the store entrance before he noticed the procession woven through the parking lot. Rod put the hearse into park, jumped out and ran over to Kirk.

"What's going on?" Kirk asked as Rod approached, a bit breathless.

"You said to the boy that we should meet you at the cemetery. But what about Parker's?" Rod asked.

"Dang it all! With all this rain and with Margie showing up, I plum forgot," Kirk replied, scratching his chin and looking back at the procession. "Okay. Go ahead on over to Parker's. I'll be over shortly."

Rod hurried back to the hearse, but before getting in, he turned toward the line of vehicles and made a motion with his arm like a cavalry officer waving his troops to "move out." The procession returned to the highway and headed to Parker's.

Across the long table at Parker's Barbecue Restaurant, Otter learned that according to Kirk, a funeral was more than just a time to grieve. It was a celebration. He added that one of the great celebrations practiced by the church was eating a meal together. It wasn't just for the food, Kirk noted, though good food adds to the celebration; it was the people enjoying each other, remembering good times and anticipating more, and being thankful for the rich gifts of life.

"Our Creator wants us to enjoy life and to share it, Otter, from beginning to end and beyond," Kirk said. Then he stood and held high a glass of iced tea. "In the great tradition of my Italian ancestors who believed that the only difference between a funeral and a wedding is that there's one less person at the funeral, let us raise our glasses to our friend Charley." Otter looked around. Just about every tea glass in Parker's was raised. "To Charley," Kirk announced, "May he continue to share in all that is good!"

Otter was cautiously impressed with this preacher who led these guys, many of them Vietnam Vets, old army buddies of Charley, in celebrating the life of their friend. Though a little weird, it doesn't seem fake at all, he thought. Some cried, some laughed at the stories shared about Charley, and they ate a lot of barbeque. But they all seemed to know what Kirk was talking about—the real worship of the Almighty was taking place around that table.

Otter had heard Dee speak of preachers back home in Lacey who had gradually sucked the life out of their congregations with constricting ideas about how life should be lived. There was little tolerance for asking the hard questions of religion. As far as Otter knew, the idea of a church being a place to celebrate was foreign to his friends and neighbors. Children grew up and left the churches, no longer held there by fear of the "burning hell" awaiting them if they didn't repent of their ways. They went other places to celebrate. As for their fears, the temporal ones of loneliness and failure topped any fear of a "burning hell."

According to his Uncle James' God, Otter had observed, enjoyment was reserved for a pretty narrow category of activities. Bible reading, praying, and singing "ol' time religion" songs were the only enjoyment to be had (Otter did enjoy the singing). But anything beyond that was likely to result in a destiny of fiery wrath.

The "burning hell" question, Otter would learn, wasn't one that Kirk asked. This left him somewhat puzzled. For Kirk, the idea of a burning hell perverted everything that Jesus and God stood for. He believed things only got better in the next life, even if a person was bent on creating hell for people in this one.

So who was right, he asked himself, Kirk or James? It mattered to Otter. He was still young and the "burning hell" question was hard to dodge. Was that what God was about? Scaring people? For Otter, doubt produced a lot of anxiety. It sure would be nice to know the truth about God.

Otter and Margie huddled under the graveside canopy out of the rain with Charley's friends. Kirk stood at the head of the pine casket that rested on a hoist above a carefully shaped hole in the ground. Rod stood at the foot. After some Bible readings and a few more stories about Charley, Kirk concluded the service in a manner that Otter found amusing.

Kirk opened the casket and started talking to Charley as if he was just stretched out on a couch in front of God and everyone, happy to see them. Finally, Kirk pulled a fork from his pocket, supplied by Parker's and placed it in Charley's folded hands.

"Save your fork, Charley," Kirk said fondly.

Otter almost laughed out loud at the sight of the fork.

What was up with the fork? Kirk had to be obsessed with food, he thought. But as Kirk gently closed the coffin, wishing his friend Godspeed, suddenly the significance of it hit Otter like a ton of bricks. He felt a lump rise in his throat as tears came to his eyes. His thoughts returned to home and the many times he had enjoyed a scrumptious meal, and when he thought it couldn't get any better, Dee or Vicky or Flora had taken his plate, spoon, and knife from the table and told him him, "keep your fork." Those few words had always signified to Otter that something good lay ahead. Something real good.

Chapter Twenty

The sun came out on the ride back from the cemetery to the funeral parlor. Otter rode shotgun with Rod again. In their conversation along the way, he learned that Rod had served in the Army at the same time as Kirk. Both had served in a Special Forces unit, the Dragon Brigade. Shortly before retiring from the Army, Rod became a chaplain's assistant. Ironically, it was at a funeral in the JFK chapel at Fort Bragg that the two men first met. As their friendship grew, Kirk learned of Rod's carpentry skills as well as his family's ties to the funeral business. When Kirk decided to open the funeral parlor, he invited Rod to join him in Dillon where he became a master mortician and a skilled coffin builder.

The hearse pulled up along the curb in front of the house, and Rod got out and opened Otter's door in the manner of a chauffeur. Kirk and Margie pulled up behind them and parked. Margie joined Otter on the sidewalk and was remarking how nice the weather had turned out when she stopped in mid-sentence. Otter was looking past her and had a sick look on his face. Kirk noticed it, too.

"You look like you've seen a ghost," Kirk said, putting his arm on Otter's shoulder. All three adults turned and looked up the street in the direction of Otter's gaze. Immediately Margie moved to put a protective arm around Otter. The red Ford Escort wagon approached, then slowed and parked behind Kirk's Mercedes.

"You know those two?" Kirk asked.

There was no reply. Otter noticed that he didn't sense the same level of fear he had experienced the last time he saw his uncle's car. Now he was surrounded by two ex-Rangers. There was no reason to fear James. But who was the other person in the car?

The Mercedes blocked Otter's view. He moved a few steps up the sidewalk to get a better look at the passenger. Margie walked slowly behind. Puzzled, Kirk and Rod stood and watched. Margie started to reach out to Otter as if to say by the gesture, "don't get too close," when she heard Otter catch his breath. He broke into a run toward the man struggling to exit the passenger-side door of the car.

"Grandpa!" he shouted. Otter reached the door as Dee managed to stand. Tears flowing down his cheeks, he wrapped his arms around his grandfather and buried his head into his chest and sobbed. "Oh Grandpa! I can't believe it's you!"

Dee held tight to his grandson and kissed the top of his head. "It's me, alright. God, I missed you!"

Margie was relieved to see that the gentleman embracing Otter was the grandfather about whom he spoke so highly. She looked back at Kirk.

"I'll fill you in later. I think everything's okay," she said.

In the emotion of the moment, Otter had completely forgotten about James. The little man just sat there behind the steering wheel, unsure just what he was going to say or do. Dee let go of Otter and shut the door of the car. As he turned, Otter saw James' face through the glass.

"Grandpa? Why are you with him?" Otter asked, nodding toward James.

"I haven't figured that out yet. All I know is that he showed up out of nowhere and saved my life."

Otter was stunned. "Saved your life?" He could not imagine that this man who seemed so cruel to him would save anyone's life, much less his grandfather's. The look of horror on his face startled Dee.

"What's wrong, Bud? It's only your Uncle James." Dee said.

"I have to tell you something, Grandpa, about Uncle James, I mean."

At that moment, Margie, Kirk, and Rod walked up to make introductions. Before Dee turned to make their acquaintance, he reassured Otter that they would talk more about it later.

Margie extended her hand to Dee. "Hello, I'm Margie. You must be Dee."

"That's right. Dee Dumpkin, ma'am. Excuse my appearance. I've been roughed up a little this past week.".

The others introduced themselves, but further pleasantries had to wait until they were inside. Dee seemed to have forgotten that he was a wanted man, but Margie was very much aware of this. She and Otter had listened to the radio in the car when they drove up from Florence that morning. Otter was clearly disturbed by the report and continued to deny that it was true.

Margie hurried them into the foyer of the old home, glancing again up and down the street to see if anyone was watching. Then she noticed that James was still sitting in the car.

"What do we do about him?" she whispered to Kirk, as she paused at the door before entering.

"Well I swan," Kirk said calmly. "I plum forgot about him. Invite him in."

Margie shot a puzzled look toward Kirk, but he was already heading inside to take care of his new guests. Walking to the edge of the porch, she raised her hand and motioned for James to come in. He didn't move. He must be sleeping, she thought. She moved down the steps and walked out to the car. "This is a terrible predicament," she thought. "Kirk doesn't know the gravity of this man's presence for Otter. Inviting him in like this could be disastrous!"

Margie approached the driver-side of the car, bending down to peer into the window. James was slumped over with his head resting against the seat. He appeared to be sleeping. She tapped lightly on the window.

He woke with a start that made Margie's heart jump. The wiry man, unshaven for two days, had a sinister look about him.

James rolled down the window. "Yessum? What can I do for you?" Margie straightened and looked up the street as a car passed, splashing water at her feet. Then she looked again into James' tired gaze.

"Won't you come in for a while and freshen up?" She was surprised by the manner of her invitation; she felt like she had just invited a friend to tea. She straightened again as another car passed.

"Naw, I don't want to impose, ma'am. I'll just catch me a nap here for a while, then I'll be on my way."

"Nonsense. It'll be dark in a while and you'll need a place to stay," she said, surprising herself again with her insistence. The southern hospitality ingrained within her was darn hard to turn off. "You must be hungry and you've got to eat somewhere. Come on in."

"Well, I guess I could eat a little something," James replied.

As he opened the door of the car, Margie caught a glimpse of something familiar in the back seat. It was her canvas bag. With a little grunt, James stepped out of the car into the street. He looked down at his clothes and felt his whiskers. "I don't look so good. You sure it'll be okay?"

"You're fine, sir," Margie assured him. She looked again to the canvas bag.

"Mr. Fisher?"

James looked up at Margie. "Yessum?"

"That bag in the back seat of your car? Is that yours?"

James looked over into the back seat. "No ma'am, I suspect that might belong to you, I think you left it at the Greyhound station back in Jacksonville."

Margie smiled sheepishly as she recalled the incident at the bus station. It wasn't one of my proudest moments, she thought.

James reached behind the seat and retrieved the bag and handed it to Margie, who was clearly thrilled.

"I can't thank you, enough, Mr. Fisher. What's in this bag means a lot to me."

James nodded his acknowledgment of her gratitude.

"Come on in and wash up, and we'll find you something to eat." Margie said. She walked ahead of

 James up the steps then held the door for him. He walked past her and gave a little nod.

"Much obliged, ma'am."

Margie set the bag on the table next to the door and looked down the hall. She was a little surprised that no one was in sight when they entered the foyer. James stood in the middle of the floor and looked up at the high ornate ceiling. Margie called for Kirk. There was no reply, though voices could be heard from the rear of the house.

"They must be back in the kitchen," she said. "Let's go see what they're up to."

From the foyer the pair moved down the long hallway to the rear of the large home. James slowed as he passed the first door on his left. A single lamp dimly illuminated the room. He took note of the three coffins on display, each a different size. Across the hall, double doors opened into the chapel. It was dark. He could see nothing but a few pews reflecting the hall light.

Kirk's head appeared from the door at the end of the hall.

"Here they are. Y'all come on back and have something to eat, shug. We had a pig-pick'n the other day and we're still eatin' from it. Can't get enough Carolina barbeque," he said, referring to the fact that they had eaten less than two hours earlier.

Margie and James followed Kirk into the large kitchen. Dee, Otter, and Rod were seated at the table in the center of the room. Otter did not acknowledge the new arrivals. Dee tried to stand, but the pain in his back led him to ask to be excused. Rod pulled two more chairs to the table.

"You won't believe what this man has lived," Kirk said

as he prepared a plate of barbeque, potato salad, and cole slaw for James.

"That little kidnapping attempt at the truck-stop you were telling me about on the way back from the cemetery this afternoon," Kirk looked at Otter and paused. The boy's eyes were full of tears. James stared blankly at the refrigerator.

Margie stopped eating. She looked up and saw Otter's face. "What's wrong? Kirk? Otter? Sweetie, what's wrong?"

"What you don't know, shug, is that this guy Gage and his two buddies had kidnapped Dee. All the time y'all were standing there at the truck stop Dee was tied up in the trunk of Gage's car!"

Margie winced. "Oh, no!" She looked sympathetically at Dee.

Dee put his hand on Otter's shoulder and reassured him it was okay.

"Bud, there was nothing you could have done about it. You didn't know."

"I did," James blurted out. James had been so quiet, that for a few seconds the room was stunned to hear something come from his mouth. Otter looked up at his uncle, then at Dee.

"What do you mean you knew?" Dee asked, shocked at James' admission.

"I heard you kickin' around in the back there. I know'd it was you. Something told me it was you in that trunk. Why'd you think I followed you?" James said, looking across the table at Dee.

For the first time Otter saw real tears in his uncle's eyes and what was undeniably an honest feeling of regret.

"You just thought you knew," Dee said. "There's no

way you could have known for sure."

"I knew. You said it yourself. I was your savior. Well, I ain't no savior, but I know the one who is, and he told me it was you." James wiped his eyes on his coat sleeve, then cleared his throat.

There was a long silence, then Kirk spoke.

"Well shug, I'll tell you the rest of the story later." He turned to James. "Mr. Fisher, I don't know if the good Lord spoke to you or if it was just your own intuition. Personally, I don't think even the good Lord knows either. He's just rejoicing that Dee is safe and reunited with his grandson."

"Amen!" Rod said enthusiastically. All eyes turned to see his wide toothy grin. Even James managed a smile.

The wave of despair had ebbed for the moment. Kirk spoke again.

"Suffice it to say, if Dee's suspicion is correct, and Gage is planning to kill the Vice President, we've got high treason going on up there at Bragg!" he exclaimed. " And on top of that, the law has accused Dee of murder. That's some kind of intrigue!"

Otter looked over at Kirk. "What are we gonna do? Is Grandpa going to go to jail?" He got up from his chair and stood by his grandfather, putting his arm around him.

"No, son, your grandpa is not going to jail for a crime he didn't commit. We'll see to that. Justice will prevail, I assure you," Kirk said.

Otter sensed the resolve in Kirk's voice. It was noted also by Rod, who gave Otter a reassuring wink. Otter stood up straight. He, like Rod, sensed a plan was forthcoming.

"I still have a few buddies up there who can help us

out," Kirk offered. "But we're gonna have to get on top of this thing quick. That Capex is set for the Fourth, and that's just the day after tomorrow."

"What's a Capex?" Margie asked.

"A capabilities exercise," Otter responded.

Kirk looked up in surprise. "You know your military lingo, young man."

Otter smiled at Dee. "Grandpa taught me all that stuff. I've even seen a parachute-drop at Sicily drop zone."

"That's good to know," Kirk replied. "We could end up at Sicily for this July Fourth exercise if we can't get this thing resolved before then. Your knowledge of the area may come in handy."

"Why can't you just call someone at Fort Bragg and report what's going on?" Margie asked, her pragmatism taking over.

"Good question," Kirk replied. "I could do exactly that. But I know these types. I know how well they're trained, and when you put that kind of training in the hands of fanatics, watch out! That McVeigh character, the guy who blew up the federal building in Oklahoma City, was just the type. And, what's his name?" Kirk looked at Dee.

"Gage." Dee said.

"Yeah, this Gage fella, if he's trained half as well as the Army claims him to be, he will not be stopped. He'll have a backup plan. If we're not careful, a catastrophe may still occur. It may not be at Sicily drop zone, but you can bet your britches he'll make a helluva noise somewhere. And on top of that, Dee here may still end up convicted of murder."

The room fell silent. Otter's excitement quickly

 turned to anxiety. He looked at Dee, who was staring down at his plate. He looked at Rod. His smile was gone.

Margie excused herself and began clearing the table when they heard the sound of the front door opening.

"Anybody home?" came a male voice from the foyer.

Margie stepped out into the hall to see a sheriff's deputy holding his hat in hand and looking straight at her. She froze.

Seeing the shock on her face, Kirk got up from the table to see who it was.

"Hey, Holt. What's up?" Kirk asked, recognizing the deputy immediately. He was a local boy that Kirk knew well, having joined him to Carla Wilson in holy matrimony just two months before. Kirk walked to the foyer and shook Holt's hand. "Have a seat. I'll be with you in just a moment." He turned to Margie and escorted her back toward the kitchen, but stopped short of the door. "Oh, shoot! I'm sorry, shug. Holt, you remember my friend Margie? She was up from Florence visiting me the weekend of your wedding."

"Sure, I remember," Holt replied courteously. "Good to see you again, ma'am."

Margie managed a forced smile, then Kirk took her by the arm and led her back into the kitchen.

"There's no cause for alarm. It's just a deputy," he whispered to his guests. Hearing the word "deputy," James started to get up. It wasn't the first time that it occurred to him he had aided a suspected murderer, but he had not taken it seriously until that moment.

"Now, now, hold on, Mr. Fisher. You just hold tight to your belief that the good Lord has a hand in all this. Everything's gonna be okay. I know this boy and I don't think there's any problem here." Kirk looked squarely into James' eyes. The look calmed James and he sat back down. "Y'all just stay put while I see what he wants."

Kirk pulled the kitchen door closed, but didn't shut it all the way. He made his way back to the foyer. Margie got up and positioned herself near the door to eavesdrop on the conversation.

"I didn't mean to disturb you this evening, Mr. Rossi, I mean Reverend Rossi, but there's a red Ford Escort station wagon out front that matches the description of one seen leaving the scene of an accident down in Ellerbee. You wouldn't know who the owner is, would you?"

Kirk walked to the window and peered past the drape.

"I didn't even notice it, Holt. You think it might be the same one seen down in Ellerbee, huh?"

"I dunno, Reverend. We don't have a plate number, just a description. But you don't know who the owner is?"

"No, I don't, friend. Wish I could help you."

"No problem. I thought you might know who it belonged to and I could save myself the trouble of calling it in. The computer in my cruiser is broke down. Otherwise I would've already checked it out myself. Well, sorry to've bothered you."

"No bother, Holt. How's that bride of yours?"

"Just fine, sir. I'll tell her you asked about 'er."

"You do that. Take care now."

Kirk held the door for the young man, then watched as he walked back to his vehicle. After closing the door, he hurried back to the kitchen. Everyone was standing, except Dee.

"I heard everything," Margie said, obviously upset.

"He's probably out there right now calling in that license number and it won't take long for them to figure out that the owner's from the same town in Florida as Dee and then they'll discover they're related, and our goose is cooked!" She crossed her arms and walked quickly to the kitchen sink, her back to the others. Otter thought she was crying.

"It's gonna be okay, shug," Kirk said, trying to reassure her and the rest of the group. "If we stay calm and think this thing through, we'll be okay."

"Well, whatever we do, it's gonna have to happen soon," Dee said. "Otherwise, I will be in jail and of no use in stopping Gage."

"And if he's in the pokey, I'm in the pokey," James added.

Rod looked at James, curious about the word "pokey." Kirk interrupted Rod's puzzled stare and asked him to see if the sheriff's deputy was still parked out front.

Kirk walked around the table to the kitchen sink and looked out the window to the back yard. He was thinking hard.

"Maybe it would be best for me just to turn myself in," Dee announced.

"Maybe it would," Kirk replied, turning to face Dee, who was now standing. "But not here. If you're gonna get arrested, it needs to be in Fayetteville. I know the chief of police up there. He's a retired sergeant major and he's efficient. He'd listen to your story and do a thorough investigation. You get arrested in Dillon and it'll be a month before they figure out just what to do. We don't have the time."

At that moment Rod's voice boomed down the

hallway. "He's back! And more sheriffs arriving too!"

Kirk thought for a moment what to do. He hadn't expected this. "Quick! You two come with me," he said, pointing to Dee and James.

"Grandpa?" Otter's chin quivered and his voice started to crack at the thought of his grandfather being arrested.

Dee hugged his grandson. "It's gonna be okay, Bud. Kirk has this all figured out. We're in good hands. Just hang on for a little longer." Dee looked over at Margie. The need in his eyes was clear. She moved to take his place, putting her arms around the boy. Dee whispered a word of appreciation to her, then followed Kirk and James down the hallway.

When Kirk turned into the dimly lit room containing the coffins, James' pace slowed. He suspected he was about to be asked to do something he didn't have the nerve to do. His suspicion was correct. As soon as he entered, Kirk motioned him to get into the powder-blue coffin.

"This one's about your size. A little short, but I think it'll fit you," Kirk said.

"Can't we just go out the back way?" James asked, hesitating to get too close to the coffins.

"Too big of a risk. You're sure to be spotted by someone," Kirk replied, trying to hurry James along. "I'm willing to bet there are more deputies about. Go on and get in."

Dee pushed James toward the powder blue coffin, and all but put James into it. The little man stretched out. For the first time he noticed his hands were shaking. He started to get up out of the casket as Kirk shut the cover. James reached up to keep the lid from closing completely.

"I ain't so sure about this," he said nervously.

"Don't worry, Mr. Fisher. You'll be fine. It doesn't lock, and trust me, you'll have plenty of air. If you start feeling a little dizzy, just push up on the lid a little and let some more air in."

Dee was already in the oak coffin, which was clearly the largest. Kirk shut the lid, then moved to shut the lid of the adjacent copper-colored one to give the appearance of uniformity. He turned off the lamp and moved to the hallway, quickly making his way back to the kitchen where Margie, Otter, and Rod awaited him.

"Where'd you hide 'em?" Margie asked.

Before Kirk could answer, there was a knock at the front door.

"Wait here," Kirk said. He calmly moved from the kitchen down the long hallway, napkin in hand for effect. The deputy was already through the door.

"Reverend," he said, "we have a problem."

Chapter Twenty-one

Two other deputies arrived and joined in the search. They began upstairs while Holt apologetically explained to Kirk that Sheriff Townsend had ordered the search and that a warrant could easily be gotten if there was some objection. Kirk reassured the nervous deputy that everything was going to be all right. After an anxiety-filled moment of silence, Holt excused himself and mounted the stairs to the second floor to help expedite the search.

Finding nothing upstairs, the deputies moved back downstairs to continue the search, asking Kirk from time to time to turn on lights or unlock a door. The old house was literally a maze.

Otter and Margie stood at the door of the kitchen and watched as the officers went about their business. Kirk saw the fear on their faces and told them to go into his office at the front of the house. There, they could watch television or play some of the video games that he kept for clients with children.

As the two made their way down the hall to the office, a beam of light flashed across the floor, coming from the room containing the coffins. The light disappeared almost as soon as they saw it. Margie took in a slow breath, then continued. As they passed the doorway, she looked straight ahead, not wanting to appear suspicious. Otter slowed and shot a quick glance inside the room, then moved on.

"Ma'am!" The deputy's voice had a sense of urgency to it. He came out into the hallway. "Excuse me, I can't seem to find the light switch in here. Would you happen to know where it is?" Margie turned and faced the young man, his flashlight formed a tight circle at his feet. She could make out the face of a young deputy. He's just a boy, she thought, not long out of high school, judging by his youthful appearance. Her mind raced. Should she assist these men in their search? She knew that the display room was lit by a series of lamps; the old house had no ceiling fixtures.

At that moment, Kirk exited the chapel with the other two officers.

"What's up, shug?" Kirk asked.

"This young man is looking for the light in the display room," Margie replied quietly.

Kirk apologized and walked across the hallway to the dark room and turned on a lamp.

"I normally keep a light on in here," he said. "Don't know why it's out."

Along with the three officers, Otter and Margie joined Kirk in the room. Kirk only turned on one lamp, leaving the room dimly lit, and giving it an eerie feeling. Margie stood in the doorway with her arm around Otter, unconsciously preparing to shield him from the shock of his grandfather's arrest, should the officers find his hiding place. She prayed that Dee and James were not hiding in the display room, but braced herself for the worst.

The room was large, having been at one time a dining room. The dark wood, Carolina cherry, was ornately crafted with built-in shelves, cabinets and closets. The deputies checked inside cabinets and behind closet doors and pulled back the skirts that covered the stands on which the coffins sat. Nothing.

Otter noticed that the coffins were closed. He studied them, trying to remember if they had been closed when he had seen them earlier in the day. He looked up at Margie. She stared at the coffins and seemed to be wondering the same thing.

More and more, it seemed clear to Otter that the deputies were avoiding looking inside the coffins. On the off chance that his grandpa and uncle were hiding inside them, he prayed the deputies would leave them untouched, assuming that no one would dare hide in such a place.

Holt moved to check what was behind the last remaining door at the back of the room. It was a wider door, obviously not a closet. He reached for the doorknob and stopped short of opening it just as the fateful question came from the youngest deputy.

"What about inside these things, Holt?" The other two deputies stood quietly for a moment looking at the coffins. They began to laugh nervously.

Kirk let out a little laugh, too. "What's wrong, son? You afraid something's gonna jump out at you?" He moved to the front of the coffins where he was joined by the three officers. Margie and Otter looked on.

"Would you please open the coffins, Reverend?" Holt asked.

"Sure thing, Holt. No problem." Kirk moved first to the copper-colored one. He raised the lid. Each officer took a turn to peer inside with his flashlight.

"Boy, that's nice!" the youngest deputy exclaimed, running his hand along the material. "What's that, satin?" He looked up at Kirk.

"One hundred percent! And talk about comfortable!" Kirk paused. He looked at Otter and winked. Otter was surprised by the gesture. What was Kirk up to? he wondered.

"Go ahead, get in and try it out. I encourage all my clients to experience how it feels while they can." Kirk feigned a serious look at the youngest of the three officers.

"Come on, Jimmy, hop in and give 'er a try," Holt urged, laughing.

"I'm not getting in that thing! You get in it if you wanna know how it feels!"

The other two officers laughed as Kirk closed the lid of the coffin and moved to the powder blue one.

"This one for a woman?" the youngest officer inquired.

"That's right," Kirk replied, "though sometimes, God forbid, I'll put an older child in one that size, or I'll use it in specialized cases."

"What do you mean by specialized cases?" Holt asked.

"You remember ol' Carl Locklear?" Kirk asked.

"Wasn't he that drunk who got hit by the train downtown a couple of years ago?"

"Yeah, that was Carl. Poor guy had both legs severed above the knees. His family opted for the shorter casket.

Saved 'em about five hundred dollars." Kirk winked again at Otter.

Kirk moved to open the coffin. Margie and Otter stiffened and held their breath. The three deputies stood ready to look inside. One reached and pushed on the lid to assist Kirk. At that moment, from the depths of the dark box, a figure appeared and sat upright. The three startled officers jumped back, the youngest unbuckling his gun holster.

"Damn! Who? What the hell is that?" the youngest deputy exclaimed.

Margie was unaware that she had hold of Otter's arm. He was pulling on her fingers, trying to loosen her grip, which was cutting off his circulation.

The whole room went up in laughter. Otter and Margie recognized the women's hose, stuffed with rags to form the arms, a pillow to form the torso, and some kind of ball to form the shape of a head. The head was attached to the lid causing the body to rise up as the coffin was opened.

"You old goat," Holt exclaimed, looking over at Kirk. "You scared the shh…" He looked over at Margie. "Sorry ma'am."

Otter and Margie laughed, albeit a little disingenuously, along with Kirk, as he explained that it was a Halloween prank he used with the kids in the neighborhood. He patted the youngest deputy on the back and reassured him that he was not the first to almost wet his pants due to the stunt.

The nervous laughter and chatter continued as the deputies moved out into the hallway, having unconsciously come to a consensus that the third coffin did not need exploring. Then, the youngest officer stopped and reminded Holt that there was the matter of the last unexplored door.

"Where does that door lead to, Reverend?" Holt asked.

"That goes into the prep room where we do our embalming."

"Any bodies in there?" Holt asked with a chuckle.

"There's one out on the table. Rodrigo, my mortician, is working on it right now. If you want to check it out, that's fine with me," Kirk offered.

Margie and Otter looked at each other. Rod had disappeared earlier, but they had not known his whereabouts.

"That the only room we haven't been in?" Holt asked.

"That's the last one," Kirk said, moving back into the room. He anticipated that the deputies would want to check it out.

"Jimmy, go check it out, then let's leave the Reverend be," Holt said, expecting nothing to turn up there either.

The young deputy followed Kirk to the back of the display room. Kirk tapped lightly on the door.

"Rod, can I come in? You're not draining yet, are you?" Kirk asked, referring to the procedure of removing the blood from a body before replacing it with embalming fluid. The young deputy turned to his colleagues. His jaw gaped and his eyes were wide.

"Come on in. It's okay," Rod replied.

Kirk opened the door and entered, followed by the deputy. The room had the appearance of a hospital operating room. Rod stood erect, wearing an institutional-green apron and black rubber gloves like a surgeon waiting for the go-ahead to operate. The stainless steel counters and cabinets reflected the light, making the room extremely bright compared to the dimly lit display room. A pump next to the table looked much like a large hairdryer suspended from a pole. It had two tubes attached, one of which disappeared beneath the sheet covering the body. The other extended to a large glass container of fluid on the floor. The deputy twitched his nose at the strong scent of a chemical in the room. On the long porcelain table lay what was unmistakably a body covered by a white sheet. Only the feet were exposed, a tag was attached to one big toe. The officer grew pale.

"You okay, son?" Kirk asked. "There's a bathroom right through that door if you need it."

"Naw, I'll be alright." After a quick glance around the room, the officer asked about the large set of double doors at the back.

"Where does that go?" Rod moved to the door and opened one of the two. It was an exterior door leading to the covered driveway along the side of the house. The warm fresh air still smelling of rain rushed in from the outside and filled the room.

"That's where we bring 'em in—the bodies—through that door," Kirk said.

The deputy managed a quick breath and nodded. He turned and retreated to the display room followed by Kirk. The two rejoined the others in the foyer.

"Anything?" Holt asked.

"Nothing in there," he replied. "Another door exits to the outside, but that's it."

"What about the body?"

"Just a dead body. That's all."

Holt looked at Kirk. "Who is it?"

Without missing a beat, Kirk responded, "It's a fella from up in Fayetteville who had a coronary here while visiting his daughter." He went on with his fabrication. "He'd been dead about twelve hours before she came home and found him. Rigormortis was already sett'n in, so Danny Thompson, the county coroner you know Danny, don't ya, Holt?" The officer nodded. "Danny recommended us. So we're prepping the body for burial back in Fayetteville tomorrow."

"That's not his car out there, is it? The red one?" Holt asked.

"Come on Holt, you can't pull that on me. Like I said, I don't know who owns that car," Kirk replied, becoming a little annoyed at the questioning. Holt obviously knew who owned the car. Otherwise, why the search? He wondered if Holt was deliberately trying to trip him up or if it was an honest mistake. Holt is a shrewd deputy, he concluded.

"Well, we've got to impound it as evidence." Holt paused then looked at the two deputies. "Y'all go on out and call for a tow truck. I'll be out in a second. I need to talk to the Reverend." The deputies left, tipping their Smokey Bear hats as they passed by Margie.

"Reverend, about going to Fayetteville tomorrow, there's no way you can postpone that trip? I'm sure Sheriff Townsend is gonna want to ask you some more questions, and the Feds will surely be interested in this…uh.." Holt pulled a small pad of paper from his pocket, "this James Fisher, the owner of the car. It appears he's a relative of the murder suspect they're looking for."

Hearing the name James Fisher, Otter bowed his head

as if the deputy had said, "Let us pray." He kept his eyes fixed on the floor. Margie stood behind him, trying her best to seem disinterested.

"Well, Holt," Kirk replied, "the interment is scheduled for tomorrow, so the body will need to be there." He paused and thought for a moment, rubbing his chin. "I suppose Rod could deliver it."

"That would be preferable," Holt replied. "I'm sure Sheriff Townsend would appreciate it."

The two agreed that Kirk would stay in Dillon to make himself available for further questioning. And with that, the deputy, without tipping his hat to Margie, left.

There was a long silence, then a great collective sigh of relief after the large front door closed shut. Kirk stepped over to the window and looked out at the deputies as they drove away. Situation stable, he thought. Suddenly, and without speaking a word, he turned and headed for the display room. Otter and Margie looked at each other, then followed. As they entered the room, they saw Dee struggling to get out of the oak coffin. He was drenched in sweat.

Otter ran to his grandfather and helped Kirk ease him over the edge of the coffin to the floor.

"Wow, I didn't know you were in there, Grandpa! Otter exclaimed.

"And a good thing we didn't," Margie interjected, "or we surely would have given you away. Phew, that was a close one! But, I'm surprised they didn't smell you!" After a tension-relieving laugh, Otter looked around.

"Where is James?" he asked.

At that instant, James came through the prep room door at the back of the room. He was barefoot and had a tag around one of his big toes. Rod followed.

"Here I am," James said, grinning.

Margie looked at Otter then at James, her mouth open in surprise.

"So you're the dead guy. Well I swan!" she exclaimed.

"That was a stroke of genius to move him out of the coffin and into the back room," Dee said to Kirk. "I was sure we were gonna be found out."

"I was too," Kirk replied. "It was a gamble to assume they wouldn't look in that last coffin, but I thought it was a bigger risk trying to hide you both in the prep room."

James spoke up. "I know something I never knowed before," he said shyly.

"What's that, Mr. Fisher?" Kirk asked.

"What a dead man must feel like when he's a lying in there on that table or in one of them coffins. It don't feel so bad!"

Everyone broke up laughing, including Otter, at the pathetic man's ridiculous observation. The quip afforded Otter still another view of his uncle. For the second time in the space of a day, he caught a glimpse of a human being. It was confusing. Who was this man? he asked himself. Despite these new insights, deep inside he could still feel the weight of his anger toward his uncle. He still needed to know what James knew and what his connection was to his mother's disappearance. He couldn't wait to talk with Dee about it.

Kirk asked the group to reconvene in the kitchen. There he laid out the plan he had for them to get to Fayetteville, exonerate Dee, and expose Gage's plot. The catch was that he might not be there to see it through. Dee would be of little use because he would be recognized immediately. For the plan to work, it would take Otter, Margie, Rod and James to pull it off.

Kirk encouraged everyone to try to get some sleep. He showed each of them to a room. Otter stayed in a room with Dee.

After Dee had showered, Margie knocked on the door and offered to dress his head wound. Once finished, she said good night and made her way to her room down the hall. Dee struggled to stretch out on the bed, and closed his eyes. By the time Otter had finished brushing his teeth, Dee was asleep. The long-awaited conversation with his grandfather about James would have to wait still longer. Otter lay down in the large bed next to his grandfather. He thought Dee's deep breathing sounded like whispers of thanks for the body-repairing rest he needed. He looked at his grandfather with admiration and wonder, trying to imagine all he had endured. He leaned over and kissed Dee on the cheek, then reached to turn off the lamp.

Staring into the darkness, Otter thought about his own journey over the past week, the people he had met who had helped him without even knowing him: Margie and Claudia, Kirk and Rod. He remembered the narrow escapes and smiled as he recalled the incident on the bus.

But what next? Otter felt the familiar mix of anxiety and excitement pervade his body. What would tomorrow bring? He closed his eyes and listened again to his grandfather's breathing. A peace seemed to replace the anxiety he was feeling, and for the first time in his life, Otter felt he was in a keeping not his own. Something or someone larger than myself, even larger than grandpa, someone with good intentions, has a hand in all that is happening, he thought. Again, in the dark, he smiled. The thought was as comforting as sleeping next to the man he loved more than anyone else in the world. Holding tight to it, he added his own whisper of thanks to the rhythm of his grandfather's breathing. Then he closed his eyes and slipped easily into a deep sleep.

Chapter Twenty-two

Kirk had everyone up early the next morning with the smell of sausage and bacon cooking. Each of his guests seemed to have slept well during the night. Otter felt ready for anything.

"They're already here," Kirk announced as he set another platter of scrambled eggs on the table.

"Who's here, Kirk?" Margie asked, a little startled by the comment. The others stopped eating and looked up at Kirk.

"The deputies," Kirk said. "Two are sitting in their cruiser just up the street. They've been sittin' out there since five-thirty this morning. I suspect the sheriff himself will be around shortly."

Kirk exuded confidence as he moved around the kitchen, serving his guests. Otter admired the fact that the retired chaplain didn't seem to be worried at all. He wanted to share the same confidence.

"By the way, Mr. Fisher, they did tow your car last night, but I wouldn't worry about it. Once this whole thing gets straightened out, they'll return it to you," Kirk said.

James stared blankly at Kirk for a moment, then resumed eating. Otter recognized the stupor and recalled that the last time he saw it was on Flora's front porch when he had narrowly escaped his uncle's clutches. Accompanying the stupor, he remembered, was the smell of alcohol—whiskey or something. He didn't detect the smell this time.

"We do need to get this show on the road," Kirk said. "I suspect that along with the sheriff we'll see a couple of MPs and perhaps some FBI fellas."

The mention of military police and FBI agents raised the anxiety level for Otter. Though it sounded scary, he forced himself to see it as an adventure.

As Otter sipped on a glass of orange juice and tried to picture the adventure in his mind, a dark figure walked into the kitchen, dressed in a black suit and wearing sunglasses. The sudden presence caused Otter to choke on his juice. Had it not been for the familiar smile, Otter would have guessed that an FBI agent had just foiled their plans. Margie burst out laughing as Dee patted Otter gently on the back to help clear his windpipe.

"Well, if *you* don't look like Elliot Ness," Margie said.

Like Margie, Otter recognized Rod right away. But who was Elliot Ness? he wondered.

"I was sure we were caught before we even started," Margie said, still laughing at Rod.

Rod was dressed in his funeral suit, looking very professional. Otter recognized it from the day before, but it was the sunglasses that made Rod's appearance seem a little shocking and mysterious. He did look like one of the famed " Men in Black."

"Everything ready?" Kirk asked Rod.

"Ready to go, sir!" Rod seemed to have reverted to his old military days, responding to his commanding officer with authority.

"Okay. Mr. Dumpkin, Mr. Fisher, you two come with me and we'll get you into a casket and get you on your way. Margie, you and Otter get your things and get going. Remember, make your way back through town the way you came in yesterday. If they stop you, just tell them you're headed back home to Florence. Once you get out to I-95, head north and stop at Pedro's. You know what to do after that."

Otter sat up. He couldn't stop smiling.

"At exactly zero eight hundred hours—eight o'clock, I leave Pedro's and head for Fayetteville to the little church on Fort Bragg Road," Margie said. She knew exactly where it was. Kirk had invited her there several times while a chaplain. It was a parish of his denomination. He often filled in for the pastor when she was away.

"Park around back and sit tight," Kirk reminded her. "My friend Helen will be there to let you, Rod, and the others in. I'm confident I can be there by late this afternoon. If not, I'll call the church."

Otter ran upstairs to get his backpack while Kirk took Margie's suitcase and canvas bag and walked with her out to her car as he had done dozens of times before. Backpack slung over his shoulder, Otter followed.

To the deputies who sat in their car, the departure must have all seemed normal enough. After the usual hugs good-bye, Margie started the car and pulled into the vacant lot next to the house, turned around and headed back through downtown Dillon, south toward

Florence. Kirk waved as they passed. Otter, trying to appear convincing, waved back, perhaps a little too vigorously, Kirk thought. For a few moments he stood watching the car as it moved past the sheriff's cruiser. The deputies noted the departure but did little more. At the intersection, the car turned right and disappeared.

Back inside, Rod was helping Dee and James into a single coffin. It was the large oak one Dee had been in the night before. Rod had removed the lining and replaced it with Otter's sleeping bag. Kirk had persuaded the two men that, without the padded lining on the sides of the coffin, they would be able to lie comfortably side by side. Reluctantly, the brothers-in-law consented, convinced that there was no other alternative.

Kirk was right. The two men fit snuggly into the coffin. After a few words of reassurance, he placed a folded towel over the side of the coffin and lowered the lid onto it, insuring plenty of space for air to pass. Rod and Kirk had placed the coffin on a gurney earlier that morning making it easy for them to move it through the prep room and out to the covered driveway to the hearse. It was a routine they had performed together hundreds of times.

Once secured inside the hearse, Kirk whispered good luck to Dee and James and closed the door. He walked with Rod to the front of the long Cadillac, briefly replaying the plan with his friend. Taking his place behind the wheel, Rod gave a little salute to Kirk, then shut the door. The engine roared. After mirrors and gauges were checked, the hearse moved slowly away.

Turning right onto Oak Street, Rod glanced into his sideview mirror to the street behind him. The sheriff's cruiser fell in behind him. Kirk had told Rod to expect it, so he wasn't surprised, though he still felt a little nervous. To help him relax, he put on his favorite cassette tape of Latino music in the recorder on the seat next to him. To the two confined in the coffin, he asked playfully, "You guys know how to do the Mambo?" It was seven-thirty.

Otter and Margie arrived at Pedro's at seven thirty-five. Pedro's was open twenty-four hours a day, so there were always tourists about. With little time to take it all in, Margie suggested that they first go up to the sombrero-shaped observation tower.

The elevator ride was a little scary to Otter, but once he got to the top he felt fine. The view of the South Carolina countryside at sunrise was breathtaking. Otter thought of Dee and how he loved sunrise on the lake. He wondered what it was like now for Dee and James in the coffin. His thoughts turned to his anticipated conversation with Dee. "If only I had said something to Grandpa about what I know about James," he whispered under his breath. "It would be a great time for a fight!" Otter smiled as he imagined his grandfather and great-uncle fighting in the coffin as the hearse moved along the interstate to Fayetteville.

Margie walked to the northeast side of the sombrero and called Otter over to see if they could locate Kirk's house in Dillon. The sleepy town of Dillon, obscured by the surrounding tall pines and hardwoods, was barely visible even from the heights of Pedro's Sombrero. A church steeple and the tops of several two-story houses reflected the morning sun.

Otter turned his attention to the interstate traffic.

 Looking north, he could see slower traffic moving parallel to the interstate on US 301. To his surprise, he saw a long dark vehicle, followed by what was clearly a sheriff's car, moving north to US 301's intersection with I-95. Otter called Margie over and pointed out the hearse and cruiser. She agreed with his identification, and the two watched as the vehicles made their way toward the clover leaf. Kirk had a hunch that the deputies might follow the hearse in order to check out his story, but suspected they would stop short of continuing on the interstate. He was right. As the hearse turned onto the ramp, the sheriff's car continued past the entrance then turned around and headed back to Dillon. The hearse moved onto I-95 and joined the other traffic crossing into North Carolina. Margie looked down at her watch. It was a quarter to eight. They needed to get going.

Before making their way back to the car, Otter spotted Pedro's fireworks outlet. "Make your Fourth of July a real blast. Get your fireworks here," Otter said, reading the sign. He persuaded Margie to let him buy some M-80s, convincing her that he and Dee had often stopped in South Carolina to buy fireworks on their way home from Fort Bragg. He felt a little ashamed that he told a lie. Dee was opposed to his having fireworks. But Otter thought they might come in handy in carrying out their plan.

Margie was waiting in the car when Otter returned with a large bag of assorted fireworks.

"I thought you were only buying M-80s?" she inquired.

"They were having a big sale on this stuff. I had almost thirty dollars left and this was only nineteen ninety-five. I couldn't pass up a deal like that!" Otter did not look over at Margie as he was talking. He could feel her disapproving eyes on him.

"Well, if I were your mother…" She stopped short. Though Otter had not divulged his secret concerning the disappearance of his mother, he had spoken of her. The fact that she had left him to be raised by his grandfather indicated to Margie that this might be sensitive territory. Otter looked at her with confused eyes, then gazed out the side window at a cat curled up in a rocking chair on the porch of the fireworks shop.

"I'm sorry," she said.

Otter put the sack of fireworks on the floorboard in front of him and shrugged. It was not the first time someone had made a reference to his mother. But it was the first time in a long time that he thought about what it might be like to have a real mother.

Margie put the car in gear and left Pedro's, making her way out to the interstate. In silence they headed north. It was five after eight. They had to make up for lost time.

Chapter Twenty-three

Everything went as planned. Margie and Otter met Rod, Dee, and James behind the little church on Fort Bragg Road. Kirk's friend, Helen, a retired legal secretary and member of the parish, was there to let them into the sanctuary. Kirk was questioned by Sheriff Townsend, then freed to go. He showed up in Fayetteville at exactly 4:30 p.m. (1630 military time, Otter noted). The next step of the plan was ready for implementation.

As they sat around the communion table eating pizza and drinking Pepsi, Kirk went over the second phase of the plan. Shortly after arriving, he had gone on-line using the church's computer in the adjacent office. There he found the Fort Bragg web site and current information on the next day's Capabilities Exercise and Fourth of July activities. The weapons capabilities demonstration would take place at 0900 hours at the firing range followed by a LAPES demonstration and parachute jump at Sicily Drop Zone at 1100 hours. If

Dee was right, Gage would launch his attack on visiting dignitaries at the weapons demonstration.

Kirk was confident that his plan would stop Gage's initial attack. What concerned him was Gage's backup plan. All soldiers, from Airborne grunts to Academy officers, were trained to have an alternative plan of action in case the initial plan failed. The Army would have to do some quick second-guessing if Gage could not be persuaded to give up his misguided attack.

Kirk's plan was basically a simple one. Later in the evening he would alert Fayetteville's Chief of Police, Homer Bigelow, that Dee was ready to turn himself in. Kirk anticipated that Fort Bragg MPs as well as federal investigative units would be brought in immediately once Dee was identified and revealed what he knew about Gage's plot.

Kirk trusted Homer Bigelow. They had first met in Vietnam at a worship service that Kirk was conducting with troops outside Da Nang. During their years of military service, he came to know the now-retired command sergeant major as a man of impeccable integrity.

At eight o'clock in the evening on July 3, Major Addison Dumpkin turned himself in to the Fayetteville Police Department and was immediately arrested for the murder of Private Terry Warren. Kirk had telephoned Chief Bigelow and asked him to come to the station so he could personally brief him on the situation. Kirk drove Dee downtown to the police station. Otter and Margie followed in her car, in case Kirk ended up staying late.

There was little fanfare over the arrest. Dee simply walked in and turned himself in. Chief Bigelow was professional, but gracious. In his conversation with the chief on the phone, Kirk assured him that Dee was not a threat. The respect between the two men was mutual.

Margie and Otter went to the waiting area while the chief led Kirk and Dee to an interrogation room.

Kirk had predicted that the MPs would not be called in until after he had had an opportunity to brief Chief Bigelow. He guessed wrong. Shortly after Kirk's call, the chief had notified the Fort Bragg military police of the impending arrest and requested that an investigator be sent over immediately. The dispatcher, a Private Hall, received the call and assured Chief Bigelow that he would make the arrangements. The investigative team had already arrived before Dee turned himself in. They were waiting in the interrogation room, a detail the chief failed to share with Kirk and Dee.

Chief Bigelow entered the room first and held the door for Dee and Kirk. Kirk was taken by surprise at the presence of the MPs. When the door closed, before any introductions were made, one of the three MPs stood up. He pointed a 9mm Glock pistol at Chief Bigelow. The chief froze. Kirk and Dee had not noticed the pistol and were already seated at the table when the gunman stood. Both men looked at the gun and then to the Chief. The shock on the chief's face made it clear that this was all a surprise to him.

"Relax, gentlemen. Sit down, Chief." The gunman nodded to the other two MPs. They stood and produced similar pistols. One moved in behind the chief and stood next to the door.

"What in hell is going on here?" the chief said sternly.

"I said, sit down, Bigelow," Gage ordered. The chief sat.

"It has to be more than coincidence that my man Hall was the one who received your call tonight, chief… I would say that it was more like Providence. And that's the second time in two weeks!" Gage looked at Dee as if he thought he would know what he was talking about. "It just goes to prove that our mission has been divinely sanctioned. That's my assessment. I thought I'd have to patch this thing back together after Dumpkin here screwed it up, but now I've been blessed with a second chance."

"That voice," Dee thought. "I know that voice." Then it came to him.

"So you're Gage." Dee interjected.

"*The* Sergeant Gage?" Kirk asked, looking across to Dee.

"You got it," Gage said. "And who the hell are you?"

"Major Kirkland Rossi, Chaplain, United States Army." Given Gage's references to divine providence, Kirk thought the sergeant might have some respect for the chaplaincy and decided to add some of his own clerical clout to the mix.

"Chaplain, huh?" Gage seemed interested. "What's your interest in Dumpkin?"

"Just a friend trying to help," Kirk replied.

"Well, padre, you got your ass in a crack when you showed up here." Gage obviously was not impressed that a US Army chaplain was present.

"Okay. Now that we've all been formally introduced, everybody shut up and listen if you want to stay alive." Gage moved around the table to the door. He looked at Dee.

"I presume, Major Dumpkin, that you've shared with your friend the padre here, and the chief, my plan to change the course of history tomorrow."

Gage was clearly impressed with himself. Kirk had had some experience with his type while serving as a chaplain. He had come to realize that sometimes there was only a fine line between the soldier who has the guts to do something deserving of a Medal of Honor and the one who is a fanatic. In Gage's case, the line was crossed. Kirk heard in Gage's voice and saw in his eyes that he really believed he was some kind of divine messenger—a messiah.

Gage looked around the room. "We've gotta make this next move look like an official transfer of a prisoner, so listen carefully," he said, his cold steel eyes demanding the attention of each man.

"It'll never work," Chief Bigelow interrupted.

"I said shut up! If you want to see another day, Bigelow, you had better make it work!"

The chief sat quiet for a moment and then dared to speak again. "All I'm saying is that every man on the force knows that this is our case. There's no way in hell that we would hand the prisoner over to Bragg."

Gage was angry. He walked over to the chief and put the pistol to his head. "Just how many of your officers know you have Dumpkin in custody? It appears to me that you've made a tidy little arrangement with him and the chaplain here to turn himself in."

Again the chief was silent.

"My suspicion is that just you and that desk sergeant out there know Dumpkin is here," Gage said. "And I'm willing to lay odds that if his life depended on it, you could convince him that we need to continue this investigation out at Bragg. And be assured, Chief, his life and yours depend on it." Gage's eyes narrowed as he looked at Bigelow. "You've got one minute to decide what you're gonna say to that desk sergeant. If he's not convinced, he's a dead man, 'cause there's no way he's coming with us."

Chief Bigelow stared hard at Gage. It was difficult for him to grasp that a soldier in the United States Army would plan such a cowardly act of aggression against his own country and threaten so many innocent lives in doing so. Sure, the nation had problems, but the US Army was the Army of a democracy and the internal problems of a democracy were not solved by aggression and violence.

"Let's go," Gage said, breaking from the piercing eyes of the chief. "The Hummer's parked across the street in the hotel parking lot. And we'll take your car, too, Chief. We want to make this look nice and official. I'll ride with you." Gage looked at his men. "Gallworth, you escort the prisoner and put him in the back of the chief's car. You and Jamison follow with the padre here in the Hummer. And no funny business, Chief. I'm not afraid to shoot every damn one of you. Whatever happens to me, my message is going to be heard loud and clear. So taking me out won't stop the inevitable."

Kirk had said that he was confident that Gage had a backup plan. Gage's statement seemed to prove him right.

Jamison used a plastic tie to secure Dee's hands behind his back. Gallworth positioned his 9mm Glock under his jacket. Gage opened the door and Jamison and Gallworth escorted Dee and Kirk outside through the lobby to the front entrance. Gage and the chief followed, stopping to talk to the desk sergeant and sign out the prisoner. The desk sergeant did not seem suspicious. The chief convinced him that the interrogation needed to continue out at Fort Bragg MP headquarters.

Margie and Otter sat in the waiting area anxious to hear some news from Kirk. Margie had her bag of nylon donuts at her side and was beginning to role a red one when Kirk and Dee appeared, escorted by two MPs across the lobby to the front door. Margie put the unfinished donut back into her bag and stood up. Otter also stood and together they started to make their way over to join them. Suddenly Otter reached out and grabbed Margie's arm. She looked back at him in surprise.

"What's wrong?" she asked.

"Wait." Otter whispered, "Something isn't right."

She looked back at the men advancing to the front door. Kirk caught Otter's eye and gently shook his head, then looked away. Neither Jamison nor Gallworth noticed. Dee, hands bound behind him, was first out the door.

"Something's up," Otter whispered. "Those MPs, I've seen them before." Margie looked back at the men, but they were already out the door.

Another MP stood with Chief Bigelow in front of the desk sergeant. The chief was saying something that Otter could not make out. When the two men turned to head for the front door, Otter and Margie looked at each other in surprise. The MP with Chief Bigelow was the Sergeant Gage who had rescued them from James' feeble attempt to kidnap Otter at the truckstop. There was no question about it.

Otter pulled Margie back down on the couch, hoping that Gage would not notice them. He didn't. But Otter noticed something curious. It was raining hard outside, yet this man was not wearing his raincoat. He was carrying it over his arm. Even more curious was that the man's standard issue MP holster had no pistol in it.

After a few moments Otter and Margie moved to the door and watched as the two vehicles disappeared up Haymont Street. Otter turned and ran to the desk sergeant. Margie followed.

"Where are those men taking my grandfather?" Otter asked.

The sergeant looked down at Otter, then at Margie. He had seen the two come in with the man just received into custody.

"I'm sorry," he said apologetically, "I thought you had already left. There appears to be some need for interrogation out at MP headquarters. Chief Bigelow said that he should return with the prisoner—I mean your grandfather—by 2300 hours."

Otter looked up at the clock behind the desk. It was ten minutes to nine.

"Do you know those MPs?" Margie asked.

"No, ma'am. They're Bragg MPs. I know some of the MPs on post but not them. Why do you ask?" The sergeant stopped writing and looked down at them. "Is there a problem?"

"Those men are planning to kill the Vice President tomorrow at the…" Margie paused, trying to remember what the event was called.

"The Capex," Otter added.

"Yes, the Capex. That Sergeant Gage and those other two have a plan to blow something up, just like that guy did to the federal building in Oklahoma City a few years back. He's got some message he's trying to get across…something about…I don't remember exactly."

The desk sergeant stared at Margie for a moment. Then he spoke.

"That's a pretty serious accusation you're making, ma'am. That kind of talk can get you in some real hot water."

"But it's true!" Otter insisted. "And my grandfather didn't kill Terry Warren. That Sergeant Gage did!"

"You got any proof?" the desk sergeant asked, still not convinced.

Both Otter and Margie thought hard. They really had nothing to go on.

"That man with the chief, he didn't have a pistol in his holster and he carried his raincoat over his arm even when he left the building. "It's raining outside! Did you notice that?" Otter screeched, his voice betraying his frustration.

"I can't say that I did," the desk sergeant replied. "But that doesn't prove anything."

"What about calling back to the MP headquarters to see if Sergeant Gage really is an MP!" Otter suggested adamantly.

"I guess I can do that," the desk sergeant replied, still not convinced that anything was wrong. He checked the number and punched it in. The voice answering on the other end wasted no time in its quick, crisp greeting.

"MP headquarters, Private Hall speaking."

Chapter Twenty-four

Once again luck was with Gage. Private Hall, a close friend of Private Jamison, Gage's right-hand man, was scheduled to be relieved from his post at 2100 hours. The two soldiers were from the same small town in Idaho, just a few miles north of Coeur d'Alene. Hall, like Jamison, was sympathetic to Gage's cause. When Gage needed some inside help from the MPs, Hall was only too happy to oblige.

Hall reassured the desk sergeant that Gage and his two men were indeed MPs. Realizing that they were going to get no further with the desk sergeant, Margie and Otter left the station.

On the way back to the church, Otter used Margie's cell phone to call Rod and James to let them know that Kirk and Dee had been abducted by Gage and that she and Otter were on their way to the church and would be arriving shortly.

They never arrived. Just two blocks from the church, while waiting for a traffic light to change, a Humvee appeared, blocking their way. Gage had suspected that Kirk had others involved who might attempt to follow and instructed Jamison and Gallworth to hang back. He was right.

The two men forced Margie and Otter out of her car and into the massive vehicle. Gallworth moved Margie's car into a parking space off the street in front of one of the closed businesses. With their prisoners, they headed for Fort Bragg.

Rod and James waited a long thirty minutes for Margie and Otter to arrive before concluding that something had gone wrong. After consulting with Helen on directions to the police station, the two were in the hearse and on their way downtown. They found Kirk's Mercedes but no sign of Margie or Otter or the car she was driving. Retracing their path, the two men headed back up Haymont Hill toward the church.

Stopped at the traffic light in Haymont, Rod noticed a car that resembled Margie's. Without waiting for the light to change, he floored the engine and the hearse squealed across the intersection. James shook his head in mock disapproval and made a little clicking noise with his tongue on the roof of his mouth. Rod ignored him.

The car was the same make and model as Margie's, but was it hers? Rod got out and walked around to the back of the vehicle. South Carolina plates. It had to be hers, he thought.

He tried the driver-side door. It was open. Margie's bag lay on the front seat.

Rod retrieved the bag and returned quickly to the hearse. Something is indeed wrong, he thought, seriously wrong.

Rod decided to head out to Fort Bragg, though he

had no idea where to start looking for the kidnappers once on post. He guessed that Gage somehow had discovered Otter and Margie and took them along as hostages, too. But where could they be?

At seeing Margie's bag, James' mind returned to the incident at the truck stop in Florence. He felt his nose. There was still a remnant of the scab from the burn caused by Otter's sudden removal of the nylon stocking from his head. Once again he felt the rage rise up within him, not because of his nephew's antics, but from the memory of the humiliation he had experienced at the hand of Gage. More than anything else, it was this rage that had driven him to follow Gage in the hope of finding an occasion to exact some revenge.

As James pictured Gage in his mind, he blurted out, "B Company."

"What did you say?" Rod asked, distracted from his own thoughts of what their options were.

"He said they were from B Company," James replied, his voice subdued as if he were in a trance. "That Gage fella, back at that truck stop, I remember he said something about B Company."

"You sure about that?" Rod asked.

James looked over at Rod and nodded his head.

"I do believe that's what he said. Not a hundred percent, but near it."

"Okay, Mr. Fisher. I got an idea."

The hearse made its way across the Army post to the JFK Chapel and the chaplains' offices next door. Rod was familiar with the compound, having spent his last year in the Army there as an assistant to Kirk. The offices were dark. It was already 9:30 p.m. Rod grimaced at his bad luck. He had hoped that he might find a familiar face staying late in the office. As they drove around to the front of the chapel, James thought he saw a light on inside.

Rod pulled the hearse over to the curb, got out, and mounted the steps to the door. James followed. The door was not locked. Inside the chapel a figure moved on the chancel near the pulpit.

"Excuse me? Hello?" Rod said. The light from a back room revealed just the silhouette of the person. The image stood still.

"Can I help you, gentlemen?" It was a female voice. The silhouette began to make its way toward the two men.

"We are looking for a chaplain," Rod said, still a little taken off guard at hearing a woman's voice.

"I'm a chaplain, sir, but I'm about to close up. What can I do for you?"

Rod was surprised at the thought of a female chaplain. He had known a couple of female assistants but no full chaplains. James was not surprised. The Pentecostal tradition he was a part of had women preachers. Why not a woman chaplain?

"I was a chaplain's assistant when I was in the Army under Captain Kirk Rossi, ma'am. Perhaps you know him?"

"No, I can't say that I do. Are you looking for him?" the woman asked, turning on a light in the entry way. The light revealed an attractive young woman in her late twenties to early thirties dressed in a class A uniform. The gold bars on her collar indicated she was a captain.

"No, not for him, well, yes, I am looking for him but…well, I am looking for another man who is with him." Rod was suddenly befuddled. James looked at him, wondering what had gotten into him to make him sound so confusing. But Rod was unsure what to reveal to the chaplain. He knew it all sounded awkward. "I am looking for a Sergeant Gage of B Company. I don't know his first name or his regiment."

The young chaplain looked at Rod, then at James. "And you are?"

"I am Rodrigo Riviera and this is Mr. Fisher. It is very important that we find Sergeant Gage."

"If you can hang on a moment so I can finish up here, we can go over to my office and check the directory. We've got services tomorrow for the Fourth of July celebration and I'm trying to finish up some last minute details," the woman said as she disappeared into a back room.

James sensed something stirring within himself. As his eyes adjusted to the dark, he was surprised to find himself admiring what he could see of the sanctuary. A cross suspended from the ceiling at the front of the sanctuary appeared in the faint light coming from the back room.

James tended to avoid churches, believing that they were full of idols that humans created to worship themselves. He confined his preaching to tabernacles—revival tents—movable sanctuaries, that according to James, moved with the winds of the Holy Ghost.

As he slipped into one of the pews to sit for a moment, his hand brushed against a small object on the seat. He picked it up and looked at it. A distant streetlight streaming through the stained glass, bathed the sanctuary in a faint rainbow of colors, offering just enough light for him to read the cover of what was a small paperback book. James smiled and shook his head.

 TWELVE STEPS TO LIFE. It was a manual published by Alcoholics Anonymous. He looked up again to the darkened cross at the front of the chapel, and whispered, "So this is what you brung me here for."

After a few moments, the light in the back room was extinguished and the chaplain reappeared. James tucked the booklet away in his coat pocket and joined Rod in the chapel foyer. The chaplain waited for the two men to exit before turning the light out. After locking the door of the chapel, she escorted them to the offices next door.

"So, when did you serve here at JFK?" she asked Rod as they made their way down the hallway to her office.

"Oh, I left here in 1991 just after Desert Storm. Chaplain Rossi, he left. So I went too. What about you?"

"I came to Bragg almost two years ago from Ft. Riley. I've been in the Army six years. two as a chaplain."

"Where are you from?" Rod asked.

"I've lived in a number of places. But I guess I call Fayetteville, Arkansas home. That's where my parents live," she said as she unlocked the door to her office.

On hearing the name Fayetteville, Arkansas, James cocked an ear toward the chaplain. He had done some evangelizing there on the University of Arkansas campus years before.

The chaplain held the door for the two men. As James walked by, he eyed the chaplain curiously. She seemed to be doing the same with him. She smiled.

"Have a seat, gentlemen, while I check on …was it Gage?"

"Yes, ma'am. Gage, B Company."

The chaplain sat down behind her desk and turned to her computer. After a few manipulations, she brought up the post directory on screen and typed in the name Gage. There were several Gages on post.

"Gage... B Company?" she asked again.

"Yes, ma'am, Joel Gage."

She scrolled down. "Gage...there it is. Sergeant Joel Gage, B Company. 504 PIR. Looks like he's the only Gage connected with Bravo Company. You want a phone number?"

"Yes, ma'am, that would be very helpful, and the Company office address if you would, please."

The chaplain scribbled down the information, tore it from a pad, and handed it to Rod. She looked at James. He was staring at her with a strange, puzzled look, almost haunted.

"Are you okay, sir? You don't look so well." She got up and poured James a glass of water from a decanter on her desk. "Here, drink this." As she handed him the glass, she tried to search his eyes.

James reached for the glass, his eyes fixed on it. His hand was shaking.

"Thank you, ma'am," he said quietly. He took the glass and drank it down in several swallows, then handed the empty glass back to her. "I just got a lot on my mind."

The chaplain continued to look at James with interest. She had a strange feeling about the whole encounter with these two men, but especially this Mr. Fisher. There was something about him that was familiar, but she couldn't identify it. And the way he seemed to avoid her eyes was more than simply the manner of a shy person.

Rod stood up to leave. James followed. Before exiting the office, Rod turned to the young woman and extended his hand. "Thank you for your help

Captain...uh..., " he shot a quick glance to the gold plate over the chaplain's pocket, but before he could read the name, she spoke.

"Dawson, Captain Darlena Dawson," she said, finishing his sentence. Rod thanked her again and turned to the door with James on his heels. Before he entered the hall he halted, causing James to bump into him. Stepping back into the office, he made his way to the chaplain's desk.

"Is something wrong, sir?" she asked, a little surprised to see him back.

Rod looked at her with fearful eyes. "Captain, something bad is about to happen and I would like to ask your help," Rod blurted out. He hesitated as he looked at James, who looked to the floor and shook his head.

"What's on your mind, sir? What bad thing is about to happen?" the chaplain asked.

Rod had second thoughts. "Nothing, I, uh, nothing." He looked again at James, then back to the chaplain. "It was nothing, ma'am. Come on, Mr. Fisher, let's go."

The two moved quickly down the hall and out the door. They crossed the chapel lawn to the hearse parked on the street. The chaplain followed, stopping at the door to watch. She was startled to see that they were driving a hearse. As the men got in and drove away, she was able to see clearly that they were also transporting a casket. How bizarre! she thought to herself. She stood motionless for a moment, reflecting on the whole encounter. Then her curiosity got the best of her. Something is not right, she told herself. She headed for her car.

Chapter Twenty-five

The chaplain followed the hearse as it made its way to B company's headquarters. She replayed in her mind the conversation with the two men back at her office. Who were they? And this Mr. Fisher? Why did she think he looked so familiar?

Once she arrived at B Company barracks, she found the hearse parked close to what appeared to be the office. The two men were still in the vehicle. She parked her car a safe distance from the hearse and watched. They got out and walked cautiously to the office entrance. It was dark and the place looked deserted. Due to the holiday, many of the soldiers were out exploring Fayetteville's nightlife.

Closer to the building a police car was parked. No officer. She couldn't make out the signage on the side that indicated what municipality it represented. What is it doing here? she wondered. It added to her suspicion that foul play was imminent or perhaps had already transpired. Call the MPs, she told herself. She decided to wait a little longer.

 Checking her watch, she saw that it was already 2230 hours. Nothing was happening. She had almost convinced herself that her imagination had gotten the best of her and was about to leave when the two men appeared again with a third, a soldier dressed in fatigues. His hands were bound behind his back and he was gagged. One of the men, Mr. Riviera, was pointing a pistol at the soldier's back, nudging him along while the other, Mr. Fisher, lagged behind.

The chaplain watched nervously as Rod moved around to the back of the hearse, barking instructions to James, who was preoccupied with his coat, to open the hearse's large back door. Once the door was open, Rod, still pointing the gun at the soldier, grabbed the handle of the casket and dragged it out of the hearse, resting one end on the ground. What happened next shocked her.

Rod opened the casket and ordered the soldier to get in. The soldier resisted. Rod held the gun to his chin and repeated his command. The soldier shook his head. Rod pushed him back, causing the man to fall into the coffin. He tried to kick his way free. James reluctantly assisted as Rod slammed the casket shut.

The chaplain had seen enough. These men were involved in some bizarre prank and she would not stand by and watch someone get hurt.

Grabbing her cell phone, she got out of her car and made her way toward the hearse.

"Mr. Riviera, Mr. Fisher?" The two men froze. "What on earth are you two up to?" she asked as she approached, still imagining that it was some sort of prank.

Rod recognized the chaplain, but said nothing. He

turned and continued what he was doing, assuming her to be no threat. Before pushing the casket back into the hearse, he retrieved the canvas bag and the small cassette tape recorder from the front seat. On his way back to the rear, he dropped the bag, spilling out several of the colored donut rings. He stuffed them back in the bag and hurried on to the casket. He opened it and said something to the soldier. Then he placed the recorder's small microphone into the casket and slammed the lid shut once again. He set the recorder beside the casket and pushed the record button. With some of the panty hose he retrieved from the bag, he tied the casket securely closed.

"I said, Mr. Riviera, what are you doing to this soldier? This kind of hazing is illegal." She was amazed that Rod continued to ignore her as he worked. He was clearly in a hurry, working up quite a sweat in his haste. James stood quietly to the side, still pulling at his coat, which, on closer inspection, seemed to the chaplain to be much too tight for him.

"Mr. Fisher, toss me another…stocking," Rod said. James was not paying attention. He removed his coat and began fidgeting with some kind of bulky vest he was wearing under his coat.

"Mr. Fisher!" Rod shouted, growing impatient. James stopped what he was doing and looked up at Rod. "I told you not to take that thing, it'll just weigh you down. Get me another stocking." James looked down at the flack jacket then up at Rod. Moments earlier there had been a scuffle in B Company's office when Rod and James entered and found Private Gallworth alone. The encounter had awakened James to the danger of what he was getting into. Fortunately they had surprised

 Gallworth, allowing Rod to take the soldier's weapon before he could use it. It was an ominous-looking automatic, the kind James had seen in movies. But this one was real—designed to kill real people. Clearly, had they not surprised Gallworth, he could easily have shot them both. And who else would they encounter with such weapons? James had asked himself. The idea of it terrified him. Spotting the bullet-proof vest, known to soldiers as a flack jacket, he took it and put it on under his coat on the way out. It didn't quite fit right.

James obediently moved to find the bag where Rod had left it. The flack jacket impeded his movement as he struggled to pick the bag up off the ground. He grunted as he leaned over and reached inside for a stocking. He could feel nothing but nylon donuts. Frustrated, he dumped the contents on the ground, revealing several nylon donuts and a long red, white, and blue braided rope. He unrolled a red one and gave it to Rod.

"Captain, I'm sorry, but I don't have time to explain," Rod said to the chaplain as he tied off the last stocking around the casket. "A lot of lives are in danger and if we don't get some information out of this guy pronto, some innocent people are going to be dead." Rod was talking with a confidence and authority that had lain dormant since his days in the military. The sense of crisis and urgency about the situation had awakened it. James noticed the change and it engendered a respect for the man that, up to that moment, he had been hesitant to give. Consequently, he found himself moving a little faster responding to Rod's commands.

"I don't know what you're talking about, Mr. Riviera," the chaplain replied, "I'm calling the MPs." She held her cell phone out where he could see it, hoping the gesture would give the threat some weight.

"Be my guest, but it will only complicate things. I have reason to believe someone in that office is in on this whole plot. Whenever the MPs are brought in, something seems to go wrong."

"What plot? What are you talking about?" The chaplain was losing patience. This was sounding less like a hazing prank and more like a serious crime. "What the heck is going on here?"

"Reverend, this guy tied up in the casket is an accomplice to murder and treason. He and that SOB Gage and the other pieces of shh…" He paused, remembering who he was talking to, " He and others in Company B murdered an innocent soldier just because he was the wrong color, and they blamed it on an innocent man. Tomorrow they plan to kill the Vice President at the Capex, him and whoever else is unlucky enough to be within one hundred feet of the blast, because he thinks women like you, spics like me, and blacks like Private Warren are the cause of our nation's problems."

Rod looked at the chaplain, his eyes glistening. "His god…"

James was startled by the hurt evident in Rod's eyes and his quickened breathing that betrayed his passionate anger.

Rod took a deep breath and continued. "I served my country proudly. But to him I am less than a dog. His god, he says, has told him to set our nation straight. That means I'm out!"

The chaplain was stunned. She knew of the murder of Private Terry Warren. In fact, she had helped make arrangements for a memorial service that had taken place just a week earlier. But treason? It was incomprehensible—here, at Ft. Bragg, surrounded by the nation's "Guard of Honor." For a moment she stood in the dark with her mouth open, not knowing what to say.

"Right now, as we speak," Rod continued, "Sergeant Gage has my boss and three others hidden somewhere here on post." He walked over to the chaplain and looked her square in the eye, then pointed to the casket. "And, according to this Private Gallworth I've got here, he's gonna waste 'em. So I gotta get information out of him the only way I know how!"

Rod turned and walked toward the hearse, signaling James to help him set the coffin back inside. The two men strained to pushed the heavy oak box back into the vehicle. Then Rod checked the tape recorder to make sure it was still on record. James grabbed the bag of nylon donuts and tossed it in just as Rod shut the door. Then they got in the hearse to leave.

"Wait a minute! Let me go with you. Maybe I can talk the private into letting us know where your friends are," the chaplain shouted. She approached to speak to him through the window. Rod lowered the window and spoke first.

"Talking won't do any good. This guy's a fanatic. He's an extremist. He'll only give in to extreme pressure," Rod said. He was looking straight ahead, his fist wrapped tight around the steering wheel. The chaplain remembered Rod mentioning that he had been trained as a Ranger in Special Forces. She knew what extreme pressure meant to him.

"It doesn't have to be like that, Mr. Riviera. He's just a kid. Let me try to talk to him, Please, let me try." She held up the cell phone. "Besides, I know people who can be trusted to help."

Rod turned toward the chaplain again. He could see she was sincere—and determined. He opened the door and got out. With a nod of his head, he signaled her to get in the car. She slid across the seat to the middle. James sat on the other side. He had been watching her closely all the while she talked to Rod.

The chaplain straightened her skirt and turned toward James. Something was different about him. Then she noticed that the flack jacket was no longer concealed. He had removed it and was now wearing it in full view over his coat. He seemed more comfortable with it on the outside. Their eyes met for a moment then he turned away. The interior light afforded her a good look at the man. His ruddy complexion, his thin slicked down hair and dark eyes—it was like a dream she was sure she knew him. On his neck she noticed a scar. He turned and looked at her. She turned away.

Rod resumed his place behind the steering wheel and shut the door, extinguishing the light and leaving them in the dark. She was sure she knew Mr. Fisher, but from where? And the scar…

Rod turned the key to start the engine, bringing the chaplain back to the situation at hand.

"Where are we going?" she asked, turning to Rod.

He put the car in reverse, backed out of the parking space and headed out onto Gruber Road. "You'll see soon enough. You've got one chance to get this guy to talk. If he doesn't, I'll bury him."

Chapter Twenty-six

Otter sat on the floor of the weight room housed within the enormous Lee Sports Complex, the largest of the several physical training areas at Fort Bragg. The weight room was located next to Lee Pool. He leaned back against a weight bench with his back to Dee. Margie sat back-to-back with Kirk. All four captives had their hands tied behind them with plastic ties.

Otter could see the pool through a partially opened door. Except for the smell of chlorine, staring at the dark, placid water reminded him of Spring Lake at night. For a brief moment it was comforting. Why couldn't they be back home? he sighed. This was all such a complicated mess.

At the door a young soldier with a pistol sat in the dark guarding the prisoners. Shortly after they had arrived, Kirk tried to talk to the young man but was admonished to keep quiet. He persisted and found himself pistol whipped, to the horror of Otter and Margie.

The weight room was a large open space containing a variety of exercise equipment as well as racks of free weights of all sizes. Several large steel disks were stacked on the floor next to Otter. He could make out the number 45 on the largest one. The floor was carpeted but still felt cool. Beginning to feel uncomfortable with the position of his body, Otter tried to shift his weight. The plastic cord around his wrists dug in to his skin, resulting in a sharp pain. It brought his mind back to the seriousness of their predicament. Gage was in control now, and his plan was still on track.

Lee Pool closed at 1800 hours. The next day was the Fourth of July, a national holiday. Public buildings on post were already closed. Ft. Bragg was ready to celebrate, which meant for the evening, nobody was around. The building was dark, illuminated only by exterior security lights that filtered through the few windows of the weight room and the faint green glow from exit signs over the doors.

As a part-time lifeguard, one of Gage's grunts had access to Lee Pool. Gage had decided that it was situated in a strategic location for hiding the prisoners and that the building was defensible if he had to resort to a fire-fight.

Ten minutes after midnight Gage arrived. He was angry. Gallworth was missing. Gage had returned to B Company barracks with Jamison to pick him up. He wasn't there. The office was open, the lights were on and the radio was playing, but no Gallworth. Gage was sure that Kirk had something to do with it. He turned on the light in the weight room, despite the risk of calling attention to his presence by passersby. In his hand he had two odd looking items. Margie, Otter, and

 Kirk recognized the nylon donuts.

"What the hell are these?" he said, crouching down in front of Otter and Margie. "You had these things with you at that truck stop in Florence, didn't you?" Margie sat quiet and looked away. Gage grabbed her by the chin and forced her to look him in the eye. "You better tell me who else you've got involved here and fast," he paused and looked at Kirk, then to Otter, "if you don't want any of your little friends here to get hurt."

Otter was livid. "You're no soldier," he shouted at Gage. "You're nothing but a traitor!" Gage raised his hand as if he were going to strike Otter across the face.

"You hurt the boy, sergeant, and I swear to you, I will hunt you down," Dee said in a firm voice. Gage laughed mockingly.

"Old man, you aren't going to do a damn thing. So shut up!" Gage's voice regained its angry tone. "Now, Miss, what's it going to be. You gonna tell me what you know or do I have to..." He stopped short. Someone was coming. Quickly he motioned to two of his men to check it out. After a few moments they returned with Jamison and two more prisoners, Rod and Chaplain Dawson.

"I found these two snooping around outside," Jamison said, "I heard a vehicle up the street gunning its engine and saw them running from it. The car appeared to be..." Jamison paused " I think it was a hearse."

"A what?" Gage asked in disbelief.

"A hearse, sir."

"Where's the hearse now?"

"It took off up Honeycutt," Jamison replied a little sheepishly, unsure how Gage would react.

"Send someone to look for it." Gage looked

disapprovingly at Jamison. He had expected his right-hand man to have already taken care of this without him having to say anything. Jamison snapped his fingers at one of the grunts. The soldier bolted out the door and disappeared.

Gage did not recognize the new prisoners, though he was quick to spot the cross on Chaplain Dawson's collar, indicating that he was in the presence of yet another chaplain.

"Well now, if that's not a sign from the Almighty, I don't know what is! Two chaplains in one night. You know these people?" Gage asked, looking over at Kirk.

Kirk shook his head, indicating he didn't.

Gage looked curiously at Dee, who seemed unusually taken by the woman in uniform.

"You know this woman?" he asked. Dee ignored him. Gage's anger flared again. He was losing his cool.

"I want some answers!" he shouted. With fire in his eyes, he stared hard at Dee then back to Kirk.

"Sergeant?" Jamison interrupted, timidly.

Gage turned to the private. "What is it, Jamison?"

"This one had Gallworth's Glock," Jamison said, referring to the automatic weapon and pointing to Rod. Gage turned to Rod.

"Where is Gallworth?"

Rod remained silent.

"I said where is Gallworth, dammit!" Gage walked over to Rod and put a pistol to his neck.

"If you know something, mister, you better tell me now."

"I buried him," Rod said defiantly.

"You what? What did you say?" Gage was incredulous. Jamison stirred nervously.

"I said, I buried him… out there in the woods."

"You buried him?" Gage could not believe what he was hearing. Now all eyes were on Rod, who stood calmly in front of Gage, as if he had just uttered some nicety.

Gage exploded. "I'll bury *you,* you sonuvabitch!" He grabbed Rod by the arm and shoved him to the door toward the pool. Then with his powerful hands, he snatched a 45 pound disk off the weight rack next to Otter. "Jamison! Bring me one of those nylon things," Gage ordered.

"What are you doing, Sergeant?" the chaplain asked, fearing for Rod's life.

Gage said nothing. Rod resisted but Jamison and the guard had already joined Gage in his efforts to wrestle the man to poolside.

"You're only going to make things worse for yourself, sergeant," the chaplain said, her voice remaining calm. Uninhibited, she followed the men to the door.

In a matter of seconds, Gage had unrolled the nylon donut, tied the weight to Rod's feet and shoved him over into the pool. Kirk could not believe his eyes. He was horrified. His best friend, who, despite his incredible arm strength, could barely swim, had just been thrown over into ten feet of water with a 45 pound weight tied to his feet! Kirk rolled over and fought to get to his feet. He strained to maneuver his massive body but could not get up. Otter and Margie stood up and quickly assisted him. At the same moment another splash was heard. Otter looked around. The chaplain was gone!

Dee got up and stepped quickly to the door, his hands still tied behind his back. Jamison, Gage, and the other grunt were not aware of his approach as they stared in disbelief at the woman who had jumped into the pool. She was struggling to bring Rod to the surface. Jamison heard approaching footsteps and turned to see what was going on. Dee planted his foot into the surprised man's chest and launched him into the pool. Immediately Gage swung around and with his pistol hit Dee hard on his jaw. He fell to the concrete floor unconscious.

"Grandpa!" Otter shouted, terrified. He rushed to Dee's side. More flexible than the adults, Otter had managed to step through his tied hands and bring them in front of him. He knelt down beside Dee who was already regaining consciousness. Despite the cut on the side of his face, he appeared to be okay.

Otter looked up at Gage, then down into the water where he saw the woman continuing to fight to bring Rod to the surface. She tried to make it to the side of the pool but was blocked by Jamison's floundering efforts to get out of the water. Finally, in order to save herself, she was forced to release Rod. He continued to struggle as he sank back to the bottom. After a deep breath, she submerged again.

Instinctively and without hesitation, Otter peeled off his shoes and dove into the water, making his way quickly to the bottom. Though his hands were still tied, he tried frantically to untie the knot in the nylon holding Rod's feet to the disk, but it was tied too tightly.

Otter got the chaplain's attention and motioned to her to go up for air. Leaving Rod on the bottom for the second time, they surfaced. Gage was pointing his pistol at them and laughing. Jamison and the other grunt had regained control of the situation with the prisoners, and at gunpoint had forced Dee, Margie, and Kirk back into the weight room.

In a deranged attempt to be playful, Gage tried to step on Otter's hands when the boy tried to rest, holding onto the edge of the pool. Otter quickly pushed off from the edge, narrowly escaping Gage's boot. Gage laughed a sinister cackle then disappeared back into the weight room. There was no way he was going to let them bring Rod to the surface, Otter thought. He looked at the chaplain. Both knew Rod had very little time left.

Frustrated that his tied hands were of little help to his feet in treading water, Otter continued to tug on the plastic ties. The chaplain saw his predicament and swam over to assist.

"You push, I'll pull," the chaplain said in a hushed voice as she inspected the plastic tie, a kind similar to ones used to secure trash bags. Otter pushed hard with one hand and pulled with the other. The chaplain hesitated to pull too hard, attempting instead to roll the plastic over the boy's wrists. His hands were red. The plastic chafed his skin. Otter bit hard on his lip as the chaplain continued her efforts. Finally, the plastic shackle slipped off his hands. He was free! Now he could be of real help.

"We've got to get him to the other side and out of the water," he said. "Maybe we can get him out before that stupid man Gage comes back."

"We can't get him across the pool with that disk tied to him, we'll have to get it loose first," the chaplain said, clearly frustrated. She was breathing hard.

"No time. I'll carry the weight, you carry Rod." Otter did not wait for a response. He took a deep breath and went straight to the bottom. The chaplain followed right behind him.

Rod's body now lay motionless on the bottom of the pool, held there by the weight. He had been without oxygen for at least three minutes. Otter reached for the weight, and at first found it difficult to lift it up. He grabbed the nylon stocking and pulled hard. The weight broke free from the bottom and he picked it up in his arms.

The chaplain had Rod with one arm around his torso. Then, with powerful scissor strokes, she began moving to the opposite side. With his arms wrapped around the steel disk, Otter began the trek across the bottom of the pool like an astronaut skipping along on the moon in slow motion. He did his best to synchronize his movement to the lunging rhythm of the chaplain's strokes.

For as long as he could remember, Otter had prided himself on being able to hold his breath under water for long periods of time. Back home on Spring Lake, Dee was always amazed at how far his grandson could swim below the surface. Sometimes it scared him when Otter disappeared under the water, seeming to never come up, only to surface some place totally unexpected.

The pool was Olympic-size. Otter was aware that the opposite side was more than 20 meters away, more than 60 feet. He had swum under water that far before, plenty of times, but never carrying a 45 pound weight. Still, he was confident he could make it.

Otter knew he was approaching his limit when his lungs began to burn. But they were almost there. I will make it, he thought. From the bottom, he could see the chaplain battling frantically to bring Rod's body to the surface and the edge of the pool. Otter strained to lift the enormous steel disk as high as he could, holding it flat against his chest and arching his back to balance it. He could see Rod's feet tied to the weight and floating just above him. The burning in his lungs was increasing, and the muscles in his legs were signaling the first sign of cramps. His body screamed at him to let go of the weight and surface for air. He resisted.

Sensing that the chaplain was not going to make the last few feet, Otter lunged upward with all his strength to get the disk high enough so Rod's head would be out of the water. Then he gave the weight another heave. There was no gain.

Otter looked up past the chaplain through the dark water to the surface. The shape of a person seemed to be crouched at the edge of the pool. Was it Gage? Was he keeping her from bringing Rod up? For the first time the thought flashed through Otter's mind that they were not going to make it, that he would have to let go of the weight to save his own life, ending any chance of Rod's survival. Suddenly he saw a flash of light and in the same instant felt his stomach collapse, forcing an involuntary inhalation of water. His body shook. The burning in his lungs ceased. Then darkness.

Chapter Twenty-seven

Otter coughed hard as he regained consciousness, his body forcing out the last of the unwelcome water. When Otter looked up at him, Dee closed his eyes and whispered a prayer of thanks. He had breathed life back into his grandson. His tears, mixed with the chlorine from the pool, caused his eyes to sting. Brushing them away with his finger, he looked down at Otter and smiled, then kissed him on the forehead.

"You okay, Bud?"

Otter nodded. "I think so." He tried to sit up.

"Just lie still for a moment, let your body rest. You were underwater a long time," Dee said, still trying to hold back the tears.

"What happened, Grandpa? Why are you all wet?" Otter asked, taking note of Dee's wet hair and the water dripping from his clothes.

"I went in the pool after you." Dee paused and took Otter's hand in his, gently inspecting each finger as if he were making sure they were all there. "After we got Rod to the side, I expected to see you come bobbing up out of the water. But when you didn't, I knew something was wrong. I jumped in and got you."

Dee was about to reveal the rest of his account when he was interrupted by the chaplain and a paramedic who had been attending to Rod. The paramedic wanted to make sure the boy was okay.

After checking his vital signs, the paramedic pronounced Otter fit and returned to help her partner with Rod. The chaplain, her wet hair pushed back from her face, knelt beside Otter.

"You're a brave boy," she said, smiling at Otter, "and an incredible swimmer!"

"You're not so bad yourself," Otter replied. "I was just holding that weight off the bottom of the pool. You were the one doing all the work." Otter rolled to his side and looked over to the gurney where the paramedics were occupied with Rod. "Is he going to be okay?"

"I think he's going to be fine, " the chaplain replied. "We weren't sure for a moment; he was under quite a long time, but he's a strong man. He'll make it."

Otter managed to sit up with help from the chaplain and looked around. The bright ceiling lights illumined the large open room, allowing him to see things in more detail. The pool seemed smaller in the light. A few feet away at the pool's edge lay the 45 pound weight. A green nylon stocking lay next to it.

The two paramedics were preparing to take Rod out to the waiting ambulance. Otter breathed a sigh of relief when he saw Rod respond with a nod of his head to something a paramedic was asking him. He really is going to be okay, he thought.

Across the pool two MPs had one of Gage's grunts in

handcuffs and were leading him to the exit. Outside the weight room a third MP had just finished speaking to Kirk and Margie. He wrote something on a pad of paper then spoke something into a radio receiver attached to his shoulder. Then he accompanied Kirk and Margie as they made their way to see Otter and Rod.

As the MP approached, Dee got to his feet, expecting to be arrested for the second time in 24 hours. At the same time, the paramedics began wheeling Rod toward the door. Rod raised his hand, signaling them to stop. He looked at Otter and motioned to him to approach. The chaplain helped Otter up and together they walked over to the gurney. She helped Rod remove his oxygen mask. Rod reached out for Otter's hand.

"You, little man, the chaplain told me what you did for me. You coulda died." Tears came to Rod's eyes. He released Otter's hand and gently touched his cheek. "No greater love, friend, no greater love," he said softly. Otter smiled. Though a little embarrassed by the attention, the gravity of what he had done was beginning to sink in.

"They want to keep him at Womack for a while, for observation," Kirk announced. "I'm going to go on over with him." He looked at the MP then back to Dee. "Margie can look after Otter if you like," Kirk added, anticipating the arrest. "I told her she can take him to Helen's." Margie nodded her confirmation as she smiled at Otter.

Then all eyes turned to the MP who had joined the group but didn't seem to be paying attention to the arrangements being made. For an uncomfortably long moment, no one said a thing. Dead silence. Dee was the first to speak.

 "I guess you'll want me down at headquarters," he said to the officer.

"Well, not this evening, sir." The officer looked at his watch. "It's 0130. It can wait.

Dee was stunned. "Aren't you afraid I'll flee?"

"What for? You're not a criminal," the officer replied.

"I'm not wanted for Private Warren's murder?" Dee looked to the MP then at Kirk.

"No sir. Private Gallworth told us the whole story on tape thanks to Mr. Riviera and the chaplain here. It seems Mr. Riviera used a little of his training in psyops to make Gallworth think they were gonna bury him in a casket out in the woods if he didn't talk," the MP said.

"What's psyops?" Margie asked, puzzled again by an Army idiom.

"Psychological Operations," Otter replied without batting an eye. They make the enemy think things that aren't true."

Margie giggled. "Thanks, Mr. Smarty Pants."

The chaplain picked up the story. "Back at B Company barracks, when Private Gallworth was apprehended by Mr. Riviera and Mr. Fisher..."

Hearing the name of Mr. Fisher mentioned, Otter looked around for his uncle. James was nowhere to be seen.

Otter caught up to the chaplain's story where Rod had retrieved his tape recorder from the front seat of the hearse.

"He put that cheap little microphone in the casket with the cord running to the outside to his tape recorder," she continued. " Just before shoving him into the casket, he told Private Gallworth he had sixty minutes of tape to confess, and the recorder was running. He said if he," the chaplain pointed to Rod, "if Mr. Riviera didn't have a confession within sixty minutes, Private Gallworth would stay in the ground permanently. Of course he was never really in the ground, just in a ditch with dirt piled on top of the coffin to make him think he was."

"That's psyops," Otter said, looking up at Margie.

The MP took up the story again. "Mr. Riviera's threat convinced Private Gallworth to spill all the beans about Sergeant Gage's Capex plot, as well as the fact that you folks were being held prisoner at the sports complex. On their way over here the chaplain called headquarters and told us what was going on, and that we'd find Private Gallworth in a casket in a ditch alongside the highway out near Sicily Drop Zone." He smiled at the chaplain appreciatively. "We found him there exactly where she said." Then he paused and looked at Rod who was listening intently. "Judging by how bad that coffin smelled when we opened it, Gallworth must have really thought he was being buried!" Then the officer spoke to the chaplain. "Too bad you didn't call us sooner."

"I think we would've been okay, sir, had Mr. Fisher not given us away," the chaplain interjected.

"How's that ma'am?" the officer asked.

"The plan was for him to drop us off here at Lee, then park the car around the corner out of sight and wait for you guys to show up. We didn't take into account that Mr. Fisher wasn't too comfortable driving the hearse. After we got out, he gunned the engine and squealed the tires. He gave away our position and took away any element of surprise," the chaplain explained. "We were spotted and apprehended before we even had a chance to help. Had we not been caught, Gage would never have thrown Mr. Riviera in the pool."

"What happened to Gage?" Margie asked.

Otter looked at Margie then eagerly at the officer. He had not heard the full account of what happened after he had gone into the pool to help rescue Rod.

"That's the weirdest thing," the officer explained. "When we arrived, Gage and Jamison were trying to get away in a Humvee. But they weren't gettin' too far. This Mr. Fisher you referred to, for some reason, he returned to the parking lot outside in that hearse. Maybe he saw you two being taken prisoner, I don't know. Anyway, he apparently saw the Hummer outside and suspected Gage might flee. So he came up with the idea to tie the hearse to the back of the Hummer. He used some sort of strange looking rope." The officer shook his head in disbelief. " When we showed up, Gage was trying to get away, just like Mr. Fisher anticipated, but all he could do was drag that meat wagon around the parking lot with Mr. Fisher inside, holding on for dear life!"

Otter looked at Kirk and squinted his confusion, "Meat wagon?" He had never heard of a hearse being referred to as a meat wagon.

The officer continued. "Before we could intervene, Gage had gotten out and dragged Mr. Fisher out from behind the wheel of the hearse. He shot the poor fella point blank. Sergeant Gage was so crazy with rage he didn't even notice we were there with guns drawn. When he shot Mr. Fisher, we immediately took him out. Jamison gave up and the others have been apprehended. I checked a few minutes ago; Gage was DOA at Womack."

There was a long silence as the shock of what had happened in the parking lot sunk in. During the pandemonium that had occurred on the inside of the building, no one had heard the shooting on the outside. At the sound of the sirens, Gage, Jamison, and the other grunts had fled the building. No longer at gunpoint, Dee, Kirk, and Margie had managed to free themselves from the plastic ties then jumped into action to help Otter and the chaplain with their rescue efforts.

"Is he dead?" Otter asked, breaking the silence. "I mean, is Uncle James, uh, Mr. Fisher dead?"

"No sir, young man, he's okay," the officer said, chuckling. "That's another strange thing. We can't figure why, but Mr. Fisher was wearing a flack jacket. For whatever reason, though, it saved his life. And to top that," the officer went on, clearly amazed at what he was saying, "Mr. Fisher had some sort of book in his coat pocket that caught the bullet square! It spread the impact area. He'll have a heck of a bruise, but nothing near as bad as it could've been." Despite all the bitterness Otter felt toward his uncle, he was glad to hear he was still alive.

The lights of the emergency vehicles continued to flash as Rod was loaded into the ambulance. The parking lot was now a crime scene. Other MP officers were cordoning off the area for investigators who would be arriving shortly.

Since Dee was not being arrested, Margie would no longer be needed to look after Otter. She decided to join Kirk in the back of the ambulance to Womack Hospital. As the paramedic was closing the ambulance door, Margie stopped him and called Otter over.

"Look over there," she said, pointing to the hearse. Even in the poor light of the parking lot, Otter could make out the red, white, and blue braided rope still tied to the bumpers of the hearse and the Hummer. It was her nylon donut rope. "It stretched about as far as it could go, but it's sure not broken! I told you it was strong, didn't I? " Margie said proudly. "Like you and your grandpa," she added, giving Otter a hug.

After the paramedic secured the door, Otter watched as the vehicle slowly moved away. He could see Margie's face looking back at him through the window. She waved goodbye.

He waved back and smiled. Margie was right, he thought, "Stretched... but not broken."

Dee approached an MP and asked if Mr. Fisher had been taken to the hospital. The officer, after conferring with another MP, pointed to the opposite side of the building to a figure sitting on the steps of a side entrance. Dee, Otter, and the chaplain made their way there and found James staring down at the small Twelve-Step book he had taken from the chapel earlier in the evening.

Otter was the first to arrive and thought he heard James singing. As the others drew near, they heard the distinct words, "...that saved a wretch like me, I once was lost but now am found, was blind but now I see." James looked up and smiled through his tears. The chaplain sat down next to him.

"I know who you are," he said, looking down at the little book. "The Lord has truly saved me today with great miracles. I was blind but now I see." He began to rock slowly as he wiped the tears from his eyes on the sleeve of his coat. "I know it's you." Legs drawn close to his chest, James hugged his knees and continued to hum *Amazing Grace*. Dee stood with his arm around Otter at the bottom of the steps.

"What do you mean, you know who I am?" the chaplain asked.

"You're Katie. I'd know you plain as day." James was crying again. "I thought you was dead," he said, shaking his head. That bastard Harlan Strock... you remember him? If you don't, that's another bless'n to thank the Lord for. I never shoulda let you come with us when you run away from your daddy and your baby, but you was bent on it then. I thought you might get a little gospel religion travel'n with us to all them university campuses and come to your senses, so I kept your secret."

"We was up to Arkansas, to the University in that other Fayetteville," James paused and cleared his throat. "One even'n when we didn't have preaching, I caught Harlan trying to have his way with you at the motel we was stayin' in. I grabbed on to him, but I'd been drinking and was useless to you. I tried my best to stop him, but that fool cut me." James reached up and felt the scar on his neck. "I was bleed'n like a stuck pig. You tried to help me, but that devil hit you and slung you down on the floor. You cracked your head on that commode. When you wasn't moving, he said you was dead." James burst into sobs.

After a moment to collect himself, James continued. "I knowed he was gonna blame it on me, so I packed up all your things, ever little thing you had. I knowed that if I didn't, the police would trace you back to me. I took it all with me and went back home to Lacey believin' you was dead." He looked up at the chaplain. "All this time I thought you was dead."

Dee pulled Otter closer to him. He couldn't believe what James was saying. He looked hard at the chaplain, who was staring at James, confused. Her face was obscured by the shadows. Then Dee turned again to James.

"What the hell are you saying, Jimmy?" he asked in a low deliberate voice. Dee released Otter and began to make his way up the steps toward his brother-in-law.

"Grandpa?" Otter said shyly, beginning to follow Dee up the steps. Dee looked back reassuringly at Otter and raised his hand, signaling his grandson to wait.

The chaplain looked at Dee, then at James, and closed her eyes. Something was happening to her head. It suddenly felt like it was going to explode. She ran her fingers through her wet hair, touching her own scar, the one left by the surgery, an operation that had saved her life, yet at the same time had taken away any memory of it. She knew that she had an unremembered past but despite attempts to recover it, with no records and no memory, she had been forced to begin a new life.

At sixteen, she was taken in by a foster family and later adopted by the Dawsons. With them she became Darlena Dawson and was able to create a new life, a good life, with the support of people who loved and cared for her.

But now something was happening to her mind. What was triggering it she didn't understand. Was it the lack of oxygen to my brain from being under water for so long? she wondered. Perhaps the trauma of the events that had just taken place, or the faces that somehow seem strangely familiar. And Mr. Fisher's story? It felt as if some memory of another life was beginning to seep through a levied past, threatening to wash away her present one. She was terrified.

With gritted teeth, Dee reached down and grabbed

James by the shoulders and jerked the frail man to his feet.

"I oughta..." But he wasn't sure what he should do. He searched the pathetic man's eyes. The pained, haunted look he saw evoked a confusing mix of feelings. Though he was angry as hell, it was hard for him to admit that James was guilty of little more than stupidity and lies. Katie was not dead. She was alive! It suddenly occurred to Dee that, in a freakish, twisted sort of way, his daughter's life was owed to James. If there is any guilt to be assigned for this tragic mess, Dee thought to himself, it belongs to me.

Dee let James go and closed his eyes. The tired little man was shaking. He straightened his coat, then slowly walked past Dee. At the bottom of the steps he halted. Then with all the effort he could muster, he looked into Otter's eyes.

"I'm sorry, son, I truly thought your momma was dead," he said softly. "I'm glad she ain't, though." He paused and studied his great-nephew's face. "I didn't mean to hurt you neither. I'm real sorry. I truly am." Then, thinking of nothing else to say, he walked across the parking lot and sat in the hearse.

Otter, too, was struck by the sincerity in James' eyes. No longer were they angry or distant eyes. They now revealed a vulnerability. It was clear that James longed for something, or someone, to fill the empty place he had finally identified within himself. His apology was totally believable.

Dee stood for a moment in front of the chaplain, not sure what to do. It was all so surreal. He was seeing his daughter for the first time in twelve years. Would the pain and bitterness that had led to their estrangement and her running away suddenly pick up where it had left off? No, he thought, we are different people. He was scared, but he was also determined not to let his fear overcome his desire to reach out to her.

"Katie? he said softly. "Is it really you, Katie?"

The young chaplain looked up with longing eyes.

"Daddy?"

Despite her confusion and the uncertainty of her feelings, she reached out to the tall, strong man. He lifted her to her feet and embraced her tenderly, tears flowing down his face.

"Oh Katie, Katie," Dee whispered, "I can't believe it. I can't believe it's you."

After a long healing embrace, Dee released his daughter, stepped back and looked at her. Across twelve years the troubled teenager had grown into a mature woman.

"How was it that I didn't recognize you?" he said, searching her face for signs of the sixteen-year-old he had known.

The chaplain shook her head and smiled at her father. She wiped the tears from her face, then looked past Dee to the boy standing at the bottom of the steps.

Remembering that his grandson was standing behind him, Dee turned to Otter and reached out his hand. The boy was hesitant at first, then slowly he climbed the steps and took his grandfather's hand.

"Katie, this is someone you know," Dee said, putting his arm around Otter.

"This is Otter, Otter Dumpkin, your son."

Epilogue

The Dumpkin home had never been so fancifully decorated as far as Otter could remember. Flora and Vicky worked all morning getting the place ready. They did wonders with the Fourth of July theme. Red, white, and blue streamers draped the ceilings on the inside of the house and swung between the oaks on the outside. Little American flags were stuck here and there, and a larger version waved gently in the breeze on a pole near the front door of the house. On the lawn overlooking the lake, several large picnic tables surrounding a long serving table were also adorned with patriotic colors.

Then there was the braided nylon donut rope. Margie had managed to retrieve it after the investigation was completed at Fort Bragg. She had sent it to Otter for his thirteenth birthday, May 22, almost two months ago, as a reminder of his strength and courage.

It was Otter's idea to place the twelve-foot length of tattered red, white, and blue rope down the middle of the long serving table as a centerpiece. Alongside it,

 Otter placed a sign that he made the night before. From both sides of the table, one could read, *Stretched, but not broken.* The compliment given to him by Margie on the last Fourth of July had stuck with him and become a kind of motto for the Dumpkin family. After reflecting on the frightening events of a year ago, he thought it served as a good symbol for his country, too.

Already a year had passed since Katie had reentered Dee and Otter's life. Following the investigation of Gage's treasonous conspiracy at Fort Bragg, Dee was officially exonerated of the murder of Terry Warren and allowed to return home. He kept in touch with Janine, Terry's wife, and did all he could to help her get on with her life. Terry's death still weighed heavy on Dee, even after a year.

For Katie—Chaplain Dawson—there was duty still to be performed. She was needed on post at Fort Bragg as one of more than 70 clergy ministering to 40 thousand troops and their families. Getting acquainted with her son would prove to be a slow process, but in the end she was confident that slow would mean less trauma for all concerned.

During the year most of the visiting between mother and son had taken place when Otter and Dee were able to take a weekend and make the trip north to Fayetteville. Katie, who still went by the name Darlena, made significant progress in reclaiming her forgotten past. Her training as a pastoral counselor was invaluable. And the Army had a wealth of trained people and resources available to her to help deal with issues that surfaced. She encouraged Dee to take advantage of the civilian equivalent. The therapy over the past year had proved healing for both Dee and Otter.

For Otter, one of the added benefits of making so many trips to Fort Bragg was their visits with Kirk, Margie and Rod. On their very first trip to see Katie, they stopped in Florence to see Margie before going on to see Kirk and Rod in Dillon. It was the last time they would stop to see her in Florence. Kirk and Margie both came to admit that there was more between them than deep friendship. On a crisp Thanksgiving Day (The idea of a Halloween wedding didn't work for Margie) they were married in the wedding chapel in Dillon. The old antebellum home had never seen as much joy and laughter and food as it did that day. The whole house was decorated inside and out with colorful waste hose stretched into shapes and rolled into donuts, transforming it into a wonder that folks from miles around dropped by to see. It was a day Otter would never forget. Never again would he think of his family as small. For Otter it became clear that this wedding was a celebration of his new family, one that had grown to include the many people that he loved and that loved him. The highlight of the day was seeing his mother, dressed in formal military attire, perform the ceremony. He could not have been more proud.

Flora was busy on the back porch frying up catfish and hushpuppies, and Vicky was in the kitchen preparing massive amounts of grits and okra along with some normal foods that average folks are accustomed to eating. All of this to feed the soon-to-be-arriving guests.

Otter was excited but at the same time a little nervous. Dee and Katie had gone to the airport in Orlando to pick up John and Laura Dawson, arriving from Fayetteville, Arkansas. Otter, for reasons he couldn't identify, chose to wait at home for them to arrive. It would be his first time to meet face-to-face the people that he had come to know as his "other" grandparents.

Dee and Katie arrived with the Dawsons at noon as other guests were arriving. Otter found them to be warm, friendly people. Laura Dawson seemed to like to hug him as much as Flora did. He didn't mind. On this day hugs were welcome. John Dawson, however, was quiet. Otter could tell he was a thinker as he watched him watching others. John was a retired history professor. In retirement he had become an avid fly-fisherman, enjoying fishing in the streams of the Ozarks. Otter looked forward to introducing his "other" grandfather to his favorite fishing holes on Spring Lake.

James was also one of the invited guests. He really was a changed man since all that had happened a year ago. During the year, a friendship had gradually been constructed between he and his great-nephew, and his brother-in-law. This was owed primarily to his recovery as an alcoholic and his faithful attendance at AA meetings. In his pocket James still carried the little AA manual he took from the JFK chapel that night a year ago. It had saved his life—twice.

Though she was still suspicious of him, Flora tolerated James' presence at the diner and on this day, at the Dumpkin home. She moved about as one of the hosts, greeting the guests. When the time came, she offered the blessing for the feast, and the celebration began.

The afternoon was filled with food and fun and even a few fireworks that Otter had kept hidden for most of a year. Katie led a variety of games with the children in attendance, including a fishing contest. Both her fathers along with Rafe assisted her with putting bread on the hooks to catch bream off the dock.

Later in the afternoon, after the homemade ice cream was all gone, Otter was anxious to begin a rowing contest he had planned for the adults. The Dumpkin rowboat and another boat borrowed from a neighbor were pulled up on the grass next to the dock. Otter announced that the first race would be between Dee and James.

The brothers-in-law were reluctant to take up the challenge at first but with the encouragement of the crowd, they agreed to have a go at it. Otter gave the two men their instructions. They were to row out to a marker he had placed about 100 yards off shore, circle it, then return. The first to arrive back to shore and pull his boat out of the water back up on the grass would be declared the winner. The two men took off their shoes and socks, rolled up their pants, and took their places by the boats. They stood ready.

"Go!" Otter shouted.

James and Dee were off in a flash, laughing all the way as they pushed the boats into the water, then quickly mounted to set the oars.

Dee was a strong oarsman but James was no slouch. The two were neck and neck for the first 50 yards when, strangely, Dee began to slow down. He stopped rowing.

James continued rowing, easily beating Dee to the marker, and was on his way back to the finish line when Dee stood up—in the sinking rowboat—and looked back to shore. Otter stood on the end of the dock grinning at his grandfather's predicament. He held up the boat's drain plug for Dee to see.

"I told you your time was coming!" he shouted across the lake. "Gotcha!"

Acknowledgements

Writing Otter Dumpkin was by no means a singular effort. Without the support of family and friends and the willing readers of the manuscript, I could not have done justice to Otter's story. Of the many people who shared their time and energy, a special few stand out in my mind to whom I would like to give recognition.

First of all, thanks to Zoe Jacobsen, Jane Drager, Emily Wood, Erin Monroe and Anna Zemke, all students at Summit School in Seattle, and to their supervisor, Bonnie Iacolucci, for reading the manuscript. Their enthusiasm for Otter Dumpkin was both moving and inspiring for me.

Thanks also to Bill Towner, Ann Dempsey and Jack Lattemann for the care they took in reading and editing the original manuscript and for their insightful comments.

To the members and staff of University Christian Church in Seattle, Washington, whose support during the writing of this book was invaluable, I offer a special word of thanks.

And to my wife Jean, I extend my deepest love and gratitude for being by my side throughout the whole process. Without her encouragement, this book would have remained only a dream.